RAVES AND CRAVES FOR *CROTA*

Winner of the Bram Stoker Award for Best First Novel!

"How could you resist a book written by someone named Owl Goingback? *Crota* is not a tale to read late at night. It's a chiller. **Convincing and fascinating.**"
—*San Francisco Examiner*

"A chase and capture scenario. The narrative high points are the accounts of Indian history and legend. **Goingback keeps the action brisk.**"
—*Publishers Weekly*

"**Engrossing.** Goingback proves he has a talent for creating heart-stopping scenes that meld realism and fantasy. **Claustrophobically frightening.** Goingback utilizes his heritage well as he turns an Indian myth into a monster of a tale."
—*Sun-Sentinel* (Fort Lauderdale)

"An **extraordinary** visionary novel."
—*Anniston Star*

"This is **one of the best** un-put-downable novels that has passed through my hands in a long time. Owl Goingback has excelled. Excitement on every page."
—Andre Norton

"Wow! I devoured *Crota*. What **a terrific read**."
—*Halifax* magazine

"Owl Goingback is one of the most interesting new
writers working today. H
oral storytelling with the
bestselling fiction, and t
perspective. **A natural**
spinning his tales fo
—Martin

OWL GOINGBACK

CROTA

A SIGNET BOOK

SIGNET
Published by the Penguin Group
Penguin Putnam Inc., 375 Hudson Street,
New York, New York 10014, U.S.A.
Penguin Books Ltd, 27 Wrights Lane,
London W8 5TZ, England
Penguin Books Australia Ltd, Ringwood,
Victoria, Australia
Penguin Books Canada Ltd, 10 Alcorn Avenue,
Toronto, Ontario, Canada M4V 3B2
Penguin Books (N.Z.) Ltd, 182–190 Wairau Road,
Auckland 10, New Zealand

Penguin Books Ltd, Registered Offices:
Harmondsworth, Middlesex, England

Published by Signet, an imprint of Dutton NAL,
a member of Penguin Putnam Inc.
Formerly appeared in a Donald I. Fine Books edition.

First Signet Printing, December, 1998
10 9 8 7 6 5 4 3

PUBLISHER'S NOTE
This is a work of fiction. Names, characters, places, and incidents either are the product of the author's imagination or are used fictitiously, and any resemblance to actual persons, living or dead, events, or locales is entirely coincidental.

For the two women in my life:
My mother, Quiet Starr,
and my wife, Nancy

ACKNOWLEDGMENTS

Special thanks go to Shirley Krigbaum, Hazel Smith and Sheriff Robert Eckert for providing information on police procedures and local area history, and to my agent, Andrew Zack, for all his hard work and dedication.

PART I

Chapter 1

The Harley Davidson's engine sputtered, chugged and tried to cut out. Buddy Jerworski looked down, watching in horror as the speedometer's needle fell toward zero.

"Shit!" he said, downshifting to a lower gear and revving the throttle.

The bike slowed, the engine sounding like a drowning swimmer gasping for air. The headlight dimmed. The engine gave a final cough. . . .

And died.

"Shit," Buddy said again as he coasted to a stop. He pulled off his helmet and goggles, staring at the motorcycle in disbelief.

This can't be happening. Not tonight. Not now—

He glanced at his watch. 5:40 P.M. In less than an hour he had a date. Linda Chapman didn't go out with just anyone; she didn't have to. With the face of a goddess, and the body of a tramp, she could take her pick of any boy at Logan High School. She usually did. It had taken him a month to work up enough courage to ask her out, and then he had nearly fainted when she said yes. Of course, the only reason she was going out with him was because he rode a Harley.

"How could you do this to me, you traitor!" Buddy shouted.

The Harley, a 1948 panhead, was his pride and joy. When he first bought it, it had been nothing more than a rusted frame, dented tank and five cardboard boxes of greasy parts. It took two years of hard work and every penny he could scrape together to restore the big bike to running condition, but it was worth it. The first day he rode the Harley to school he became the envy of all the other kids. He was the king, the streets and parking lots his kingdom.

But Buddy wasn't feeling so kingly now. He slapped the bike's gas tank in anger. A hollow twang sounded.

Oh no.

He leaned forward and unscrewed the gas cap. It was too dark to see down inside the tank. He shook the bike, but heard nothing. No splashing . . . no gas.

"Great. Just great. Buddy Jerworski, you're an idiot."

He had no one to blame but himself. If he hadn't been so anxious to impress Linda, he wouldn't have taken the bike out for a test spin. Even then, it was inexcusable to take off without first checking how much gas was in the tank.

I'm dead.

He replaced the gas cap and buttoned his denim jacket. The temperature was dropping fast. Not much longer until it got dark. Turning, he gave a long and rather hopeful look back down the dirt road. If only a car would come along, he might be able to hitch a ride. He'd driven down Cemetery Road many times after dark, but never walked it. He wasn't looking forward to doing it, either. It was spooky enough in the daytime.

Lowering the kickstand, he leaned the bike to the left and stepped off. He was still a good four miles from town—too far to push a five-hundred-pound motorcycle. He couldn't just leave it, though. Harley Davidsons were major theft items, especially an original panhead. Maybe he could hide it.

Fastening his helmet and goggles to the seat, Buddy pushed the Harley off the road and down into the ditch, carefully laying it over on its side. Climbing up the bank on the opposite side of the ditch, he entered the woods in search of fallen branches to cover the bike. Three trips later, an armload of leafy branches a trip, he was satisfied that his motorcycle wouldn't be spotted by anyone driving by.

Darkness set in as he labored, turning everything beyond the narrow graveled lane into overlapping layers of shadows. The forest came alive with the calls of cicadas, tree frogs and a boisterous bobwhite. Overhead, the first stars of the evening poked their heads through an ebony blanket.

He wiped his hands off on his jeans and checked his watch: 6:15 P.M. He would need a miracle to make it to Linda's on time. He turned around and looked both ways down the road, hoping for the welcome sight of an approaching car. The road was empty.

"Just my luck," he said aloud, the ache of despair gnawing his stomach like a hungry rat. Visions of Linda Chapman's firm little body pressed tightly against him began to fade as reality set in. Shoving his hands deep into his jeans' pockets, he started walking.

Why me, God? Why is it always me?

Buddy had taken only a few steps when he heard sounds of movement coming from the woods, near where his bike was hidden. The noise startled him. He stopped and turned around, but didn't see anything.

It's just a rabbit, you dumb shit. No reason to get upset. Just a rabbit crashing through the underbrush. The woods are full of them.

But it sounded too big to be a rabbit.

Okay then, it's a dog. Probably some farmer's mutt out chasing rabbits.

Bending over, he gathered up a handful of rocks from the road's edge, just in case the dog had a bad attitude. The sounds drew nearer, causing his imagination to conjure up visions of vicious bulldogs and slobbering Dobermans.

Buddy decided to avoid any possible confrontation between himself and the dog—or dogs. Tossing the rocks in the direction of the noise, he turned and started jogging down the road, heading toward town.

He'd gone no more than half a mile when,

rounding a curve in the road, he glanced behind him and spotted something moving near the road's edge.

What the hell is that?

Buddy came to an abrupt stop, watching as something big and dark crossed the road behind him. He caught only a glimpse, just a blurred shape, before it disappeared in the darkness cloaking the ditch on the left side of the road.

Cocking his head to the side, Buddy listened carefully. Above the singing of cicadas and frogs he could hear the sounds of leaves crackling and sticks snapping. The sounds grew louder, closer. Whatever was in the ditch, it was coming his way.

Jogging now was out of the question. The thing that followed him was big, a lot bigger than any bunny rabbit—bigger than a dog. His heart started to jack-hammer with fear. He took off running.

The road curved to the left, then back to the right, straightening out as it reached the iron bridge that spanned Lost Creek. Halfway across the bridge he stopped to look behind him. What he saw caused his legs to weaken.

He was still being followed, the mystery animal less than half a mile away. No longer content with moving amongst the underbrush, it ambled down the middle of Cemetery Road.

The animal did not move with the hurried run, stop, sniff, run-again movements of a dog. Instead it walked straight down the center of the road, never looking around, confident in its surroundings. Unchallenged. The movement of a predator.

"A bear!" Buddy sucked in air. There weren't supposed to be any bears in central Missouri, especially not in this part of the state. The last time anyone had seen a bear in Hobbs County was almost fifty years ago. But it had to be a bear; it was too damn big to be a dog.

As he stood on the bridge watching, the bear must have looked up, for all at once a pair of large, slanted eyes shone in the darkness. They didn't just reflect light; they seemed to glow, as though each was an amber lens behind which burned a brilliant flame. As far apart as the eyes were, the head must have been enormous. And an enormous head could only be attached to an even bigger body.

Buddy had seen enough—more than enough actually, more than he wanted to see. He turned again and fled.

Four miles to town. I'll never make it. How close is the nearest house? Two miles? A mile and a half? Maybe I can climb a tree, wait it out till someone comes along. Can bears climb trees?

He rounded another curve in the road at a dead run, his side hitching with pain. Off to his right was the old Catholic cemetery, its weedy ground and ancient markers guarded by a crumbling wall of stone and a black iron gate. The gate stood open, as it always did, bent on its frame.

The cemetery! I can hide in there!

He sprinted into the cemetery and raced up the graveled drive. Past the Johnson family crypt, with its matching pair of winged angels; past the burial plots belonging to the Kellings, the Smiths and the Brandymeyers. He reached the center of the cemetery, pausing to catch his breath at the giant metal cross—a cross that always seemed to glow at night, no matter how late it was or how cloudy the sky.

From the cross he made a mad dash for the oldest section of the cemetery, hoping to hide amongst the crowded gravestones and overgrown weeds. Passing the first row of markers, he dropped to his hands and knees and crawled. Three rows later he stopped, his back resting against a cold granite headstone.

Buddy placed a hand over his racing heart. It felt like a drug-hyped rock drummer was doing a solo on the inside of his chest. Any faster and he'd have a coronary for sure.

Be calm. Be calm. I think you lost it. You should have lost it; you just broke every track record ever set at Logan High. Buddy Jerworski—track star.

Had he lost it? Had the bear given up the chase? There was only one way to be sure. Like it or not, he had to take a look. With trembling hands, he shifted his weight forward and peeked over the crumbling tombstones.

The teenager's heart sank. The bear with the funny yellow eyes hadn't given up. On the contrary, it had followed him into the cemetery. He watched, hardly breathing, as it paused at the Johnson tomb to examine the cornerstones and steel door. The bear stopped again at the giant metal cross, sniffing the monument's base like a dog at a fire hydrant.

Was the bear sniffing for him? Maybe. Maybe not.

Either way, it obviously wasn't pleased with what it smelled. He watched in awe as the creature rose up on its back legs and slapped the cross.

Ka-wap!

The monument tilted to the left.

"Je-sus Christ!" he whispered.

It's a bear. It's gotta be a bear. That's it—it's the biggest fucking bear in the world, and it doesn't like crosses. I'll bet you it doesn't care much for teenagers either!

The bear turned its head, dropped back down on all fours and continued toward him.

Panic-stricken, Buddy looked around for a way out. Behind him dense woods closed in on three sides of the cemetery. He considered making a dash for the trees, but it was much too dark to hope for a speedy flight through the forest. That left only one direction to choose from. Only one way out.

Keeping low, he studied the front half of the cemetery. Rows and rows of granite grave markers stuck up from the ground, flowing down the hill like dominos. Buddy noticed they stopped about fifty feet from the stone wall guarding the front of the property. At the far right corner of that wall stood a metal utility shed, where lawnmowers and grave-digging equipment were kept. Buddy knew the shed would be locked, no help there, so he focused his attention beyond the wall. Across the road, a pale light shone in the darkness—the soft filtered glow of a bedroom lamp from an upper-story window. Old Man Sharkey's house!

Damn! Why didn't I run that way?

Could he make it? It was a long run: down the cemetery's drive, across the road, over an old wooden bridge at the beginning of Sharkey's driveway, then up the hill to the house. There was also the problem of getting around the bear. The damn thing was only a few rows of headstones away from him.

Was it a bear? Doubt suddenly entered his mind. He couldn't see it clearly in the darkness, and only assumed it was a bear because of its size. But bears weren't that big, were they? Sure, there were a few monstrous grizzly and polar bears in the record books, but Hobbs County, Missouri, was not their natural stomping grounds. And what about the eyes? Whoever heard of a bear with glowing eyes? Come to think of it, whoever heard of *any* animal with glowing eyes?

Buddy didn't want to think about the eyes. When he did, it caused his body to go cold with fear. He couldn't afford to freeze up. Time was running out. But how long should he wait before making his move? If he waited too long he might find himself hopelessly trapped. Then again, maybe the thing would walk right past him, leaving the area between him and the road open. Did it know where he crouched? Could it smell him?

Looking back toward the front of the cemetery, he noticed the leaves on the trees opposite the road start to shine. The gravel lane in front of them grew noticeably brighter.

Headlights! A car was coming!

He glanced to his left. The bear was only about one hundred yards away, and coming closer. It was now or never.

With teeth clenched, he jumped up from his hiding place and started running.

Buddy heard a crash to his left.

I've been spotted.

Faster he ran, faster than he had ever run in his whole life. Head down, arms pumping, tennis shoes kicking up dirt, Buddy flew down the hill. He reached the driveway, slipped on the loose gravel, almost went down. The road ahead of him brightened. The car was closer. Too close!

The vehicle was coming too fast; he was still too far away. It would pass by before he reached the road. The driver wouldn't even see him.

Buddy screamed and poured on a burst of speed. He reached the road, stumbling out of control into the blinding glare of lights.

There was a roar, a choking cloud of dust and the screech of brakes.

Sickening pain slammed into his hip, exploded through his body. He went airborne, his feet racing to pass his head.

He landed on his back with a thud, the air violently expelled from his lungs. Blackness rushed over him.

The blaring of a horn faded, leaving a sharp ringing in his ears. He thought he was going to pass out, but he didn't. His eyes uncrossed, blinked and focused on the headlights above him. He didn't move, didn't even try.

"Oh my God," said a voice somewhere in the distance.

A door opened, and closed again. Gravel crunched as someone came around to the front of a pickup.

"Jesus H. Christ," the voice said, closer now. A man's voice. Deep. Rough. "What are you, crazy? My God . . . Listen, kid, take it easy—don't try to move. I'll get an ambulance. Is anything broken? Where does it hurt?"

The questions drifted through Buddy's mind like cloud formations. He tried to focus on what was being said. A moment passed before he could speak.

"I'm okay," Buddy answered, his voice barely a whisper. "Really, I'm okay." He wiggled his toes and slowly straightened his legs. His right leg was numb from the impact but didn't appear to be broken.

Thank you, God.

"I didn't see you," the man said. "You ran right in front of me. You sure you're okay?"

"Yeah, I'm sure." The pounding in his head started to ease.

"Here, let me help you up."

A pair of hands reached down and slowly pulled Buddy to his feet. The face staring down at him was tanned, deeply lined and covered with a coarse brown beard. The bill of an orange hunting cap protruded like a porch above a pair of dark brown eyes. The name *Jim* was sewn over the left pocket of a camouflage shirt.

Buddy bit his lip, fighting back tears as the numbness in his hip and right leg faded out to some very real pain. Once the swelling set in, which it would, he probably wouldn't be able to walk for days.

"What the hell's the matter with you, anyway?" Jim asked. "You trying to get yourself killed?"

"Something . . ." He swallowed and tried again. "Something's chasing me."

Remembering why he'd been running, he turned and looked toward the cemetery. The metal cross still leaned at a funny angle, but there was no sign of the bear. The truck must have scared it away.

Like a levee breaking, the teenager's strength suddenly drained out of him. He slumped against the hood of the truck.

"What?" Jim asked. He loosened his hold.

"Something was chasing me," Buddy repeated, thanking God for the warmth of the engine, and the lights.

The burly man stepped back and looked both ways down the road. "What? Where? I don't see anything."

"I think it's gone now. You must have scared it away." He straightened up. "Listen, mister, I'm telling you the truth. It chased me into the cemetery. That's why I was running."

Jim eyed him suspiciously. "You on something, kid?"

Buddy's shoulders slumped. Why did every adult in the world think teenagers were always *on* something? Just because he ran in front of a truck didn't mean he was stoned.

"No, I'm not *on* anything," he answered, his voice cold. "And I haven't been drinking, either. I'm telling you, something chased me into the cemetery. I saw your headlights and made a run for it."

"Okay, okay. I believe you," Jim said. "Settle down a little. You say something was chasing you. What was it?"

He shook his head. "I don't know . . . a bear, maybe."

Jim grinned. "Son, I hate to say it, but there aren't any bears around here."

"Try telling that to the bear," Buddy said sharply.

"Listen, kid," Jim said, staring at him. "I've been hunting in these parts for over twenty years, and I'm telling you—" He hesitated. His voice softened. "All right, if it'll make you feel any better, I'll have a look around. You wait here."

Buddy almost laughed; he wasn't about to offer to go with him.

Jim walked back around to the driver's door of his truck and reached in through the open window. He pulled a lever-action hunting rifle from the gun rack. He also grabbed something out of the glove box. Walking back to where Buddy stood, he cocked the rifle and flipped off the safety.

"Here," he said, handing him the paper sack. "You look like you could use some of this. Just don't go telling anybody I gave it to you."

The bag contained an unopened pint bottle of Jack

Daniel's. Buddy removed the bottle and broke its paper seal. Tipping his head back, he took a big swallow. The whiskey burned his throat and forced tears to his eyes, but it made some of the weakness go away. He started to take another sip but decided against it and slipped the bottle back into the sack. He'd better not get drunk; he still had a motorcycle to get home.

He watched as Jim walked about three hundred feet down the lane, carefully looking to the cemetery side of the road. He didn't go into the cemetery, nor did he stray beyond the glow of the truck's headlights. A few minutes later he returned.

"You on the level about this?" he asked, laying his rifle across the hood of the pickup.

Buddy nodded.

"Well, whatever it was, it's gone now." Jim scratched his beard. "I'll give the wildlife agency a call in the morning to see if anyone else reported seeing anything unusual. Maybe it *was* a bear." He started to turn away, then stopped. "By the way, what in God's name are you doing out here at night anyway?"

"My bike broke down about a mile back, and—"

He stopped. All of a sudden there was a strange crackling in the air about him, like the sensation during an electrical storm when lightning is popping everywhere and the air is filled with electrons.

"You feel that?" he asked. The hairs on his arms stood straight up.

"Yeah," Jim nodded. "Must be a storm brewing."

Buddy looked up. The sky was clear.

A sharp breeze came up, blowing dust across the road and making the branches of the trees swing and sway. Oddly enough, only the branches of the trees in their immediate area moved. Trees farther away stood strangely motionless, as if no wind caressed their foliage.

Terror grabbed him by the gut. He knew, without really knowing how he knew, that the thing from the cemetery was close by—that it was coming for them. He wanted desperately to run, but his legs refused to obey.

"What the fuck—" Jim picked up his rifle and stepped away from the truck. He was watching the branches of the trees on the opposite side of the road.

"It's coming . . ." Buddy whispered, his voice cracking. He wanted to hide, to cover his eyes so he wouldn't see, but he couldn't move.

"What did you say?" Jim turned back around. Something rose up behind him.

Amber eyes blazed in a head of monstrous proportions. The creature was close enough now that Buddy could see every detail of its powerful body, every line of its hideous face. It was definitely *not* a bear.

He tried to scream a warning, but only a soft hissing of air escaped his constricted throat.

Jim, hearing movement behind him, spun around. Black claws sliced the air.

Something splashed across Buddy's face and upper body. Warm. Wet. He licked his lips, tasted blood.

Jim dropped the rifle and took a staggering step

backward. He turned around and stared at Buddy, stared through him, his eyes wide and glazed. He tried to speak, but didn't—couldn't—because he no longer had anything to talk with.

Jim's coarse brown beard was gone, as was the lower half of his face and part of his throat. Only thin strips of muscle and tissue remained where once his lower mandible had been. His windpipe lay exposed in the severed throat, gurgling with blood as it struggled to draw in air. There was one final dying gasp as the big man fell forward.

Buddy looked away from Jim, his gaze riveted on the monster just beyond. A funny bubbling noise erupted from his stomach as his bowels turned loose, filling the seat of his pants. He knew that he was going to be more than just late for a date. He screamed.

Chapter 2

William "Skip" Harding awoke, muttered a curse and grabbed the telephone before it could ring a third time. Katie, his wife, murmured something incoherent as she turned away and drifted back to sleep. The phone call wouldn't be for her; it never was. Switching on the table lamp beside the bed, Skip turned his alarm clock around to face him.

Christ, it's only 3:15. This had better be good.

"Hello," Skip answered, his mind still fuzzy with sleep. Fragments of a strange dream faded back into his subconscious. Something about Indians. And arrows.

"Hello . . . Sheriff?" said the voice. "I'm sorry to disturb you at this hour, but . . ."

Skip recognized the acute, nasal-pitched voice as that of Undersheriff Lloyd Baxter, a veteran with the Hobbs County Sheriff's Department for over eight years. Lloyd was tall and scarecrow-thin, with a set of gangling arms that always showed a few extra inches of wrist at the cuff. Despite his irritating voice—caused by a constant case of bad sinuses—

Skip knew Lloyd as one of the best men on the force. He would never call this late at night unless it was something important—something that couldn't wait.

"Go ahead, Lloyd. I'm all ears."

Skip sat up in bed and fumbled a filterless Camel out of the crumpled pack lying on the nightstand. He lit the cigarette with his "girlie" lighter—a refillable butane with a picture of a gorgeous redhead on the side of it; when the lighter was turned upside down the woman's black bathing suit slowly disappeared. The lighter was a birthday present from the boys at the station. He used it only because it drove Katie crazy when he pulled it out in public. Driving your wife a little crazy could be good for a relationship, even if sometimes it got you a black eye in the process.

Skip didn't pay much attention to the lighter clutched tightly in his beefy hand. What he was hearing over the phone cleared his head of the last of its nocturnal fogginess. It also put a vile taste deep in the back of his mouth.

"I'm out here on Cemetery Road, in front of the cemetery," Lloyd continued. "Seems we've got a double homicide on our hands. Two Caucasian males. One's a juvenile. Somebody did a number on them, cut them up pretty bad. I think you ought to get down here."

"Right, I'm on my way," Skip whispered.

He carefully placed the receiver back on its cradle, trying to make as little noise as possible. He didn't want to wake Katie because he didn't want to explain what the phone call was about. No sense in her losing a good night's sleep too.

Slipping out of bed, he experienced a slight shudder of delight as his feet came in contact with the polished wood floor. He loved the feeling of a wooden floor; it brought back memories of childhood. Despite Katie's arguments to carpet when they renovated, the floors in their house remained just as bare as the day they moved in.

Grabbing his brown uniform pants off the back of a chair, he removed a matching shirt from the walk-in closet. After that came a pair of white athletic socks and his favorite cowboy boots. The boots, scuffed and worn to the point of falling apart, were his most comfortable pair for walking—something he was sure he would be doing a lot of before the night was through.

As he buttoned the collar of his shirt, his fingers brushed against the shell gorget he wore. About the size of a half dollar, the shell disk was decorated with the carved images of a spider encircled by a rattlesnake. Two holes were drilled in the top of the disk, just big enough to slip a piece of leather cord through. Years ago he had found the gorget while walking along the banks of Lost Creek. His grandmother had told him it was good luck, and he had worn it ever since.

He tucked his shirt in and removed his gun belt from where it hung on the brass coat tree. His gun was a Colt Trooper .357 magnum with a four-inch barrel, loaded with semi-jacketed hollow points for extra stopping power. He buckled up, switched off the table lamp and stepped quietly into the hallway. Halfway down the hall he stopped to check in on William "Billy" Harding, Jr., as he always did before going out.

The nine-year-old slept soundly, one leg protruding from the protective warmth of a G.I. Joe blanket. He and Katie had wanted a child so badly. When Billy was born it was their dream come true. He meant everything to them. He was everything worth working for, worth living for.

Skip inched the door open a fraction farther. The light from the hallway danced across Billy's bed, falling upon the hearing aid lying upon the night table. An icicle stabbed deep into Skip's heart.

Billy was barely four when he took sick. At first they thought it was something minor—the flu perhaps. But despite all precautions, the boy's temperature continued to climb. He was so pale, so deathly ill when they rushed him to the emergency room at the county medical center. The doctor who examined him seemed genuinely concerned, but that didn't soften his diagnosis any: rheumatic fever.

The days that followed were a blur: the I.V.'s, the shots, the pain of watching Billy suffering, the feeling of helplessness as infection set in. Skip and Katie were both so drained in the end that the final blow wasn't as bad as it should have been. It didn't really sink in until much later. He still remembered the doctor's exact words: "I'm sorry, Mr. and Mrs. Harding, but the fever has damaged your son's eardrums. Your son is deaf. . . ."

Not only had Billy lost all hearing in his right ear, and most of it in his left, but he had also lost the ability to speak. He wasn't unable to speak; he just no longer seemed willing to try, as if the sickness had caused a mental block.

Of course, the disabilities could never change the way they felt towards their son; nothing could ever change that. It just wasn't fair to the boy. Still, he'd adapted fairly well to the situation. He made good grades in school and got along great with the other kids. The hearing aid helped some. He could pick up an occasional, high-pitched sound in his left ear. He'd also developed an extraordinary ability to read lips, which made it next to impossible to keep secrets from him.

With a sigh, Skip closed the door.

Before leaving the house, Skip grabbed the Winchester 1200 riot gun from the hallway closet. A light layer of dust coated the shotgun. It had been a long time since he had reason to carry the Winchester with him. Logan was a peaceful town, Hobbs a quiet county. At least it had been until a couple of hours ago. Slipping the chain on the back door, he stepped outside. It was going to be one hell of a night.

Finishing the last of the brackish coffee, Skip tossed the Styrofoam cup on the floorboard. He'd stopped off at Nancy's Cafe long enough to grab a quick cup before heading out of town. The diner had been quiet, it usually was early in the morning. A pimple-faced teenager was working the counter while a waitress named Rosemary, who had green teeth and a stained yellow apron, sat in one of the booths, sucking on a Coca-Cola. The cafe's only customer was a grimy young man with a scraggly beard and a few too many tattoos. He'd given Skip an "I'm just waiting for the bus" look and gone back to eating his hamburger and fries.

A couple of sheets of plywood had covered two of the cafe's front windows. The tiny restaurant was the only place in town to suffer any damage in Friday's earthquake. Skip supposed everyone had gotten off pretty lucky, considering the quake was a six on the Richter scale. Rumor was it had rattled windows as far away as South Bend, Indiana.

The center of the quake was the New Madrid fault, located about a hundred miles southeast of Logan, near the town of the same name. It'd been a little over a year since the fault last acted up. Nothing serious then, either, just a few tremors. But back in 1811, New Madrid shook a good one, rocking America with its most severe earthquake ever—powerful enough to cause the Mississippi River to reverse its course and flow northward for several hundred miles. For years experts had been predicting a repeat of the 1811 quake.

Skip hoped the scientists were wrong because the city of St. Louis was built over a system of underground caverns. Back when the city was known as Port St. Louis the caverns had been used for the refrigeration of meat, cheese, wine, hides and other commodities. Since then most of the caverns had been sealed off and long forgotten; many of the city's residents didn't even know they existed. They'd find out about them if there was another major earthquake, however, because half the city would be in the basement.

Turning off Cherry Lane onto Cemetery Road, Skip reached down and shifted his Bronco II, smiling at the way the four-wheel-drive truck gripped the road. Five minutes later he spotted the blue flashing lights of the two patrol cars that were already on the scene.

When dealing with a homicide the first officer to arrive at the scene has the responsibility of securing the area. Lloyd was an experienced officer and knew what to do, so it didn't surprise Skip to see both patrol cars strategically positioned crossways in the road. In between the two cars sat a dirty gray pickup. An area of approximately one hundred feet on each side of the pickup was roped off with bright yellow barrier ribbon. The entrance to the Catholic cemetery was also sealed off. Lloyd stood on the side of the road, talking to one of the deputies. He walked out into the road as Skip drove up and cut the engine.

"What've you got so far?" Skip asked as he stepped out of his truck. He was anxious to take charge of the situation before any press could show up.

"What we've got is a mess," Lloyd said. "I've never seen anything like it."

Skip reached behind him and grabbed his flashlight off the seat, closing the truck door. "Who found them?"

"I did," Lloyd said. "I had Murphy secure the area while I reported in on the car phone. I didn't dare use the radio; too many people have scanners nowadays. I didn't think you'd want everyone in on it before you got here. Lord knows they'll find out about it soon enough."

Skip looked across the road to the two-story brick home of Bob Sharkey. "Anybody been up to talk to the old man yet?"

"I already sent Murphy up there," Lloyd said. "Turns out the old boy slept through the whole thing."

Skip turned to Corporal Randy Murphy, who had joined them in the center of the road. "Get ahold of Logan PD and tell them I need a couple of units to seal off this road. Nobody comes in, nobody goes out. I want this area airtight. Then get in touch with the office and have Sally call Mitchell and Brown in. They won't like getting out of bed before sunrise, but that's tough shit. I'm gonna need every man I can get to carry on a halfway decent search out here. Also, I want you to see if we can borrow a light cart from Milland Trucking. They always keep a few backups on hand. We're also going to need an ambulance out here to transfer the bodies. Tell the driver to stay off the siren and lights; there's no need to hurry. You got all that?"

Murphy nodded, did a flashy about-face and trotted off.

Skip smiled. Murphy had been on the force less than three years. Though still a little inexperienced, he was bright and eager to learn—qualities that would one day make him a damn good lawman.

Lloyd stepped closer, his voice dropping to a whisper. "I won't bullshit you, Skip; this one's bad. You didn't just eat, did you?"

Skip appreciated the concern. "Not unless the diner's coffee counts as a meal."

Lloyd frowned, turned and started walking toward the pickup. His rigid behavior got Skip to thinking that maybe things were a lot more grim than what he let on over the phone.

They were.

On first impression Skip thought he might be dealing with a case of hit-and-run. A spray of dried crimson was splashed across the pickup's hood and front bumper. Under their powerful flashlights the blood stood out in stark contrast against the faded gray paint of the old GMC. A small furry animal lay dead on the road just in front of the truck's bumper. Skip gently prodded the tiny creature with the toe of his boot.

His bowels turned to ice.

Instead of legs and a tail, the underside of the fur revealed a semicircle of gleaming white molars, complete with cavities and fillings. Bile burned its way up Skip's throat as he realized that what he had mistaken for roadkill was actually the bearded lower jaw of a man.

"God Almighty!"

Straightening up quickly, the sheriff took deep breaths until he felt the pounding in his head start to ease. He hadn't gotten sick, but he had come damn close. Wiping tears from his eyes, he turned to Lloyd. The expression on Lloyd's face showed he understood exactly how Skip felt.

"It gets worse," Lloyd stated solemnly.

Not wanting to disturb any possible evidence, they walked the long way around the truck to the ditch on the opposite side of the road. There was a body in the ditch.

The dead man lay on his back, arms and legs sprawled helter-skelter. His shirt was soaked with blood, so were his jeans. A name tag was sewn over the left pocket of the shirt, but it was so stained with blood it couldn't be read. One thing was sure, there was no way of identifying the man from his face—or what was left of it. Skip felt his stomach do a slow roll as he thought of the man's missing jaw and beard lying back in the road.

"Not very pretty, is it?" Lloyd asked.

"No, it's not," Skip coughed. He was reminded of the bodies he'd pulled out of a '69 Camaro ten years earlier. The driver of the car had tried to beat an Amtrak train through a crossing, and lost. The driver, along with his two female passengers, had ended up looking like spaghetti. Skip had nightmares for weeks.

"You got a name to go along with the body?" Skip asked.

Lloyd pulled a blue spiral notebook from his shirt

pocket. "Driver's license says he's James P. Hoffman, age forty-three, Route Three, Warrenton. Height, weight, hair and eye color all match up. The truck's registered in his name."

Skip nodded. He looked around. "You said there were two. Where's the other one?"

Slipping the notebook back into his pocket, Lloyd directed the sheriff to the opposite side of the road. They crossed another ditch, stopping at the base of a stout hickory tree. Something shiny at the base of the tree caught the light—a pile of gray and pink internal organs. Slippery snakes of intestines, a heart and other parts. Skip felt his throat tighten as Lloyd aimed his flashlight up into the leafy branches above them. Skip's stomach trembled. He couldn't stop; he heaved.

Lloyd stood quietly by while he threw up. When he was finished Skip wiped his face with a white handkerchief and turned back around.

The second body was that of a young man, sixteen, seventeen years old at the most. The boy was hanging upside down in the tree, fifteen feet off the ground, his back wedged tightly in the fork of a lower limb. The teenager had been gutted as one would gut a steer. His chest was a dark red cavity flanked by a white picket fence of ribs.

Though his clothes were saturated, the kid's face was free of blood. His eyes were open, staring; his lips drawn back in an expression of terror.

Skip shuddered. With the body upside down like it was, it looked like the corpse was grinning at him.

"Jesus Christ," he whispered under his breath. He turned and looked at Lloyd.

"I told you it was bad," Lloyd said.

"You didn't exaggerate," Skip replied. "Why in the hell would someone do something like this, Lloyd? To kill a person is one thing, but to go through all the trouble of gutting them and hanging them in a tree . . . it just doesn't make sense. Why risk it?"

"Maybe the killer was leaving a message," Lloyd suggested.

"You thinking drugs?" Skip asked.

"Maybe. It's hard to tell. He must have pissed somebody off real bad to get himself field-dressed like that."

Lloyd's choice of words said it all: the kid had been field-dressed. It was the same thing you did to a deer: hang them upside down so the blood drains, and gut them right there on the spot. Skip had done it lots of times, so had Lloyd. After seeing this, however, it was doubtful if either of them would want venison any time soon.

"Okay, so let's say it was drugs," Skip continued. "Where does the other guy fit in? He doesn't look the type to be involved in drugs. He looks too redneck."

"Who knows?" Lloyd shrugged. "Maybe he just picked the wrong place to be at the wrong time."

Skip nodded. Lloyd's theory made as much sense as any he could come up with.

"We'll start with the other body first," he said. "We're probably going to need a hook-and-ladder to get the kid down." He looked back up at the body.

"Jesus, how in the hell did they get him up there in the first place?"

"Beats me," Lloyd answered, glancing up at the body hanging above him. "Are the cases still in your truck?"

"Yeah . . . it's unlocked."

The cases Lloyd was referring to were two aluminum cases loaded with everything necessary to carry on a thorough crime scene search. In larger departments the job of crime scene examiner is usually undertaken by a specialist. Hobbs County, however, was still pretty rural, with its biggest town, Logan—also the county seat—having a population of just over fourteen hundred. Fortunately, prior to his moving to Logan, Skip had worked for six years as a crime scene specialist with the St. Charles Police Department.

Cases in hand, the two men approached the mutilated body in the ditch from a roundabout way. There was always the possibility that evidence could be trampled upon, therefore they avoided the direct path from the gray pickup. Kneeling at the edge of the ditch, Skip opened the larger of the two cases. The smaller one contained a tire and footprint casting kit, which wouldn't be used until later.

Skip reached in, removed a leather-bound notebook and handed it to Lloyd. It would be the undersheriff's job to take notes as they went along. Lloyd frowned. He knew what a tedious job he was being stuck with. Everything had to be recorded: the exact time of arrival, exact location of the crime scene, light and weather conditions, the names of the officers contacted, along with the names of anybody else on the scene at the time. That was just for starters. In addition you had to jot down a detailed description of the victim and his clothing. You had to list his name, age, height, weight, complexion, color of hair and eyes and, when possible, his social security number and birth date. If you didn't have writer's cramp by then, you would by the time you described the victim's wounds in terms of exact location, type and size. Finish up with a general description of the crime scene and you almost had it.

Reaching back into the case, Skip pulled out a Pentax 35mm camera and flash assembly. Taking the necessary photos was almost as tedious as the notes. There had to be photos of all approaches to the crime scene, as well as photos of the surrounding area. Shots had to be taken showing the location of the bodies and their position in relation to the areas in which they were found. Close-ups of the bodies showing all wounds were also necessary. In addition, any evidence, stains, or other distinguishable marks had to be photographed. To top it all off, every photo taken had to be described in detail in the notebook, listing such things as the type of camera and film used, the f-stop, shutter speed, distance focused, direction the camera faced and the time the photo was taken.

Grinning, Skip handed the camera to Lloyd.

"You're an asshole," Lloyd grumbled.

"Rank hath its privileges."

Leaning over the ditch, Lloyd started flashing away, photographing the body from various angles. He paused after four shots to record the photos he'd taken. Then he took three more shots directly over the body, looking down. These shots were close-ups to show the wounds in detail.

While Lloyd was playing shutterbug Skip walked slowly around the area, searching for anything which might give a clue to the murderer's identity or the motive behind the killings. Such clues could come from something as obvious as a dropped billfold, or from something as unlikely as a matchbook cover or a pocket comb. Often the clues were microscopic, like fibers or fragments of clothing, paint chips and even human hair.

He was also on the lookout for footprints and tire tracks, as well as any broken branches or twigs that might indicate which direction the killer came from or fled to.

About twenty feet from the body in the ditch, Skip found a .30-.30 lever-action rifle lying in the weeds. Slipping on a pair of gloves and being careful not to smear any fingerprints, he picked up the rifle to examine it. There was a round in the chamber but the gun had not been fired. Carrying the rifle back to Lloyd's patrol car, he wrapped it in a plastic trash bag and carefully placed it in the trunk.

Skip continued his walkaround for another fifteen minutes or so, but he didn't find anything else of interest. Rejoining Lloyd, he slipped slowly down into the ditch to begin his search of the body itself.

He started with the head and worked downward, looking for trace elements: pieces of hair, fiber, or other small materials clinging to the body. Finding such items sometimes made all the difference in whether a suspect went free or fried in an electric chair. Of course, trace elements weren't worth a damn unless he had a suspect to go with them. It wasn't like he could send them off to the FBI and get back the name and address of the murderer, no matter what they showed on television. But if he ever had someone sitting on ice with whom he could compare the items, then there was a chance of making a connection.

Finding nothing out of the ordinary on the body, he carefully slipped a small paper bag over each of the victim's hands, holding them in place with rubber bands. It usually wasn't a good idea to take elimination fingerprints or scrape the fingernails in the field. That job was saved for the environmentally controlled atmosphere of a morgue. The paper bags would protect the hands from contamination. Plastic bags were never used because they caused condensation that could ruin many trace elements.

Completing the detailed search of the body, Skip and Lloyd placed it in a disposable body bag. The bag would ensure that no physical evidence was lost during the trip to the morgue. Once at the morgue, the body would become the property, and problem, of the county coroner.

In homicide cases the area directly under the body is given the greatest attention. While wind may blow away items of trace evidence originally on or around the body, evidence under the body will usually be trapped and protected.

After removing the body from the ditch Skip studied the ground where it had lain. The vegetation in the ditch was mostly sparse weeds, with no litter to speak of. He still took a soil sample from the area where the victim's head had been, placing it into a small cardboard box. The box would be mailed to the criminalist's laboratory in St. Louis first thing Monday morning. It was amazing some of the things the boys in the lab could come up with from a handful of dirt.

By the time they'd finished with the first body the ambulance and additional officers were on the scene. Skip instructed the ambulance driver to sit tight until they finished with the second body. He then assigned deputies Mitchell and Brown the job of scraping a sample of blood from the front bumper of the pickup, threatening instant death should they touch anywhere else on the vehicle before it was dusted for fingerprints.

As expected, getting the second body down out of the tree proved to be a pain in the ass. With the ditch in the way, they had to scrub the idea of calling for a fire truck. Their only alternative was to climb the tree, search the body where it was, then lower it to the ground with ropes. Skip was greatly relieved when Corporal Murphy volunteered for the job.

Climbing the tree was only part of the headache. The body was wedged so tightly between two limbs it took Murphy twenty minutes to work it loose. Twice during that time, he slipped, narrowly escaping putting himself on the disabled list. Finally, after an hour of struggling, the body was down. Skip still wondered how someone had managed to get it up there in the first place.

To reward Murphy for a job well done, the sheriff allowed him to accompany the bodies back to the morgue. It wasn't as bad a detail as it sounded. Once the bodies were dropped off, Murphy would have to wait at the hospital for a ride. One probably wouldn't be available for a couple of hours. In the meantime, he would just have to find something to keep himself busy—like talking to the nurses on night shift. Rumor had it several of them were quite fond of men in uniform.

After the ambulance pulled away, Lloyd and the two deputies started a thorough search of the gray pickup. They began by carefully dusting for fingerprints along the exterior surface of the vehicle. Once they finished the outside, they would sweep and vacuum the interior, carefully labeling anything found in the process. While they were busy with the truck Skip decided to take a walk through the cemetery to see if anything could be found there. He carried the tire and footprint plaster casting kit with him in case it was needed.

He suspected the killer, or killers, might have been in the cemetery prior to the murders. What tipped him off was the way the large metal cross leaned to the left. He'd driven by the cemetery earlier in the week and the cross had been straight as an arrow. Could the victims have been witnesses to an act of vandalism? His suspicions grew as he approached the monument.

Halfway up the right side of the ten-foot cross was a basketball-sized dent that might have been made with a sledgehammer. He would have to get a photo of it, and possibly a scraping or two for the lab. Unfortunately, the grass around the monument was too thick for there to be any footprints. He did, however, come across a clear print about fifty yards beyond the cross. Judging by the tread pattern, it looked like it might have been made by the kid in the tree. It still wouldn't hurt to make a cast. If nothing else, it would verify that the kid had been in the cemetery prior to, or at the time of, his death.

Squatting down, Skip pulled a tiny notebook from his shirt pocket and jotted down a brief description of the footprint, noting the time and location for the record. He was also supposed to take a photo of it, but he didn't exactly always do everything by the book.

Putting the notebook away, he carefully removed a twig from the indentation. He then set about preparing it for casting by spraying it with a light coating of silicone spray. To prevent it from being damaged by the propellant gases in the aerosol can, he used a piece of cardboard to deflect the spray onto the impression. After that he placed a metal casting frame around the print, gently pressing the frame into the surrounding soil.

While the silicone was drying he prepared the plaster of Paris in a rubber mixing bowl, using a wooden spatula to mix the water and plaster together. He could always tell when he had the combination just right: it looked like pancake batter. *It probably tastes like shit.* Holding the bowl close to the impression, he let the mixture slowly trickle onto and over the spatula. Pouring the mixture directly on the print could ruin it.

He poured just enough to fill the impression and create a stand of plaster about a half-inch deep. As the plaster hardened he made reinforcing material by cutting a piece of wire screening into two-inch-wide strips.

After reinforcing the cast he added the remainder of the plaster, giving the cast an overall thickness of about two inches. The cast would be hard enough to remove in thirty minutes. It would then be allowed to dry for another thirty minutes before brushing away any clinging soil with a soft brush. After brushing, it would be wrapped in clean paper and packaged in a firm container.

Skip wasn't sticking around for the cast to harden. He was anxious to get down to the morgue. He had a hot date with a couple of cold bodies.

Chapter 3

Skip detested everything about the morgue. He hated its lingering smell of embalming fluid and disinfectants; the stark whiteness of its ceiling, walls and tiled floor; the way the bright fluorescent lighting made colors appear grotesquely too vivid, too real. Most of all he hated the two stainless-steel worktables that sat in the center of the room, a constant reminder that all those who came to the morgue were on a one-way trip. But these things went virtually unnoticed in the presence of Fred Granger.

The sheriff couldn't picture Fred as being anything other than a coroner, except maybe a mad scientist. The aging veteran of the cadaver scene was tall and wiry, with a fringe of unruly white hair on each side of an otherwise bald head. The threadbare white smock he wore was as much a part of him as his thick, wire-rim glasses. To top it all off, Fred had a walk like Groucho Marx's and an endless supply of morbid jokes and war stories. Fred's bedside manner may have been unusual, but you never heard any of his patients complain.

When he wasn't at the medical center Fred could usually be found in the back room of the Pine Hills Funeral Home, which was owned by his younger brother Eric. While Eric took care of the business side of the funeral home, selling mahogany caskets and comforting loved ones in their time of need, Fred tended to the dead. He enjoyed working with the bodies of the recently deceased, considering each a mystery, a giant jigsaw puzzle with arms and legs. He loved to poke around in them, trying to figure out what had led to their state of eternal rest. And he was very good at his work.

Skip paused in the morgue's outer office to pour himself a cup of coffee. Fred always kept a pot on hand for *live* visitors. There was also, Skip knew, a pint of brandy stashed in the bottom desk drawer. Checking his watch—it was almost 7:00 A.M.—he took a deep breath and entered the examining room. Fred Granger was just opening the first body bag.

"We need to double-check the bags and clothing for evidence before you toss them," Skip said as he stepped into the room.

Fred looked up, flashed a grin, and nodded toward two paper-lined trash receptacles that had been set up to store the victims' clothing. As usual, Fred was way ahead of the game. Skip felt like a fool for opening his mouth.

"And how was your evening, Sheriff?" Fred asked. There was just a trace of sarcasm in the question.

"To put it mildly, it was a bitch," he replied. "How's the funeral business?"

Fred forced a frown. "It's been rather dead lately."

It was an old joke that Skip had heard a thousand times, but it did bring a smile to his face. Something to relieve some of the nervous tension Skip always felt when first entering the morgue.

"My, my. You do have your hands full, don't you?" Fred clicked his tongue as he pulled the bag away from the first cadaver. It was the faceless body of James Hoffman. "What did he do, take a bite out of a grenade?"

"Something like that. We found him and his buddy out on Cemetery Road."

"Oh?" Fred's eyebrows arched a little, making him look comical.

"Yeah, they were in front of the cemetery. If I didn't know better, I'd say you and Eric must have buried a couple out there that didn't want to be buried."

"Now, Skip, you know we've never put anything in the ground that looked this bad." He gave Skip a sober look. "You got the rest of him?"

"Yeah, it should be in one of the other bags."

Fred looked around and spotted the two black plastic bags sitting in the corner of the room. "Which one?"

"The little one. Here, I'll get it for you."

"Thank you, Sheriff. You're a gentleman and a scholar."

It was Skip's turn to fake a frown. "Just don't let it get around."

As Fred began examining the wounds on the body

of Jim Hoffman, Skip carefully removed the paper bags from the victim's hands. Using a clean, small-bladed knife, he scraped along the inside of each fingernail. The scrapings were deposited in a small white envelope to be sent to the lab in St. Louis.

Finished with the hands, he started going over the dead man's clothing, paying particular attention to his shirt collar, pants cuffs and pockets. But a couple of bagger-lice and some pocket lint was all he found.

"You ready to get him undressed?" Fred asked.

Skip nodded.

Undressing the dead man proved to be quite a task. Besides being on the healthy side, the body was stiffening up, making the work that much more difficult. As each item of clothing was removed—shoes, socks, shirt, pants, underwear—it was carefully wrapped in clean white paper, labeled and placed in the first trash receptacle. Once the body was undressed Fred went back to examining the wounds, while Skip took elimination finger and palm prints.

"Take a look at this," Fred said, pointing at two symmetrical cuts on the left side of the victim's neck, each about a half-inch in length. The first cut was just below the left ear; the second was on the throat, just above the Adam's apple. The victim's face disappeared just above the cuts.

"Looks like they were made by a weapon of some kind," Skip commented, not sure what Fred expected him to see.

"Could be," Fred nodded. "The damage to the

skull indicates the jaw was torn away in a left-to-right movement."

"Torn away?"

"Yeah. I've got some damage indicators on the right side. Stretched muscles, torn ligaments, bruised flesh . . . that sort of thing."

Skip pulled out a notebook and wrote down what Fred said. "Cross out chain saw. Crowbar, perhaps?"

"It's a thought, but not likely." Fred pointed again to the two cuts. "The weapon that took this man's face off had two distinct points set approximately five inches apart. But it was probably curved like a crowbar, because instead of slicing through the back of the neck it hooked under the lower jaw."

Fred turned the dismembered lower jaw over. "The marks are more pronounced here. Notice the scratches on the jaw bone and the tears along the gum line, just aft of the lower incisors. See how several of the incisors are pushed forward? This would indicate that the points, or prongs, of the weapon were at least three inches long, perhaps longer.

"The base of the tongue is also shredded badly and has been torn free from where it attaches to the lower jaw. I'd say the weapon entered through the left side of the victim's face, at an area parallel to and a little below the jawline, passed through the mylohyloid, which forms the undersurface of the chin, and out through the mouth."

Turning his attention back to the body, Fred paused to allow Skip time to catch up with the notes he was taking.

"Another thing, both the external carotid artery and the superior thyroid artery were severed, which would account for the actual death of the victim. As much blood as those arteries pump, he was probably dead before he hit the ground."

Fred crossed the room. Reaching a counter near the wall, well away from the body, he lit up a cigarette. Skip jotted down what he said, closed his notebook, and joined him. Both men knew that it was going to be a long morning; there was still another body to do. It had already been a long morning for the sheriff.

The undressing and initial inspection of the second body—the teenager—was carried out like the first, with Skip checking for trace elements and taking notes. No wallet or I.D. was found on the deceased, but the sheriff's office had received a missing persons report with a description matching the victim's. Still, he couldn't be completely certain if it was the same person until someone identified the body.

As they removed the last of the clothing Skip's attention was drawn to a tattoo on the kid's left shoulder. It was a black 74, about an inch in height and two inches across.

"What's that?" Fred inquired.

"Biker tattoo. It stands for seventy-four cubic inches, the size of the old Harley engines."

"Harley Davidson? This kid don't look like a biker to me."

"He doesn't look like one to me either," Skip

agreed. "He's too young . . . too clean-cut. Maybe he's a wanna-be."

Fred's eyebrows knitted. "Say again."

"A wanna-be. That's what you call someone who likes to dress like a biker, act like a biker but doesn't have the balls to get on a bike. Who knows, maybe he's got a subscription to *Easy Riders* magazine."

"Maybe," Fred nodded.

Either way, the tattoo could prove useful for putting a name with the body. Skip would give a call back on the missing persons report and see if the youth missing had such a tattoo. He hoped not, because he hated breaking bad news to local citizens. What could he possibly say to soften the blow? *Good news, we've found your son—he's at the morgue.*

The teenager's chest cavity was a gaping red chasm under the harsh fluorescent lights. Blood stained the kid's skin from his navel to his knees, with a good portion of it settling around his groin. There was no blood on his face, which meant he'd been killed prior to being hung upside-down in the tree.

"Look here," Fred said, breaking Skip's train of thought.

The coroner pointed to three cuts just above where the kid's collarbones should have been, but were no longer. They traveled downward for an inch before reaching the missing section of body. The marks were identical to those found on the other body. Skip opened his notebook as Fred started in with an oral description.

"Once again we have encountered marks, cuts, if you will, made by an unknown instrument with a pointed or pronged cutting surface. The cuts travel downward before disappearing, indicating the killing blow was administered in a downward motion. We lose track of the cuts just above the clavicle, and I believe it is here that the weapon sank deep into the flesh, because the clavicle failed to either deflect or stop the stroke. The fact that the clavicles are no longer present would also indicate that the weight of the weapon, and or the force of the blow, must have been considerable."

Fred paused long enough to allow him to catch up. "The rib cage also seems to have had no noticeable effect on the blow. A strip six inches wide is missing from the clavicle to two inches above the navel. Most of the ribs have been torn free from where they connect to the thoracic vertebrae, and the sternum is missing completely."

"So you're saying . . ." Skip interrupted. Fred was starting to sound a little too technical. Once the old man got started, he could talk for hours without stopping.

Fred looked across the table and smiled. "Sorry, I guess I was starting to get carried away. It's just . . . I've never come across anything quite like this before."

Skip looked down at the body and sighed. "One thing's for sure, when word gets out about this I'm going to have half the bloody town down on my back. Can you give me anything preliminary to go on . . . anything at all?"

Fred removed his glasses and wiped them on a handkerchief. "This is just an educated guess, mind you, but I think your killer is at least six feet four inches tall and built like a gorilla. Had to be tall to make the cuts at the angle they are, and had to be stronger than hell to do this kind of damage. After seeing this kid, I can tell you that the weapon used is at least six inches wide, with curved prongs a half-inch wide and from three to six inches long."

"Sounds like a potato rake," Skip commented.

"Exactly," Fred nodded. "Only picture a potato rake that's been welded to a heavy metal bar, something to give it enough momentum to do a lot of damage."

"Sounds pretty frightening," he said.

"Not nearly as frightening as the psycho wielding it. You said you found him in a tree?"

Skip nodded. "About fifteen feet off the ground."

"Damn." Fred shook his head. "Why would anyone want to do something like that?"

"It's hard to say. Maybe he was involved in drugs."

Fred cocked an eyebrow. "You want me to run a chemical analysis on him?"

"It wouldn't hurt," the sheriff replied. "Go ahead and run one on both of them."

"Your wish is my command," Fred grinned. He turned and looked at the remaining plastic bag. "I guess we'd better have a look through this boy's insides while we're at it."

Skip shuddered. There was no way he was going to probe through the ghastly contents of the last bag. "I think I'm going to have to pass on that one, Fred," he said.

"Oh?" The coroner sounded disappointed. "Well, I guess you do have enough to keep you busy writing reports for the next couple of hours."

"More like the next couple of days."

Fred nodded. "If I find anything else of value, I'll give you a call."

"I'd appreciate that," Skip said.

Fred pushed his glasses up higher on his nose. "Do me a favor?"

"What's that?"

"Nail the son of a bitch that did this."

"I'm gonna try, Fred. Believe me, I'm gonna try."

Chapter 4

The deer couldn't have been dead for very long—four, maybe five hours at the most. It probably died sometime during the night. If he guessed right, it had been killed between midnight and sunup.

An eight pointer. Nice rack.

Kneeling next to the deer's hind legs, Jay Little Hawk examined the ragged cut running lengthwise down its underbody. Whoever did the slicing was either in a hurry or didn't know what they were doing. He suspected the latter, seeing how the scent glands weren't removed. Just as well the poacher dumped the carcass, because the meat wouldn't have been fit to eat. Sloppy job. Damn sloppy, if you asked him. Such a waste.

Grabbing the legs, Hawk flipped the deer over. He liked to retrieve the bullet whenever possible. Sometimes it made the difference between a poacher going free or going to jail. Odd, he could find no sign of a gunshot wound on the right side either. Maybe he'd overlooked it.

Running his hand slowly along the sleek hide, he

felt for a knot, bump or small patch of dried blood. Just because the wound wasn't visible didn't mean it wasn't there. Sometimes a piece of tallow becomes dislodged, plugging the hole like a cork in a wine bottle. The animal still dies, but all the bleeding is internal. But even with his fingers, he could not locate the bullet hole.

That was strange. There had to be a wound somewhere. Deer just don't stand still and let you field-dress them. Flipping the animal back over, he rechecked its other side but found nothing. He even examined the deer's anal passageway, thinking somebody might have made a one-in-a-million shot. A trace of greenish dung was all he found for his troubles.

He just couldn't figure it out. Unless whoever brought the buck down had been directly underneath it when they fired—which wasn't likely—there was no evidence the deer had been shot at all. Surely somebody hadn't just stumbled across the buck after it was already dead and decided to field-dress it. No one was that stupid, were they?

The more he thought about it, the more it bothered him. In his ten years as a game warden he'd seen his share of poachings, but what he saw today just didn't sit right with him. There was something odd about the whole thing, something he couldn't put his finger on.

Why had the deer been cleaned, then abandoned? Was it just a botched operation? Did the person or persons involved get scared and dump it at the last minute? The ground beneath the buck was soaked with blood, so it was obviously gutted where it lay. If that was true, then where were the internal organs? Like the bullet wound, they were nowhere to be found. He'd never heard of someone keeping the innards and discarding the body, but from the looks of things that's exactly what they'd done.

Wiping off his hands with dried leaves, Little Hawk walked over to a fallen log and sat down. He pulled a pipe from the pocket of his flannel shirt, filled it with tobacco and lit it with a kitchen match. A cloud of cherry-scented smoke rose above him. He watched the cloud, pondering the mystery before him.

His discovery of the deer was accidental. Hawk wasn't looking for poachers; it was his day off. Even on his days off, he liked to spend as much time in the woods as possible, enjoying the sights and sounds of Mother Nature. He'd acquired his love of the forest early in life, as a boy living on the Cherokee Indian Reservation in North Carolina. The Great Smoky Mountains had been his playground, the animals and birds his playmates.

On the eve of Hawk's twelfth birthday, his parents were killed in an automobile accident. With no other relatives in North Carolina, he'd been sent to stay with his grandfather, who lived on the reservation of the Western Cherokee near Bartlesville, Oklahoma. His grandfather, though strict, was caring and wise. He was also a tribal shaman, and it wasn't long before he began teaching his skills and knowledge to Hawk.

The knowledge hadn't come easy. Hawk spent years learning tribal history, customs, ceremonies and medicine. He endured the stifling heat of the sweat lodge, the numbing hunger of fasts and the loneliness of the vision quest. But it was all worth it. Not only did he learn how to walk in balance, but the Great Spirit blessed him with the ability to cure certain illnesses, to see things others couldn't and to walk upon a spiritual plateau unknown to the white man.

Hawk left the reservation at the age of nineteen—two months after the death of his grandfather—to enlist in the army. It wasn't an easy choice, but he had to do what his inner voice told him. With a promise that he would one day return, he boarded a dust-covered Greyhound bus for Tulsa.

The army was good to him despite sending him to Vietnam straight out of boot camp. Truthfully, he didn't mind going to Vietnam. His tour "in country" proved to be an excellent opportunity to sharpen the survival skills taught to him by his grandfather. Those skills paid off on two different occasions, saving his platoon from walking into VC ambushes. Each time he'd been alerted to the enemy's presence by a tiny warning signal going off deep inside his head, an uncanny sixth sense that saved him and his buddies from certain death.

While Hawk sat and silently reflected on his past, a fluffy white cloud drifted lazily across the Missouri sky, momentarily passing in front of the sun. As it did, the shadows in the tiny clearing shifted slightly, causing him to notice something he'd overlooked earlier, something he never would have suspected.

Curious, he got up and walked back over to the deer. Running his hand over the body confirmed what the shadows pointed out. The animal's neck was broken.

What the hell?

Along the banks of Lost Creek, where the water is shadowed deep blue by the hills on each side, grow tiny patches of wild ginseng. Some know about the fabled plant and search for its twisted roots amidst clumps of wild blackberries, poison ivy and flowering sumac. In the town of Truesdale there is a place where you can get twenty dollars for a pound of the dried root. The root is resold to a commercial health food store in St. Louis, where it is falsely labeled as "Korean ginseng" and sold to skinny, pallid-faced customers looking for the easy way to fitness and health. Even at twenty dollars a pound, few search for the plant; for it takes many roots to make a pound and it just isn't worth braving the mosquitos, yellow flies and water moccasins to get to it.

Hawk also gathered the tiny roots of the wild ginseng plant—known as "Little Man" to Cherokee medicine men—but he didn't do so to sell it. He made more than enough money as a game warden to suffice his every need. Instead he boiled the roots with other wild plants to create a herbal tea helpful in relieving the agony of rheumatic joints. Not that he suffered, but there were others who did. He also gathered the black mud from along the creek bed, and the green moss from the larger rocks, to make a compress better for healing open wounds than anything a doctor could prescribe.

Placing a freshly dug root into the cloth sack he carried, Hawk whispered a few words of thanks and dropped a glass bead into the hole as payment to the plant's spirit. He then washed his hands in the icy cold water of the creek. The water was crystal clear, with a faint taste of minerals to it. Both the coldness and the peculiar taste were the result of the creek running underground for several miles. About two miles farther south of where he stood the creek would again disappear from sight, traveling through one of the area's many subterranean caverns. Where it eventually ended up was anybody's guess, hence the name "Lost Creek."

Thinking about caverns and subterranean passageways reminded him that he ought to check on the Devil's Boot while he was in the area. The "Boot," named for its unusual shape, was one of Hobbs County's better-known caves. In fact, it was the only one anybody had ever bothered to name.

Located halfway up the side of a steep hill, in the center of a limestone and granite bluff, the cave's entrance was a modest hole about seven feet high and fifteen feet wide. The opening was protected by an overhang of grayish rock and partially blocked by a rubble of fairly large boulders. The first chamber was about twenty feet wide and nearly the same height, its floors covered with a layer of sand and fine gravel.

A tunnel at the back of the chamber led into the hillside thirty feet or so. There it connected to a larger chamber whose floor happened to be twenty feet straight down. The second chamber was shaped like the bottom of a man's boot, giving the cave its name.

Over the years, the cave became a very popular attraction with the local teenage population, so much so that its floors were constantly littered with empty beer cans, wine bottles and discarded condoms. Some energetic individual even constructed a wooden ladder from the tunnel down into the second chamber. With the difficulty of reaching the second chamber made easier, Devil's Boot became *the* place to hang out for the Budweiser-and-marijuana crowd. All that ended a little over two years ago when an eleven-year-old boy slipped on one of the ladder's rungs and fell to the rocky floor below. He died en route to the hospital.

The sheriff's office stepped in after the accident, sealing the cave's entrance with boards and sheets of plywood. A sign was posted, warning people of the dangers and forbidding any trespassing within the cave. Both sign and boards were enough to deter any future would-be spelunkers from entering the cave—at least they had been. As Hawk rounded a bend in the path leading to the cave's entrance, he noticed that sign and boards were no longer in place.

* * *

It took Jay Little Hawk thirty minutes to hike back to his jeep and return again to the Boot. It wasn't just because the boards weren't in place that he had gone to get his flashlight. It was more on account of the odor coming from the cave—a sickly sweet kind of smell, like a mixture of sour grapes and shit. There was no mistaking the odor: it was the smell of death.

In addition to the foreboding stench, an eerie quietness hung over the area. A great hush had fallen over the forest dwellers—a hush, Hawk thought, with all the nervous energy of the calm before a storm. Now a white man, his ears attuned to different sounds, might not have noticed the strained silence. If he did, he might have mistaken it for the peaceful serenity of the country. Having been raised in the old ways, Hawk knew that what he was experiencing was anything but serene. A message had been laid out for him by his timid forest friends, one as plain as any conceived of paper and pen. A message of warning.

He cocked his head slightly to listen. No doubt about it, something was wrong. Was it a warning not to go into the cave?

Switching on his flashlight, he carefully stepped over and around the boulders, boards and sheets of plywood at the cave's entrance. Except for a few discarded beer bottles, the first chamber was empty. Aiming his light at the floor, he noticed a disturbance in the dust. A path led from the entrance back into the tunnel. Someone had been in the cave, but he couldn't tell how long ago it had been.

Moving as silently as a cat, he slipped into the

narrow mouth of the tunnel. He kept his back pressed against the rocky wall; his flashlight extended before him in his left hand. Twenty feet farther in, the tunnel took a sharp turn, cutting off the light filtering in from the entrance. Switching off his flashlight, Hawk momentarily enjoyed the sensation of being in darkness so deep he couldn't see his hand in front of his face.

By turning the light off, he forced himself to use his hearing. People often depend too heavily on their eyesight, ignoring the other senses God gave them. But Hawk had spent years tuning each of his senses. He was as much at ease in the dark as he was in broad daylight.

Holding his breath, he listened for sounds that might have gone unnoticed. To his left, he could hear the faint scraping of legs as insects scurried over the rocky wall. From somewhere near the entrance came the chirping of a cricket and the soft rustling of dried leaves being tossed about by the wind. If there was someone else in the cave, he would have heard them. It may have been only a slight shift in position, or the soft raspiness of an expirant breath, but it would have been enough to alert him to possible danger. He heard none of these, however. He was alone.

Assured that he was not placing himself in jeopardy, Hawk switched the flashlight back on and continued forward. Reaching the point where the tunnel connected up with the second chamber, he shined the light down into the rocky room below.

The second chamber looked much the same as

when last he saw it. The floor was littered with beer cans, pop bottles, and burger boxes; the rocky walls were decorated with graffiti. The wooden ladder was still in place, the floor near its base still stained a reddish-brown from the blood of the boy who'd fallen from the slippery rungs. The sheriff's department had tried to wash away the bloodstain, but it had already set into the porous rocks.

The shape of the second chamber made it impossible for him to see all of it from the upper level. Obviously, someone had been in the cave recently. Why else would the boards sealing the entrance have been removed? Whether they had ventured into the second chamber remained to be seen. One thing, the sickly-sweet odor was stronger now, more pronounced. Had it happened again? Had someone sneaked into the cave, slipped from the ladder and gotten hurt? Hawk dreaded what he might find in the chamber below.

Turning around backward, he stepped onto the first rung. The ladder was still sturdy, but he moved slowly, making sure his smooth-soled cowboy boots didn't slip. Fifteen rungs later he was safely on the ground.

The second chamber was three times the size of the first, and darkness swallowed the beam of his flashlight before it reached the back wall. Hawk studied the floor as he crossed the room. Someone *had* been in the second chamber.

Glancing back up, he was surprised that he hadn't reached the back wall yet. The chamber was big, but it wasn't that damn big. Nevertheless, instead of reflecting off a graffiti-covered wall of gray, the flashlight's beam disappeared into total darkness. Hawk suddenly realized what was wrong. He hadn't miscalculated; he should have been standing at the back wall, but it wasn't there. Instead, he faced an opening about seven feet high and nearly twice that wide, its base choked by a pile of fallen rock.

Had the wall collapsed because of Friday's earthquake? Curious as to what lay on the other side of the opening, he scaled the hill of stone.

Beyond the opening was a narrow passageway about six feet high and seven feet wide. The passageway appeared to connect up to another, even bigger chamber. A foul wind blew from that chamber.

Hawk started to step into the passageway when he was overcome with a feeling of numbing terror. He froze. Only twice before had he experienced such a sensation. Each time it had come as a premonition, a warning of great peril. Even then, the feeling had never been as strong, or as clear, as it was now.

Switching off the flashlight, he again allowed the darkness to engulf him. He slowed his breathing and listened for any sounds that might offer a clue to the danger he faced. All was quiet; the only sound was the beating of his heart.

Remaining motionless, Hawk forced his mind to relax, clearing it of all thoughts. He turned off the little voice inside his head, becoming like a lake whose surface only rippled slightly from the cool night wind. His mind no longer transmitted; therefore, it could receive.

Almost immediately, Jay Little Hawk knew the danger he felt was not a stationary thing. Nor was it something that had entered the cave after him. Whatever the danger was, it came from deeper within the cave, from the very bowels of the earth—and it was coming his way.

As Hawk's feeling of terror increased, something touched his mind. A presence so evil and foul that it was beyond the description of words.

Stifling a gasp, he opened his eyes and stared into the blackness before him. He couldn't see what was coming, yet he knew it came for him. For the very first time in his life, Hawk knew what fear was. For the very first time he fled.

Chapter 5

In the inky depths of eternal night, in the total blackness of subterranean passages, where blind things slither and crawl, he awoke. The creature with glowing eyes of amber, whose name had long since been forgotten by man, stirred from his restless slumber and hissed a breath of anger.

He had gotten little pleasure from the two men he slew the night before. Their blood had been watery, lacking in the taste that comes from courage and a strong heart. The killings had left him less than satisfied, the bloodlust still strong in his veins. Nor had there been time to enjoy more than a few bites of the deer he killed, barely making it back to his lair before daylight.

Rocking back on powerful haunches, he dug a black claw into his left flank, scratching at an itchy patch of scaly hide beneath the sparse reddish hair. He thought about the days before men. The good days. There had been such battles then. The ground had shaken with the roars of great beasts, dim-witted but full of courage. Their blood had been hot and spicy. Tasty.

But then came the great light. With a tail longer than the mightiest creature, it ruled the night sky, turning darkness into day. He'd hidden from the light, seeking refuge in a cave, sleeping while the sky darkened and the world grew cold.

He'd slept a long time, a very long time. When he finally awoke the world was different. White, cold and barren. Gone were the great beasts and the thrill of a challenge. Gone too were those of his kind. He was all alone in the world, the last of his species, the last of an era. Had he been given the gift of tears, he would have cried. Instead, he turned his back on the frigid world and returned to his cave, entering a state of deep hibernation, remaining that way until the day of the great shaking.

With a growl as cold as ice, the creature arose and left his lair. Darkness had again fallen on the outside world. It was time to hunt, time to eat.

With speed surprising for his size, he navigated the twisting passageways of the subterranean world. He paused when he reached the ladder leading from the second chamber of the Devil's Boot up to the first, for he still had difficulty climbing it. But he hesitated for only a moment before starting up.

He paused again when he reached the mouth of the cave, taking time to look out over the landscape. A long time had passed since he was free to hunt. Sniffing the air, he let a fat gray tongue roll against his upper fangs. The scent of prey flavored the night wind. Not close, but not far either. It was time to kill.

If anyone had been walking near the back pasture

of Roy Owens's farm at that particular moment, they would have noticed a disturbance amongst his herd of Hereford cows, a restlessness unusual for such a calm, quiet evening. Mooing woefully, the cows crowded together for protection. Standing a little apart from the herd, Roy's prize Hereford bull, Bubba, sniffed the air, blew snot and pawed nervously at the ground. The Crota was coming.

About the same time Skip Harding was finishing up the last of the reports he had to write—hours after Jay Little Hawk fled the Devil's Boot—Richard Cummings was settling down to a dinner of scrambled eggs with grilled potatoes and onions. His wife, Jewell, would have frowned at such a combination for dinner—it always gave him gas—but she had passed away a little over two years ago and he'd been living alone ever since.

Actually, he wasn't alone in the truest sense of the word. While no human companion shared his modest, two-bedroom mobile home and five acres of wooded land, there was Bruno. And although the lop-eared pit bull may not have been the greatest at carrying on a conversation or playing checkers, he helped to fill the painful void left by Mrs. Cummings's absence. In fact, the dog filled it rather nicely. Bruno never complained when Richard didn't shave and take a bath each and every night. Nor did he fuss when Richard drank more beers than he really should, or had a few friends over on Saturday to watch the ball game. To top it all off, Bruno enjoyed scrambled eggs and potatoes for dinner. No, Bruno was all the companion Richard needed, all the companion he would ever need. On a scale of one to ten, he actually rated higher than the late missus, God rest her soul.

He and Bruno had grown very close over the years, each able to sense the other's needs. So when halfway through dinner Bruno started to growl in his low, rumbling voice, Richard knew that something was wrong.

"Shhh . . . take it easy. What's the matter, Bruno? You hear a fox?" Setting down his fork, he reached a reassuring hand beneath the table.

Richard peered out the window over the table but couldn't see anything in the darkness. Nor did he hear anything out of the ordinary. That didn't mean there wasn't someone messing around out there. Bruno had been right too many times in the past for Richard to doubt him now. Just last Wednesday they'd caught a carload of teenagers using his driveway as a place to park and get a little drunk.

Bruno stood up, the muscles in his haunches and neck tight with anticipation. He cocked his head, listening to sounds only he could hear. His growling grew louder.

"Okay, boy. I believe you. Let's say we go have a look outside."

Getting up from the table, Richard followed the dog down the narrow hallway to the back door. Opening it, they both stepped out onto a small, wooden back porch. Bruno's growling became more threatening.

"Who's out there?" Richard yelled.

There was no reply. The only sound was the wind gently caressing the leaves of the tall oak trees.

"I'm warning you, you'd better answer!"

Still no reply.

Bruno tensed; his muscles tightened.

"Sic 'em, boy!" Richard ordered.

Bruno exploded off the porch. Running low to the ground, he raced down the path leading through the woods to a small pond. Richard followed at a fast walk. He reached the edge of the woods in time to see the dog disappear around a curve. No sooner had Bruno slipped out of sight than the peaceful quiet of the night was shattered by the furious snarls of the pit bull on the attack.

Bruno had something!

Richard smiled. There wasn't anything on four legs or two that the dog couldn't handle. He'd only gone a few steps farther, however, when the snarling turned into high-pitched yelps of fear, and then into animal screams of pain.

Something had Bruno!

Richard hurried down the path, stopping when he reached the curve where he'd last seen the dog. There was no sign of him.

"Bruno!" he called.

All sounds of a confrontation had stopped. A strained silence descended over the forest. The crickets held their breath.

"Bruno . . ." he called again. "Here, boy." Richard heard the snapping of sticks, the rustling of dry leaves. Something moved a few yards ahead of him. The noises were heavy and loud, too loud to be made by a dog.

"Bruno?" Goose pimples broke out along his arms. The skin around his temples grew tight. "Damn it, Bruno. Are—"

Something sailed through the air, crashed to the ground in front of him. Richard jumped back, startled.

"What the hell?"

He took a hesitant step forward. The thing before him moved, lifted a head in his direction. It whimpered and cried, its body glistening in the moonlight. Richard took another step.

Not a possum. Not a coon.

Richard leaned closer, and suddenly realized what the creature was. He screamed.

"No! Please, God, nooo!"

He staggered back, clutching his chest. He hadn't known what it was at first. How was he supposed to know that the bloodied, raw body before him was his beloved pit bull, Bruno? The dog had been literally skinned alive, looking like something fresh from the womb, all wet and shiny, pink flesh white in the darkness.

Richard's heart constricted in pain; his eyes watered. The blood rushed from his head, causing his legs to fold up under him like an accordion. He tried to catch himself from falling but failed. Arms outstretched before him, his left hand struck Bruno's bloody body and slipped off.

Pain flashed white behind his eyes as Richard struck the ground. The impact caused him to bite his tongue. He tasted blood. Stunned, he didn't move, content to lie there and feel the pain. But then he realized that his left hand was lying across Bruno's side.

He jerked his hand back as though burnt. The sudden movement launched another explosion of colors through his brain. Richard didn't care. He pushed himself up into a kneeling position. There was blood on the palm of his hand. Bruno's blood. The air about him stank of it. The smell entered his nostrils, gagging him.

He shook his head to clear his mind, to keep from getting sick. There was nothing he could do for Bruno. As he watched, the pit bull's life ended with a wheezy gasp and a final shudder. The dog's tongue rolled limply out from between his heavy jaws. A froth of pinkish liquid followed.

Dead. Bruno was dead.

A strange, crackling noise drew his attention away from Bruno. It sounded like someone crunching a giant bag of potato chips, or electricity sparking from the end of a live wire. The noise came from every direction at once. Richard looked about, searching for the source of the crackling, but the darkness refused to reveal its secret. Then, a scant twenty yards away from him, something emerged from the trees.

Oh, my God.

The creature was huge, monstrous, the biggest thing Richard had ever seen—bigger even than the bears he and Jewell saw at the St. Louis Zoo back in '73. It stood on the trail, staring at him with a pair of glowing yellow eyes. Snake eyes.

For some strange reason Richard felt that the creature was studying him, sizing him up for one reason or another. He also had the feeling it was going to do the same thing to him that it did to Bruno.

Run!

With a gasp of fear, Richard struggled to his feet. The thing with the glowing eyes came toward him.

He had to get out of the forest, had to make it to his trailer or he was a dead man. Even then, he couldn't be sure if he would be safe. Could the trailer's thin aluminum walls keep out such a beast? He had no other choice: there was no place else to hide.

Fighting terror so powerful he could taste it, Richard began to stagger down the path when a pain suddenly pierced his laboring heart, an excrutiating burning that stabbed deep into his chest. A familiar agony, one he had experienced three years earlier. Richard was having a heart attack.

"Please, no. Not now. Not now . . ."

His bottle of heart medicine sat on the nightstand beside his bed. He hadn't thought he would be needing it. His heart had been fine for years. But the shock of seeing Bruno killed—seeing the monster—was too much.

The pain struck again, harder, spreading from his shoulder down to the tips of his fingers. An invisible knife driven deep into a heart that was already scarred and weak. Richard grabbed his left side and doubled over. He tried to tell himself that the pain was no worse than a bad case of gas, but that wasn't true. It was much worse.

Gathering his courage, he glanced behind him. The creature still followed, but it wasn't any closer. Maybe he would make it to his trailer after all. Perhaps there was hope yet . . .

A dark thought crossed his mind. Why wasn't it any closer? He was barely moving, his walk a mere shuffle. The creature should have caught up with him, but it hadn't. Why?

Suddenly, he knew. The thing chasing him was making a game of the chase.

Holding his side tighter, ignoring the pain, Richard did something he hadn't done in years: he ran. He ran with all his might until he reached the tiny clearing behind his mobile home. Then it hit him—the fiery pain of a bursting heart. Like a speeding meteor it exploded through his chest and down the veins in his arms and legs, ripping out capillaries and artery walls along the way.

The muscles in the left side of his face constricted, forcing the corner of his mouth to turn down in a sneer. Saliva drooled over his lower lip. His left arm and leg went numb. He fell forward, his face striking the hard stones of his driveway. He was only twenty feet from the back door, close enough to see through the kitchen window. He could see the Felix the Cat clock that hung on the wall, its eyes moving slowly back and forth. Tick tock, tick tock.

Richard started crawling, his right hand digging into the ground, pulling his failing body along. He had to bite his lower lip to keep from crying out, but he refused to give up.

The back porch drew steadily nearer. Another ten feet and he would reach it, another five after that to the door. He was going to make it!

From behind him came the rush of movement. Richard heard a low growl. Or was it a laugh? He didn't have to look to know that he wasn't going to make it to the back door. Ironically, his last thoughts weren't of agony, suffering and death, but of the plate of scrambled eggs and taters growing cold on the kitchen table.

Chapter 6

Jay Little Hawk's eyes were closed, his breathing shallow. Torrents of sweat streamed off his naked body. In his right hand he held an eagle feather; in his left he held his medicine pipe. A bucket of cold spring water sat by his side; next to it was a small wooden bowl containing the smoking mixture—kin-nikinnick—he used in his pipe.

Ignoring the intense, almost stifling heat in the sweat lodge, he dipped the feather in the bucket and sprinkled water over the heated bricks before him. The bricks hissed and crackled as a billowing cloud of steam rose toward the curved ceiling.

No taller than a man's chest, the sweat lodge was made of twenty-eight bent pine saplings covered with tightly stretched blankets of assorted colors. The floor of the sweat lodge was bare earth, covered with scrap pieces of old carpet. In the center of the lodge a circular pit was scooped out. In this pit were laid eight fireplace bricks. Hawk had heated the bricks to the point of exploding in a small fire just outside the lodge.

Taking a deep breath, Hawk began to recite a prayer taught to him by his grandfather. As he did he tossed a twisted braid of sweetgrass onto the steaming bricks. The sweetgrass was an offering to the spirit world, a gift to those he would ask for help.

Allowing time for the sweetgrass to smolder and burn, scenting the air with its haylike fragrance, he began to fill his pipe.

The clay bowl of Hawk's pipe was about an inch in diameter and a little over two inches deep. The clay came from the hills of North Carolina, as did the wood used in making the twenty-inch stem. The rectangular stem was wrapped in buckskin and gray rabbit fur, with a golden eagle feather hanging beneath the point where it joined the bowl. At the base of the bowl four lines were drawn to represent the four different directions—the four winds.

Lighting his pipe, Little Hawk prayed.

It was almost dark when he emerged from the sweat lodge. Shivering slightly from the crisp air, he quickly dried himself with a towel and pulled on his jeans and shirt. He paused briefly while slipping on his socks and boots to watch the last sliver of sun sink behind the towering hills to the west. The hills, some of the tallest in Hobbs County, were separated from the one his modest two-bedroom cabin perched atop by a steep valley. In the middle of the valley flowed a stream whose waters were still pure enough to drink. From where he stood, he could just see the little stream, its surface glowing like molten lava with the reflection of the sunset.

Hawk's greatest pleasure in life was to sit on his back porch, a fresh cup of coffee in hand, watching the day fade into twilight. Unfortunately, he found little pleasure in it this evening. His mind was still troubled over his experience at the Devil's Boot. Never before had he felt such evil. A white man might have passed it off as a bad case of nerves, or an overworked imagination, but Hawk knew better. He'd been a shaman for too long, seen too many things, to go waving off what had touched him as a flight of fancy.

So he had come home and entered the sweat lodge to cleanse his spirit of the vileness that had touched it, and to prepare for the ordeal of a vision quest.

Hawk's first vision quest came during his manhood rites, at the ripe old age of thirteen. After a ritual sweatbath his grandfather took him to a barren hillside on the southern tip of the reservation. For four days and nights he stayed in a deep pit—alone, scared, cold, without food and with little water. He lost weight and grew so weak that he was unable to walk. But the vision he sought eventually came. With it came a new understanding of the purpose of his life, as well as an insight to the path he would follow.

In twenty-five years he had gone on only five vision quests, each time seeking answers to difficult problems in his life. Hopefully the answers he sought this time would come to him as they had in the past. Maybe they would come tonight.

Wrapping his pipe in a soft piece of leather, Hawk threw his blanket over his shoulder—a gift from his grandfather, the same blanket he had worn on his first vision quest. In the center of the bright red blanket was sewn a yellow turtle. The blanket offered more than just warmth, it offered comfort and reassurance, for in just about every Indian tribe the turtle is a powerful spirit. *Nobody messes with the turtle.*

Hawk followed a narrow path to the opposite side of the valley. Reaching the top of a hill, he stared down into a dark hole measuring roughly six feet deep and four feet across—somewhat smaller than he usually dug them. The size didn't matter, however; it's what would happen once he entered the vision pit that was important.

Setting his blanket and pipe on the ground, Hawk lowered himself into the hole. Once in, he retrieved both items, wrapping the blanket around his shoulders. With pipe in hand, he walked slowly around the pit in a clockwise direction. The walking had no religious significance; he was just making damn sure nothing had crawled in during his absence. Sitting on a rattlesnake or bobcat was an experience he could do without. Satisfied he was the sole occupant of the pit, Hawk sat down with his back against the dirt wall, facing south.

With his right hand he dug a small hole in the ground at his feet. In it he placed a pinch of kinnikinnick as a gift to Mother Earth. Next he filled the pipe, silently praying as he packed the tiny leaves into the bowl. He lit the mixture with a match, offering the pipe to the Great Spirit, Mother Earth and the four directions. Raising the pipe above his head, he prayed aloud. He said a prayer for all the living things on earth, for all things have spirits and these spirits can offer aid when asked in the proper manner. But aid is offered only to those worthy of receiving it. Hawk sincerely hoped he was worthy.

It was hard to say when the vision actually started, though it couldn't have been more than a couple of hours after entering the pit. The first indication that something was happening was a gradual lightening of the area around him. While the area outside the pit remained unchanged, Hawk suddenly could see everything inside the pit, as if someone were holding a soft light over his shoulder. He could see the brown, skeletonlike fingers of a tree root protruding from the opposite wall, and the loose dirt that had fallen back in when he climbed into the pit. Even a shiny black beetle was clearly visible as it scampered up the wall of dirt and rock.

The unusual illumination was followed almost immediately by the soft, rustling sounds of something walking slowly toward the pit. At first Hawk mistook the sounds for the padded footfalls of some small woodland creature. As he listened, however, he became aware that they never seemed to get any closer, or any farther away. Nor did they falter or stop at any time as they moved in a clockwise direction around the pit.

The muffled footfalls continued for what seemed

twenty minutes before gradually fading to silence. They were replaced by the sound of two wooden sticks being beaten together. A hollow sort of sound, it seemed to echo, or to be answered, from three different directions. No doubt these sounds signaled the arrival of the spirits.

Whispering a prayer of strength, Hawk refilled and lit his pipe. He'd just taken his second puff when he became aware that he was no longer alone. Though he couldn't see anything, he could distinctly hear the labored breathing of someone, or something, directly across from him. He also detected a faint, musty odor. He sniffed. The smell was like freshly plowed fields after a summer rain, the aroma of rich bottom lands along the Missouri River, the deep black soil of Mother Earth.

Moments later he detected another presence in the pit with him. Hawk could actually feel someone sitting to his left, his body touching his. No sooner had this unseen something been felt than it was joined by yet another visitor to Hawk's right. The three different presences formed an invisible wall around him, leaving only his back—which was pressed firmly against the dirt wall—unguarded.

Breathlessly he waited. He knew the spirits were likely to do one of three things before offering to help him in his vision quest: they would either surround him with a warm feeling of happiness and love, as they had done on his first vision quest, or they would mischievously play with him, *or* they would test him to see if he was worthy of their consideration. They chose to test him.

All at once, a pair of disembodied eyes appeared in the darkness before Little Hawk. Just eyes. No face. No body. Nothing else. Floating about three feet above the ground, they blinked, danced and rolled in invisible sockets.

The eyes came closer, stopping a few inches away from his face. Hawk didn't move. To show fear at such a time would mean to fail, to be considered unworthy of any assistance from the spirit world. Worse yet, it would mean he wasn't fit to be a shaman.

An invisible hand grabbed his right thigh. Through his jeans he could feel the touch of bony fingers and sharp nails. Another spectral hand mockingly caressed the left side of his face. The stench of foul breath engulfed him, the smell of the grave seemed to rise from the black earth, sending his mind reeling with nausea. From somewhere beyond the pit a piercing scream shattered the night. The scream was followed by a laugh so hideous it made his arms and legs break out in quivering gooseflesh.

The sound of sticks being beaten together returned, this time louder, faster. Not far from the pit an unseen animal—if it truly was an animal—snarled and hissed.

The eyes in front of him faded and disappeared. The hand gripping his thigh released its hold. From beyond the pit came a howl. With breathless anticipation, Hawk waited to see what would happen next.

A shapeless patch of translucent white vapor suddenly swooped into the pit, disappearing into the ground at his feet. Hawk sat very still. Seconds later, the vapor reappeared from the ground.

Like steam from an overheated radiator, the vapor spewed forth. It boiled, rolled, condensed and took on shape. As he watched, the vapor transformed into the spirit of an Indian warrior.

The spirit warrior was about Hawk's height, maybe a little taller, his rugged beauty marred only by a sadness in his eyes. He wore his hair parted down the middle, his two long braids wrapped in leather and fur. Shell earrings adorned his ears, a string of bear claws hung around his neck. A breastplate of bone was worn over a beaded shirt of tanned buckskin. His leggings and breechcloth were also beaded, his moccasins were not.

Though Hawk could see the warrior clearly, he could also see through him. The spirit looked down upon him for a moment or two, then slowly raised his right hand in a sign of greeting. Hawk returned the greeting. The spirit smiled, nodded, changed back into mist and soared upward into the night sky.

No sooner had the first spirit left than a second warrior appeared. Like the first, he too extended the sign of greeting before sailing up into the sky. A third soon followed . . . and a fourth.

One after another they came, an endless parade of spirits flying upward to touch the stars and heavens above. All told, over thirty warriors appeared before

Hawk, each greeting him before vanishing into the darkness.

Never had he been so honored. In fact, as far as Hawk knew, few Indians had ever experienced such a wonderful sight. Though Hawk's heart was happy, his mind was troubled. To have so many spirits show up at a vision quest was highly unusual. It could only mean that something of great importance was to be learned tonight, something which could have a direct effect not only on him but on all his people.

Twenty minutes had passed since the last spirit appeared. With the passing of the warriors, the presences in the pit—as well as the sounds beyond—faded away. All was silent. Hawk was beginning to wonder if the vision was over when a white moth fluttered into the pit. Knowing it was too cold a night for moths, he immediately recognized the tiny insect for what it truly was: a messenger.

Circling the pit, the moth alighted upon Hawk's left shoulder. No sooner had the moth landed than a voice began to whisper in his ear. The voice was familiar; he knew it well. It was the soft, gentle voice of his grandfather.

The voice of Hawk's grandfather, coming from the mouth of the moth, began to tell an incredible story, a legend involving a famous Indian warrior, his brother—a prophet—and a creature from the dawn of time.

Chapter 7

In the dense shadows of a forest, at the edge of a vast field, a nightmare crouched . . . and waited. It was only thirty minutes since the Crota had last killed, but it seemed like a lifetime to the monster. The bloodlust still coursed through the creature's veins.

The cows huddled at the far corner of the field, their bodies pressed tightly against a barbed-wire fence. They bellowed in fear and cast worried glances at the darkness around them. But the Crota wasn't interested in the females—not yet, anyway. There would be plenty of time later for the easy slaughter, for the feast. For the present, he was only interested in the thrill of a challenge.

With a savage snarl, the creature moved into the open. The air about him crackled and popped with vibrant energy—his energy.

Muscles tensed and rippled under a faint sheen of sweat as the Hereford bull ripped open the ground in great furrows. The earth shook beneath the thunderous challenge of the animal. Eyes blazing, back arching, the bull blew streamers of snot from flared nostrils. Around the pasture the night grew deathly still. The whippoorwill hushed its song, and the cicadas were mute. Everything waited; everything watched. Overhead, the moon hid its face in fear behind a passing cloud.

Tapping the ashes into an old coffee can, Roy Owens slipped his pipe into the breast pocket of his overalls and stood up. Anna would be setting supper on the table any minute and he still needed to wash up. There were only two things his wife ever fussed at him about: smoking his pipe in the house, and being late getting to the supper table.

As he opened the door separating the screened back porch from the rest of the house, his attention was distracted by the bawling of the cows. He usually couldn't hear them when they were out in the back pasture, but the wind happened to be blowing from that direction. As he listened, the cries of the cows grew louder. Something was upsetting the herd. Maybe they had caught wind of a bobcat. He'd better go check on them.

Anna was wiping her hands on a flowered dish towel when he stepped into the kitchen. Hearing the clomp of his work boots on the tiled floor, she turned from the stove.

"Roy, you about ready? Supper's almost on the table."

He didn't answer. Crossing the room, he opened the door of the hallway closet, taking out a red flannel shirt and his favorite cap (bright green with a John Deere emblem on the front). He never went anywhere without his cap.

"Now where are you off to?" Anna inquired. A frown tugged at the corners of her mouth. She was probably worried about the meat loaf getting cold. It took all afternoon to fix it the way he liked it.

"Something's got the cows spooked," he answered. "Probably that bobcat again. I'd better go check."

He slipped a flashlight into his back pocket. Fumbling past the jackets and other clothing in the closet, he pulled out his old single-shot twelve gauge. A half-full box of number-eight shells went into the leg pocket of his bib overalls.

"Well, you hurry back," Anna fussed. "The meat loaf won't be worth a flip if it gets cold."

"Hot or cold, it's still the best meat loaf in the state," he said. "Who knows, maybe I'll bring you back a new fur coat."

Anna laughed. "Out of one bobcat? It'd have to be an awfully small coat."

The bellowing was even louder when he stepped back outside. Even Old Bubba had gotten into the act. The deep bass voice of the big bull was easily identifiable from the rest of the herd. From the way it sounded he was mad as hell about something. Had to be that damn bobcat again.

"This ought to take care of the varmint," Roy said, patting the side of the shotgun. "Here, kitty, kitty."

* * *

The Crota crouched no more than twenty feet from Bubba, the muscles in his hind legs twitching with excitement. He inhaled deeply, taking in all of the night scents, savoring the sweet smells of sweat and fear. Bubba blew a final warning, then charged.

With head low to angle his deadly horns straight ahead, Bubba raced toward the Crota like a locomotive. The distant trees echoed his thunderous charge.

With a roar, the Crota lunged to meet the bull. They collided in the middle of the field.

Crash!

Bubba tried to run down his opponent, trample him beneath his hooves, but the Crota stopped his charge with ease. Finding that he could not overpower the monster, the bull turned and ducked, his left horn piercing the Crota's upper thigh. Blood flowed.

The Crota hissed in anger. Razor-sharp claws flashed like lightning through the air, ripping bloody furrows in the Hereford's sensitive nose. Bubba bellowed and twisted violently, trying to shake off his attacker. The Crota hung on. Leaning sideways, he bit off the bull's right ear, bringing him to the point of madness.

Hearing the commotion, Roy began to run. From the sounds of the fight, he knew it wasn't any bobcat Bubba was tangling with. Maybe someone was trying to rustle his prize bull.

He reached the edge of the back pasture at the same time the moon slipped out from behind the clouds, giving him a clear view of what was happening. What he saw caused him to doubt his sanity.

"Mother of God!"

Old Bubba was no more than thirty yards away. His body shuddered and shook as his back legs strained, his hooves digging into the soft earth. Foam dripped from the bull's mouth, and great clouds of white blew from his nostrils.

Standing erect, front legs wrapped around Bubba's horns, was a creature the likes of which Roy had never seen before. It was as big as a grizzly, maybe bigger, its scaly, reddish-brown hide spotted with tufts of red hair. Framed with a mane like a lion's, the head was a demented cross between a bear, a boar and a dog. Under a wrinkled snout, a wide, lizardlike mouth opened to reveal pointed teeth. But the most frightening feature was the creature's eyes—slanted, with black slitlike pupils, glowing luminescent yellow in the moonlight.

Roy was so entranced by the scene before him he forgot about the shotgun cradled in his arms. He watched as Bubba twisted and ducked, seeking a vital spot on the monster. There was a sharp crack as the thing countered the move by breaking off one of Bubba's horns.

The sight of the creature tearing off Bubba's horn, like someone pulling the wing from a Sunday chicken, brought Roy back to his senses. Muttering a curse, he raised the shotgun to his shoulder and fired.

The blast of the shotgun was answered by a roar

so hideous it made Roy's legs go rubbery. It must have had the same effect on the cows, for they suddenly quit their bellowing.

With a movement almost too quick for Roy's eyes to follow, the monster let go of Bubba's remaining horn and dropped to the ground. The bull, carried forward by his own momentum, passed directly over the creature. As he did the Crota slashed upward and back, deadly claws sinking deep into the bull's unprotected belly.

A shower of blood sprayed the ground beneath Bubba. Blood gushed from his nostrils. Then, as the bull shook in agony, his guts tumbled to the ground like a nest of steaming snakes. Bubba, the blue-ribbon winner of six county fairs, was killed.

Sweet mother of God, that thing killed Bubba.

With mounting fear, Roy realized that up until the time he shot at it the monster had been toying with the bull, playing with it as a cat would a mouse. He also realized that the monster may have been playing with Bubba, but it wasn't going to play with him.

Dear God.

Frantic, Roy fumbled for the box of shotgun shells in his pocket. The monster rolled over, got to its feet, turned its head and watched him.

Dear God. Dear God. Dear God.

In his haste to reload the shotgun Roy spilled the box of shells on the ground. He dropped to his knees, trembling fingers snatching madly at the loose shells. The monster roared. Roy had just gotten a shell into the chamber when the thing charged.

* * *

Anna Owens stood in the doorway, listening to the sounds coming from the back pasture. She'd been a country girl long enough to know that no bobcat could ever cause that kind of ruckus, nor could a pack of dogs. Something was wrong, very wrong. For the first time in years she wasn't worried about supper getting cold. She was frightened. If only Roy would hurry up and come back, she'd never again fuss at him about smoking his pipe in the house.

The shotgun blast made her jump, but not nearly as bad as the roar that followed it. The silence after that was but a brief one, broken by a scream that made all the blood drain from her face. It wasn't the cry of an animal. The scream was human.

Tears clouding her eyes, she grabbed the telephone and dialed the Hobbs County Sheriff's Office. She didn't wait to answer any questions; she just gave her name and address, then hung up. There wasn't time to give any more; she had to hurry. Roy might be hurt.

The thought of her husband lying injured flooded her mind as she raced down the path leading to the back pasture. She hadn't even bothered to grab her wrap, but the night chill went unnoticed.

Reaching the pasture, she found everything as quiet as . . .

As quiet as a graveyard.

Why is it so quiet?

"Roy?" There was no answer.

Crossing the field, she headed toward the back

fence where the water trough and feeder were located. That's where the cows usually gathered after dark. Find the cows and she'd find Roy. A third of the way across the field she paused, puzzled.

To her left a small dark mound rose above the weeds. She'd been in the pasture thousands of times, yet she didn't remember seeing such a mound before. Curious, she left the path and walked toward it.

"Roy?" she called. Still no reply.

Anna was afraid to call again. There was something about the silence that scared her, something far worse than the scream she'd heard only minutes before. A cold feeling of dread settled deep in her stomach.

Halfway to the mound, she tripped over something and went sprawling. Pain flashed up her arm as her left wrist twisted beneath her.

"Ow!"

Sitting up, she vigorously massaged her wrist with her right hand.

Anna stopped rubbing.

The palm of her right hand was wet and sticky. The wetness smeared across her wrist. The palm of her left hand was also wet, as was the grass about her.

How odd.

It was too early for the dew to set in, and it hadn't rained in days.

Looking about her, she noticed that the grass where she sat looked darker than elsewhere in the field. It obviously wasn't water that wet her hands and soaked through the back of her dress.

A shudder danced along Anna's spine. She didn't want to think about what could be wet, sticky to the touch, and look black in the darkness. She quickly stood up.

Back on her feet, she retraced her path, searching for what she'd tripped over. She'd only taken a few steps when she came across a green John Deere cap lying in the weeds.

Roy's cap.

Roy never went anywhere without his cap. So what was it doing here? She reached down to retrieve the cap when she realized there was something in it. . . .

"Oh, God! Oh, God! No! No . . ."

Jamming a fist against her mouth, she stifled the scream trying to tear from her throat. Roy's severed head stared at her with unblinking eyes, questioning, demanding. His mouth hung open in a silent scream.

The world began to spin slowly sideways. Anna didn't want to faint. She pushed her fist even tighter against her mouth and bit down. There was a funny taste on her lips. A salty taste.

Horror seized her heart as she realized that the wetness on her hand was now smeared across her mouth. The salty, sticky wetness of blood. Roy's blood.

Anna staggered back, gasping for breath. She tried to spit the taste of blood from her mouth but it wouldn't go away. The world around her blurred into dizzying shades of gray. She didn't know whether she was going to be sick or pass out. Roy's head peeked at her through the weeds. It looked as though he was standing in a hole.

Suddenly, from her right came a series of sharp cracking sounds, like someone ripping nails from boards. Not really wanting to see what caused them, but knowing she had to, Anna turned and slowly walked in the direction of the sounds. She moved as if in a dream.

Another one of the mysterious mounds lay near the back fence . . . and another . . . and another. They were a little smaller than the first mound. As Anna drew closer she discovered that the mounds were the bodies of her cows. But even though she now knew what the mounds were, she didn't flee. She knew she should, but she couldn't. Her legs wouldn't obey her. They refused to allow her to turn around and go in the opposite direction, or to even stop where she was. She could no more escape than could a rabbit after it has heard the piercing cry of a winged hunter. When Anna finally did stop she was standing no more than ten feet from the source of the peculiar cracking noise. The sound was that of bones being splintered and crushed between powerful jaws.

Pausing in the midst of his feeding, the Crota regarded the intruder with open curiosity. He made no move to attack, for he did not feel threatened by the woman standing before him. Instead, he leaned forward and pulled another rib bone from the body of the dead cow. The sound of the bone snapping made him happy. Throwing back his head, he laughed.

Chapter 8

Corporal Randy Murphy turned off of Cemetery Road onto the driveway leading up to the home of Mr. and Mrs. Roy Owens. He drove slowly, angling the cruiser around potholes and using the spotlight to light up the front of the house.

The Owens's residence was a single-story, white and beige, ranch-style house with a screened-in back porch and adjoining carport. A white Buick was parked in the carport. Beyond it a gray tarpaulin covered a bulky shape which was probably a tractor. Randy pulled around to the rear of the house and parked. The flashing blue lights of his patrol car reflected eerily off the aluminum siding of the house, giving everything a carnivallike atmosphere.

The door separating the back porch from the house stood open, providing a view of an empty hallway. The curtains on the kitchen window were also open, but Randy didn't see anyone in the kitchen either.

The dispatcher said the woman who called sounded frantic—terrified, even. She'd hung up after giving only her name and address. Randy didn't like that. It was dangerous responding to a call when you didn't know the situation. A fellow could get his head blown off. He kept thinking of the previous evening's murders.

"Well, here goes nothing."

Grabbing the six-cell flashlight from beside him on the seat, he slid out of the patrol car. He just didn't like the look of things. His instincts told him something was wrong.

Reaching the porch, Randy unsnapped the safety strap on his holster, freeing his Smith & Wesson 9mm automatic. He knocked loudly on the screen door.

"Hello . . . Sheriff's Department. Anybody home?"

Inside sat two wooden straight-backed chairs with a small dropleaf table between them. Metal shelves, crowded with Mason jars of fruits and vegetables, lined one end of the porch while a chest-type freezer took up most of the space at the opposite end. Not getting a response to his knock, he tried the door. It was unlocked.

Randy crossed the porch to the open doorway of the house and peeked in. The narrow hallway ran about ten feet to his right, ending at a closed door behind which was probably a bedroom. To his left the hallway passed a bathroom, another bedroom and a sewing room before opening onto a combination kitchen-dining room. He stepped into the dining room and looked around. Matching cabinets and counters of brown were set off by yellow-flowered wallpaper. The only sound was the soft, steady hum of the refrigerator.

"Hello . . . anybody home?"

No answer.

Two place settings were arranged on the table, knives, forks and napkins at the ready. A meat loaf sat on a glass serving platter in the center of the stove, flanked by pans of creamed corn and mashed potatoes. He lightly touched a fingertip to the meat loaf. It was cold.

Beyond the dining area was the living room. The color TV opposite the two recliners was still on, but the sound had been turned all the way down. Beyond the living room, a door opened onto the master bedroom. It too was empty.

Retracing his steps, he checked the other rooms but found nothing out of the ordinary in any of them. Everything appeared to be the way it should be. No sign of a disturbance. The only thing missing were the owners.

Randy stepped back outside, glad to be free of the strange quiet inside the house. But it was just as quiet outside. Having been raised on a farm, he found the silence disturbing. Even on the calmest of nights there were sounds: birds, crickets, frogs. And surely someone would have heard his siren when he drove up, even if they were elsewhere on the farm.

Leaning in through the open window of the patrol car, Randy called the station to tell them of the situation. He also let them know he was going to have a look around the area. The dispatcher confirmed the message, advising him that Unit One was in the area if he needed them. He said he didn't think so, and signed off.

His first stop was the barn. The bright red building sat about three hundred yards from the house. Opening a side door, he was greeted with the musty scents of animals, hay and manure. He was cautious to look where he stepped.

The ground level of the barn was divided into a pen for livestock, and a storage area for feed and . . .

Whoooo . . . !

Randy spun around, his right hand going for the handle of his gun.

Who . . . who . . . whoooooo!

The sound came from above him. He aimed his flashlight at the ceiling. There, perched on a rafter in the back corner, was a pair of barn owls, their snowy white faces twin moons in the darkness. He let out a sigh of relief, annoyed at the way his heart raced.

"Stupid birds," he muttered.

Whooo!

"You. That's who," he said, retracing his steps back outside.

Since no livestock was in the barn, the animals must be in a pasture somewhere. Perhaps, he thought, something had happened to one of them and the owners had gone to administer aid. If so, maybe they were still out in the field and weren't aware of his arrival. On the back side of the barn he spotted a well-worn path leading into the woods. There were cattle droppings on the path, so maybe it led to a field not visible from the barn or house. It was worth taking a look.

The woods he entered ended about as quickly as they began. The path did indeed lead to another pasture. The grassy field, wet from the first of the evening dew, shone like a multitude of diamonds under the bright moonlight. The scene might have been picturesque if it weren't for the uneasy quietness cloaking the area. And there was a funny smell carried on the wind. Having worked at a local slaughterhouse, Randy recognized the unpleasant, rusty odor as the stench of blood and raw meat.

Drawing his pistol, he advanced forward, swinging his flashlight to illuminate the area before him. He'd walked about fifty feet when he came across the shredded, bloody remains of a man's red flannel shirt.

Randy knew better than to touch the shirt. Instead he walked a wide path around it and continued on. A few yards farther on he discovered the owner of the shirt, or at least what was left of him.

"Shit!" he exclaimed, jumping back.

The body was terribly mutilated—the head missing, the right arm torn off at the shoulder. Huge gashes, like wounds caused by a machete, were cut into the chest and stomach at right angles to each other. Spirals of steam rose from these gashes, ghostlike in the night air.

It's still warm. Couldn't have been too long since this happened.

He turned and looked around, searching for a

piece of machinery—a thrasher or brush hog, perhaps—that the man must have fallen into or been run over by. No such machinery sat in the field. But there had to be. What else could chop up a man in such a way? Randy looked down at the body. It looked like something fished out of a gator pit.

Chewed.

He stepped back. The darkness seemed to close in, suffocating him. The man hadn't been run over by a piece of farm machinery. He'd been murdered—hacked to death by someone, or something. Maybe the killer was still around, watching.

Randy's grip tightened on his pistol as a tingle of fear danced along his spine. He hadn't brought along his portable radio, which meant he would have to return to the patrol car to call for backup. Did he dare? Calling for assistance was standard procedure. But what if the killer was still around? Returning to the car might allow the maniac the chance to slip away unnoticed. To leave the field could be a mistake. He had to look around first and secure the area.

Turning away from the mutilated body, he walked slowly toward the back fence. Less than a minute later, he came across a second body.

Like a beached whale, the bull lay on its left side, legs sticking straight out. The animal's eyes were open, but only the white of the irises showed. The tongue protruded gray and limp from the mouth. Next to the body, between the front and back legs, were the bull's internal organs.

"What the hell is going on here?" he asked aloud.

His voice sounded much too loud. The silence made him nervous. Shining his flashlight in the direction of the back fence, he was startled to see someone standing there.

"Sheriff's Department! Identify yourself!" Randy yelled, his voice cracking. There was no disguising his fear.

The figure near the fence didn't acknowledge the command or make any attempt to flee. The distance was still too great, and the night too dark, to tell who it was.

"Who's there?" he called again.

No reply.

If it was the killer, then why didn't he make a run for it? Was it a trap? Could it be an attempt to lure him closer, bringing him within range of a gun or knife? A string of questions flashed through his mind, any one of which, if answered wrongly, could cost him his life.

Keeping his eyes on the suspect, he circled toward a stand of pine trees on his right. He intended to use the trees for protection in case gunplay erupted.

Halfway to the suspect, the corporal halted. He was suddenly experiencing a feeling of being watched. Never in his life had he felt such a sensation. It was as if some hidden danger had set off a series of tiny warning signals in his head. Was someone else in the area? Did the person by the fence have an accomplice? Was he walking into a trap?

Keeping the unmoving suspect within his peripheral vision, he swept the wooded area near him with the bright beam of his flashlight. The feeling of being watched grew stronger. Holding the light steady, he tried to peer through the underbrush, but it was so thick that visibility ended ten feet into the trees. If someone was there, he could pass right by them and not know it.

Close enough to get a knife in the back.

Randy turned his attention back to the party standing at the fence. He could see it was a woman, though her back was turned to him. Did her hands, unseen, clutch the metallic smoothness of a pistol? A knife?

"Hello!"

No answer.

Randy crouched, ready for action. He approached from the side.

He could see her a little better now: brown hair worn tied up, a plain blue, short-sleeved dress. No coat or jacket.

"Lady, are you all right?" Dumb question. It was obvious she wasn't. He stepped in front of her—

And gasped.

She was standing there, stiff as a board, arms limp at her side. Her face was a waxen mask without expression. Her eyes, open and glassy, were rolled back into their sockets.

"Ma'am?" He stepped forward and gently touched her cheek. There was no response.

She's in shock.

"Jesus, you're cold. We've got to get you to a hospital, and fast. Here . . . put this on." He removed his insulated jacket and slipped it over her shoulders. He might as well have been dressing a department-store mannequin. She didn't move; she didn't talk. In fact, she barely breathed.

"Listen, I've got to get you inside where it's warm—"

A strange crackling interrupted his train of thought. It was like a sudden buildup of static electricity.

"What the hell is that?"

He stepped away from the woman. The feeling of being watched returned, grew stronger. His heart thudded madly as a wave of black fear washed over him. He knew it wasn't just the two of them. Without knowing how he knew, Randy knew the killer was still around. Maybe it was a foolish thought wanting to come face to face with the killer. Maybe he'd bitten off more than he could chew.

The crackling grew stronger, the feeling of fear more intense. From the woods to his left came sounds of movement. The sounds drew nearer.

His flashlight fell unnoticed to the ground. Bracing himself, he gripped his pistol tightly in both hands, arms extended, elbows slightly bent, his finger on the trigger. He took a deep breath, and waited.

A dry twig snapped. A shadowy figure emerged from the woods, accompanied by a bobbing light. Another figure appeared. Another light. The first light swung his way. The crackling stopped.

The two figures came closer, took on definition. Arms, legs, faces and identities appeared. Randy let out a sigh of relief and gently lowered his gun. His hands were shaking so badly he could barely get the pistol back into its holster. One of those approaching stopped near the body of the mutilated man. The other kept coming.

"You okay, Murphy?" Lloyd shone a flashlight into Randy's face.

"Yeah, I'm fine," he lied, bending down to retrieve his dropped flashlight.

Lloyd nodded. He looked at the woman. "Who's this?"

Randy shook his head. "I don't know. She was just standing here. I think she's in shock. Maybe that's her husband lying over there. She might have seen it happen."

"How long ago did you find her?"

"Three, four minutes at the most. I heard you guys coming, thought it might be the killer coming back to take up where he left off."

Lloyd nodded. "You call for an ambulance yet?"

"Not yet. I didn't bring my portable with me."

"That explains why we couldn't reach you. Next time make damn sure you have your radio with you before leaving your patrol car."

"Right, I—"

Lloyd unclipped the portable radio from his belt, turning up the volume. "Dispatch, come in. This is Unit One. Over."

"Go ahead, One. Over," the radio squawked in reply.

"Roger, be advised we're gonna need backup and

an ambulance out here. We've got another J-Four on our hands. Also, you'd better get hold of Skip. We're gonna need him out here too. Over."

"Roger, One, will advise. Over."

Lloyd clicked the radio back off. It would have been better to call the report in over the telephone. Now everyone in the county with a scanner—and who had access to a list of department codes—would know there had been a non-accident-related death. Of course, everyone would know by morning anyway.

Hanging the radio back on his belt, he turned to Randy. "It'll take the ambulance at least twenty minutes to get here, probably take the sheriff a little longer than that."

"What about her?" Randy asked.

"The most important thing is to keep her warm until the ambulance arrives. Talk to her, that might snap her out of it. In the meantime I'm going to do a walk around and start securing the area."

"Go slow, that fucker might still be out here."

Lloyd nodded and hitched his gunbelt higher up on his hips.

Randy turned his attention back to the dazed woman. She hadn't moved an inch since he'd first laid eyes on her.

Jesus, she's really out of it.

How could anyone stand so still for so long? He thought about trying to get her to sit down, but changed his mind. He wasn't a doctor and wasn't about to take the chance of causing any injury. You wouldn't move a traumatic person at the scene of an automobile accident, and he wasn't going to do it here. No, Lloyd was right; all he could do was sit tight, and hope that whoever had stalked this field earlier wouldn't be back.

PART II

Chapter 9

MONDAY, SEPTEMBER 17

The sharp smell of grilled onions assaulted Skip as he entered Nancy's Cafe. The diner was busy, as it always was at lunchtime. Yellow-clad waitresses scampered roachlike around the room, delivering greasy condiments and filling empty coffee cups and tea glasses. Behind the Formica counter, burgers sizzled on a blackened grill while french fries bubbled and browned in golden vats of scalding oil. The murmur of voices mingled with the clanking of silverware and plates to create a sound that made him feel like he was inside some giant machine.

Pausing in the doorway, he removed his hat and aviator sunglasses. Two sweat-soaked carpenters were hard at work putting a new sheet of plate glass in the front window. They labored under the watchful eye of Nancy Remes, the diner's Oriental owner. She flashed Skip a quick smile, then went back to the task of supervising. If the carpenters had thoughts of doing a half-assed job, or of padding their list of expenses, they might as well forget it. Nancy was a shrewd businesswoman, not one to be easily fooled. Skip often wondered how a scrappy little lady from the Philippines ended up owning a burger joint in central Missouri. Maybe it *was* a small world after all.

Stepping over the tools near the entranceway, Skip made his way toward the booths in the back. As he passed the counter several customers turned curious faces his way. He ignored them. The last thing he wanted was to get trapped in a conversation. And he sure as hell didn't feel like being asked any more questions concerning the mutilations—questions he couldn't answer.

Katie was seated at their usual booth. She wore the gray shirt-and-jacket combination he liked so much. Her brunette hair was swept up, business-style. A thin gold chain hung about her neck.

Much too sexy to be a loan officer.

Noticing Skip's arrival, she put down her ink pen and closed the tiny black notebook she'd been writing in.

"You look dreadful," she said, as he folded himself into the seat across from her.

"Thanks. I'll have you know I *feel* dreadful too."

A frown shadowed her face. "You need to go home and get some rest."

No sooner had he gotten home last night than he'd had to rush out to the Owens place. He didn't get back until well after midnight and was gone again before the sun came up.

"I wish I could," he said, stealing a sip of her

water. He shook his head. "It's like a three-ring circus out there. I've got county cops showing up, city cops, politicians, veterinarians, off-duty firemen, reporters, news crews—you name it. Every damn one of them has an opinion about how I should do my job. I've had to borrow a couple of units from Warren County just to handle the gawkers. The traffic on Cemetery Road is practically bumper to bumper."

"I'll bet they're riding you pretty hard," she said.

Skip pulled a pack of cigarettes from his shirt pocket, lit one and blew smoke at the ceiling. "I'm the sheriff; who else they gonna ride?"

"They could be a little more patient." Her voice was firm. "Everybody knows you're doing the best you can."

He laughed. "Patient? Hell, I'm lucky they haven't started screaming for my badge. Three people brutally murdered, a score of cattle mutilated. That's not something that sets easy with a town this small. Christ, the Jerworski boy was only sixteen years old."

Buddy Jerworski's mother had positively identified the body. They had also found Buddy's Harley Davidson a couple of miles from the cemetery, hidden in a ditch beneath some branches.

"I'm telling you, people are scared," Skip continued. "And when people get scared they do stupid things. Several of the ones we turned back this morning were toting guns. I'm afraid someone innocent is going to get shot, maybe one of my deputies."

She laid her hand over his. "Any clues yet?"

"Nothing. No tire tracks, no footprints, no witnesses. Beautiful, huh?"

"What about Mrs. Owens?"

He shrugged. "The doctor says it's too early to tell. She might pull out of it; she might not. Right now she's a vegetable."

"Poor thing." Skip saw her frown. She was probably thinking how horrible it must have been to find her husband the way Mrs. Owens did, or what she would do in the same situation, which would only remind her how dangerous his job could be. They had talked before about him going into a different line of work—argued, actually. She hadn't forced the issue too much, knowing how much his job meant to him.

Marcella, the youngest of Nancy's three waitresses, arrived with Katie's order. She handed Skip a menu and flashed him a smile. He eyed Katie's tuna salad sandwich, thought about ordering the same, but decided on a cheeseburger with a side order of onion rings. Marcella jotted down the order, winked and strutted away. The wink didn't go unnoticed.

"Got something going on the side, have you?" Katie said. Marcella's flirtation was only harmless fun, and Katie knew it.

Skip cleared his throat. "It's the uniform, dear. Honest."

"I bet."

"Honey, you're the only woman in my life, I swear. I will love you 'til the day I die."

She smiled uneasily, hooking her index finger

under his chin. "That's an interesting choice of words."

Lloyd entered the diner noisily, greeting customers as he walked over, a stack of folders tucked neatly under his left arm.

"Greetings, Lloyd," Katie said, looking up from her sandwich.

"Hello, good-looking," Lloyd replied. "How about you and me running off to Mexico together?"

"Careful . . . I'll tell Barbara on you."

"Oh God, don't do that. She'll beat the hell out of me."

Skip motioned for Lloyd to join them. Katie slid over to make room.

"Do you know the mayor's looking for you?" Lloyd asked Skip.

"Let him look. You didn't tell him where I was, did you?"

Lloyd swiped a pickle off Katie's plate. "Are you kidding? I told him you had to run over to Warrenton and wouldn't be back for a couple of hours."

"What'd he say to that?"

"Let's just say he wasn't too happy."

Skip grinned. "Good. I hope it ruins his day." He looked at the folders. "What did you find out?"

"I spoke with Fred Granger a few minutes ago. He's still going over Roy's body with a fine-tooth comb."

"You mean he's going over what's left of it," commented Skip.

Katie's sandwich paused midway to her mouth.

"Yeah," Lloyd continued. "So far it looks like the same M.O. as the last one." He slid the folders across the table. "I got on the phone and called around like you asked. It seems there have been some sixteen hundred cases of cattle mutilation reported in twenty-eight different states."

Skip whistled in surprise.

"I couldn't get the specifics on all the cases, but I did get some information on the mutilations in Kansas, Arkansas and Minnesota. Fascinating stuff. No clues or physical evidence ever found around any of the bodies; nobody saw or heard anything; sexual organs, eyes and tongues surgically removed. In a couple of cases they found a filmy white substance that couldn't be identified stretching from the carcass to the ground."

Katie put down her sandwich.

"And nobody saw anything?" Skip asked.

"Not anything they could put their finger on. They did have a rash of UFO sightings—"

Skip held up his hand. "Hold it right there. Flying saucers and little green men?"

Lloyd frowned. "I just read the stuff, I don't write it."

"I'm sorry. Go ahead."

"Like I was saying," Lloyd continued. "At the time the mutilations occurred there was a rash of UFO sightings, but a connection could never be proven. There's also a couple of reports about unmarked helicopters buzzing ranch areas and leading the air force on a merry chase."

"Helicopters, huh?" Skip rubbed his chin thoughtfully. "I suppose it's a possibility. That would explain why we haven't found any tire tracks, or why nobody saw any suspicious vehicles in the area. You said some of the cattle had certain internal organs surgically removed?"

Lloyd pointed at one of the folders. Skip opened it and glanced through the computer printouts and fax copies.

"Sexual organs, mainly," Lloyd said. "In some cases the hide where the incisions were made looked burned. The most incredible thing is the total absence of blood remaining in the bodies. Do you have any idea how hard it would be to drain a full-grown cow of all its blood?"

Skip admitted he didn't.

"Hell, it would be next to impossible. First off, we're talking about a good sixty pints of blood. Even with a portable hand pump it would take you at least ninety minutes. Another thing, once you remove a third of the blood the veins collapse. The only way it could be done is by injecting a saline solution into the heart while the animal is still alive. The solution increases the heart rate and makes the blood pump faster."

"But the blood wasn't drained from the Owens's cattle," Skip stated. "And they were ripped apart, not surgically operated on."

"Yeah, I know," Lloyd nodded. "I think these files are all UFO nonsense, but they make great reading."

"Anything else?" Skip asked.

"Did I mention the devil-worshiping cults?"

Katie gave Skip a look. "No, you didn't," Skip said deliberately.

"Actually, they're not sure if it was devil-worshipers or not. There was one incident where a circular altar was found not far from where a couple mutilations had occurred. A couple of the stones used to form the circle had pentagrams and other religious signs on them. One had the word *Isis* painted on it. Isis was an Egyptian goddess, or something like that. It's all in the files."

Skip shook his head. "Well, Lloyd, I want to thank you: this really clears everything up. Jesus, if I didn't already have enough to think about, now I've got to consider bizarre cults and little green men from Mars."

"Sorry about that."

"Seriously, though, I would like to look into this cult thing a little more. Round up a few volunteers and go through the cemetery again. Look for unusual stone formations, names, carvings—anything that might indicate a cult is involved. I'm gonna see if I can't tear Doc Scriber away from his office for a couple of hours to take another look at those cows."

Lloyd started to rise.

"Oh, yeah," Skip said, remembering something. "There's been a reporter from the St. Louis *Post-Dispatch* hanging around the office. Take him with you. Keep him busy and out of my hair for a while."

Lloyd frowned. "Thanks a whole hell of a lot."

"Anytime," Skip smiled.

Lloyd left at the same time the waitress brought Skip's order to the table. Funny, but he didn't feel nearly as hungry. Maybe thoughts of cattle mutilations and a quarter-pound cheeseburger didn't go so well together. Electing to stick with just onion rings, he folded a napkin over the burger, laying it quietly to rest.

He said to Katie, "Look, I don't want Billy leaving the yard."

"You think there's any danger in town?" she asked.

Skip let out his breath. "I don't know. Three people dead in less than twenty-four hours and we don't have a clue to go on. At first I thought it might be drug related, but now I'm not so sure. Maybe it is some kind of cult. Lord knows what kids today are into."

"You think it's kids?" Katie asked.

He shook his head. "No . . . not really. I don't think kids could have done it; the murders are too vicious, too insane. Our killer isn't a kid. He's a monster."

Chapter 10

7:15 P.M.

The cow lay on its right side, legs stretching straight out. It had been split along its underside from about six inches back of the udder, right through the udder, with two teats on one side and two teats on the other, clean to the brisket between the front legs. The head of the cow had been split open lengthwise, the separation running between the upper and lower jaws, which looked as if they had been pulled in opposite directions, causing the entire head to rip all the way back to the base of the skull.

There were twelve bodies in all, eleven cows and one bull—thirteen if you counted Roy Owens at the morgue. *All the king's horses and all the king's men couldn't put Ol' Roy back together again.*

The poem came to Skip as he stood staring down at the mutilated cow. He almost smiled. Not that he found anything funny about the murder of Roy Owens, but wasn't it strange how the mind could conjure up humor in times of tragedy? Maybe it was a cushioning effect, the brain's way of softening the terror and protecting the sanity. Maybe he was just tired.

It'd been a waste of time coming back out to look for fingerprints. There weren't any. Nor would it do any good to look for footprints, because the ground was too torn up to make out individual tracks.

Closing the crime lab kit, Skip decided to walk around the outer perimeter of the field. He didn't expect to find anything, but he'd been at it for hours and wanted to get away from the rancid smell of blood and death.

The farther he walked, the fresher the air became. He'd almost forgotten what it was like to take a breath and not smell the stench of raw meat. He walked three hundred yards or better before stopping. Lighting a cigarette, he turned to survey the area.

From where he stood the crime scene looked like an oasis of light in a valley of shadows. Within that circle was Philip Scriber, the county veterinarian; five deputies; half a dozen public officials and two newspaper reporters. Skip felt detached from the activity taking place inside the circle of lights. Alone. He knew his detachment wouldn't last forever—there was still a lot of work to be done—but he was damn well going to enjoy his brief moment of solitude while it lasted.

Exhaling slowly, he gazed up at the sky. The muscles in his neck hurt; so did the ones in his lower back. He wasn't getting any younger. It wouldn't be too many more years before he started thinking about retiring. He laughed aloud. If he didn't come up with a suspect soon, he'd be retiring sooner than planned.

Rubbing the knotted muscles in his neck, he thought about Katie and Billy. They were probably sitting down to supper right then—TV dinners, most likely. Katie didn't like to cook when it was just the two of them. Billy didn't mind, to him a frozen dinner was just as good as a steak anytime.

"Shit . . . back to work."

Crushing the cigarette butt in the ground, he started back. It was already dark enough that he had to strain to see where he was walking. The last thing he needed was to step in cowshit. But getting a little manure on his boots was the least of his troubles.

Crouching in a dry creek bed, the Crota could barely contain his excitement as he watched Skip cross the field. The thought of killing another human delighted him. There wasn't much of a challenge in it, but he was still charged up from the previous evening's slaughter and felt an insatiable desire to kill again. His muscles tensed in preparation for the attack. He licked his lips in cool anticipation.

Skip suddenly looked up. Odd, but he had a peculiar feeling he was no longer alone.

He looked around but saw nothing to make him suspicious. Probably just a case of the jitters. Jitters or not, he found himself wishing he hadn't strayed so far from the others. The island of light in the distance looked comforting, safe.

The sheriff quickened his pace. He'd taken only five steps when a wave of intense nervousness halted him mid-stride.

"Damn it, you bloody idiot," he told himself. "There's nothing out here—only darkness, trees and cowshit."

His words of reassurance didn't help. His nervousness increased. Loosening his .357 Magnum in its holster, he listened carefully to the sounds around him. Everything was quiet. That, more than anything, convinced him something was wrong. Where were the night birds? Why had the crickets, so boisterous earlier, stopped their chirping?

Curious, he turned away from the direction of the crime scene. His eyes swept quickly left, then right, as he searched for the source of his uneasiness. Off to his right, the ground was broken by the jagged black scar of a dry creek bed. Just beyond it was the rusted barbed-wire fence marking the end of the pasture and the edge of the Owens property. The creek bed ran parallel to the fence for about thirty yards before making a sharp turn and passing beneath the wire strands, continuing on in the wooded countryside beyond.

Skip was suddenly intrigued by the creek bed. He'd noticed it earlier but hadn't paid much attention to it. Could the killer have used it to gain entrance to the pasture? Perhaps it had served as an escape route. He would have to have it searched for clues come morning.

He took another step forward . . . and froze. There was something lurking in the creek bed; he was certain of it. Something crouched in the darkness, watching him. Had the killer returned to the scene of the crime? Without giving it a second thought, he drew and cocked his pistol. Lucky he did.

With a roar, the Crota lunged.

What the fuck is that?

Skip dove to his left, leaving only empty air for razor-sharp claws to slice. He hit the ground rolling, turned, got his feet under him and jumped back up.

Jesus Christ . . . It's big . . . fast. Not a man. Not a bear. A monster!

He braced his right foot, steadied the pistol in both hands and fired four times at the hideous creature. The Magnum echoed like a cannon across the field.

Bullets slammed into the monster's scaly brown chest. Blood flowed. The creature shook its head and howled in rage. Moonlight flashed off murderous fangs.

The slugs should have dropped it, but they didn't. Skip was in trouble and he knew it. Before he could flee, the Crota charged.

He held his breath and fired two more shots, but the bullets didn't stop the monster, didn't even slow it down.

I'm dead!

A massive hand lashed out, black claws splitting the air. He tried to duck out of the way, but a glancing blow caught him across the left side of his head. Pain rocketed white-hot down his body, and blood trickled where claws had split his scalp.

Everything went a dizzy gray as Skip was knocked to the ground. He landed on his back, staring up at a spinning sky, listening to the footsteps of death approaching.

"This way! . . . Someone grab a light!"

He heard the shouts of others racing to his aid, but he knew they were too far away to reach him in time. If only he could stay alive for a few more seconds. The pain . . .

Skip closed his right hand; it was empty. His gun lay lost somewhere in the weeds, empty. Movement from his left drew his attention. The Crota came into view.

Sweet Jesus.

Fred Granger was right: the killer was big, real big—twice the size of any bear Skip had ever seen. Yellow eyes glowed like candle flames above a wrinkled snout. But even though the eyes glowed, they were cold, deadly, like those of a rattlesnake. Saliva dripped off gleaming fangs, licked away from the lips by a round, gray tongue. The creature's front paws slowly clenched and unclenched, its black claws clicking together like bones.

The Crota stared down at him, above him now, then threw its head back and laughed. The laugh, like that of a hyena, was so frightfully hideous it caused Skip's bowels to loosen. And it was the laugh, more than anything else, that filled him with an intense desire to live, and stirred him to action.

Ignoring the pain, he slipped his right hand deep into his pants pockets, frantically searching for something—anything—to defend himself with. His fingers almost numb, he fumbled over keys, coins and a roll of Life Savers, finally coming into contact with the metallic smoothness of his bathing-beauty lighter.

Above him, the face of the Crota leaned closer, blocking out the pale moonlight. The creature's foul breath filled his nostrils, gagged him. Its eyes bore into him.

Skip fought back the nausea, fought back the dizziness. He tore the lighter from his pocket, spinning the striker wheel with his thumb, thrusting his hand straight into the eye of the beast and screaming a cry of defiance. A five-inch flame rose from Skip's hand, lighting the face of the creature.

The Crota hesitated, taken aback. Curiously, he studied the flame, raised a hand to swipe it away. But something stopped it, something caused its eyes to widen, something made it afraid.

Skip was still screaming, his eyes burning into the creature's, when the creature shrieked and jumped backwards, roaring and shaking its head from side to side, its red mane billowing. A taloned foot lashed out, missed Skip by inches. He rolled clear, but the pain made his vision blur. The Crota lashed out again . . . and again. Shots rang out in the distance.

Skip managed to roll a few more feet before unconsciousness engulfed him.

* * *

"Daddy, are you okay?"

His eyes flickered open. He must have dozed off. Funny, he didn't remember going to sleep.

"Daddy, can we play now?" Billy stood looking down at him, casually tossing a baseball in the air and catching it in his old pitcher's mitt.

Skip blinked. He sat up and looked around. Behind the child stretched a blighted field of thorny gray weeds. He turned his head. The field of thorns stretched endlessly in all directions.

What time was it? He wasn't wearing his watch, and when he tried to look up at the sun he found he couldn't. He must have pulled a muscle in his neck. He should be more careful; he wasn't a young man anymore.

"Can we, Daddy? Can we?" Billy's voice was almost a whine.

"Okay, okay," Skip answered. "Just give me a minute to get my socks and shoes on . . ."

Odd, why wasn't he wearing socks and shoes? He rarely went barefoot. Maybe he'd left them back at the house. But surely he hadn't walked across the field without them.

He wiggled his toes. He'd better find his shoes before his feet got cold. The one thing he couldn't stand was cold feet. Billy continued to toss the ball into the air.

Skip started to look for his missing shoes, but he could no longer turn his head to the left or right. How strange. He would have scratched his chin in puzzlement, but his arms wouldn't move either. Very strange indeed.

"Billy, do you know where Daddy's shoes are?"

Billy didn't answer him—couldn't answer him—because he was unable to talk. That was also strange; Billy hadn't spoken a word since he'd lost his hearing. So how could he have spoken only moments before?

"Billy, didn't you just—"

Skip meant to ask his son about his sudden ability to speak. Instead he fell silent as Billy took a bite out of the baseball, his teeth tearing through the tough fabric covering as though it were made of marshmallow. Blood spurted from the ball, splattering the boy's shirt and pants. Skip watched in awe as a long gray tongue snaked from Billy's mouth to lick the crimson from his chin.

Billy popped the rest of the baseball into his mouth, chewed it and swallowed. He licked his fingers, looked down at his father and smiled. A double row of gleaming fangs crowded the tiny mouth.

As he watched, Billy's eyes changed, the pupils going from soft brown to black slits. The irises, no longer white, glowed yellow.

Skip tried to move, but he couldn't. He was completely paralyzed.

Billy's flesh rippled like waves on an ocean as something tore at it from inside, struggling to be free. His face stretched, split and fell apart. His head swelled and burst in a shower of crimson from the strain. His body grew to four times its normal size, shuddered and broke apart like pieces of a jigsaw puzzle, leaving a monster to stand where a boy once was.

The towering creature stood upright on its hind legs, its taut muscles covered with brown scaly skin and patches of red hair. Its broad, snouted face was framed by a flowing red mane, similar to a male lion's, while its glowing eyes were underlined with a wide mouth of fangs and heavy black lips. Its ears, if it had any, were hidden beneath the mane. The creature was a male, its penis also framed by coarse red hair. Menacing black claws protruded from the four long fingers of each hand, as well as from the four toes on each foot.

The monster seemed to block the sun as it stood before Skip, still holding Billy's baseball glove. Looking down, it asked with a growl, "Baseball, anyone?"

Skip glanced down. His shoes glided effortlessly over the path. "That's funny, I could have sworn I was barefoot."

"What was that, dear?"

He was startled by the voice.

Katie walked beside him, her hand in his. She wore a blue, backless summer dress—the same dress she'd worn on their first date—her hair tied up with a matching ribbon.

"What did you say?" she asked again.

"Oh, nothing. I was just talking to myself."

She squeezed his hand and smiled. Skip caught a whiff of perfume. The fragrance was enticing, started to give him an erection. Katie must have noticed, for without another word she veered from the path, leading him to a small clearing.

With a sultry, graceful movement, she let the straps of her dress slip slowly off her shoulders. She wiggled slightly, and the dress fell away. She wore nothing underneath.

Skip's excitement grew. He fumbled at the buttons of his shirt and his belt buckle. His shoes and socks were already off, though he didn't remember removing them. Finally, the last of his clothing slipped away and he stood naked before his wife.

She looked down, smiled and removed the blue ribbon, letting her hair fall about her shoulders. Skip stepped forward and gently lowered her to the ground.

His hands caressed and groped as his mouth slid hungrily over her breasts. Her nipples stiffened from the touch of his tongue. She moaned softly.

Arching her hips, she guided him into her in one smooth movement. She was warm, very warm. Skip gasped with pleasure. She thrust against him, her fingernails digging tiny furrows into his buttocks.

"Faster . . . faster," she whispered, her breath heavy with desire. Her eyes went dreamy . . . closed. When they opened again they were no longer soft and brown; they were big and yellow.

Skip went limp instantly. He tried to pull away, but he was held in an embrace like a vise. The thing that was his wife smiled at his futile struggles. Her smile grew wider and wider, stretching until the flesh at the corners of her mouth ripped open. Blood trickled over her lips and down her chin.

He could feel the body beneath him changing, growing in size, becoming hard. Smooth legs became scaly and rough. The fragrance of perfume became the odor of raw meat. Fingernails dug deeper into his backside. Blood flowed wet and warm between his legs. His wife's hair was no longer brown and silky but coarse and red.

Her head moved forward, mouth opening to reveal fangs. The fangs bit deep into Skip's left cheek, tearing flesh and crushing bone. He screamed from the pain. The pain . . .

The pain was a thunderous throbbing, an echoed roaring with no beginning or end, interlaced with fiery twinges that burned like great lightning bolts through his brain. Splotches of pastel hues and streamers of scarlet drifted across his mind like surrealistic cloud formations. With great effort, Skip forced his eyes to open, then quickly shut them as a sea of blinding light flooded in.

"I think he's waking up. Get the doctor."

The words sounded as if they came from the other end of a long tunnel. They were barely audible above the roaring in his ears. He opened his eyes again. The room spun before him, nausea gripping his stomach and throat. Slowly, gradually, everything settled into place.

He was in a hospital. There was no mistaking the scrubbed white walls, or the portable TV suspended from the ceiling. A white curtain was pulled halfway around his bed, blocking off the view of the rest of the room. Through an open doorway beyond the curtain, he could hear the chatter of two nurses making the rounds.

A young man wearing a green surgeon's gown and a gold Rolex watch stepped into view.

Dr. Livingstone, I presume.

"Welcome back to the world of the living, Mr. Harding. I'm Dr. Richards. How are you feeling?"

Skip started to reply, winced from the pain and decided to remain silent. Gently he touched a fingertip to the left side of his head and felt bandages.

The doctor picked up a clipboard hanging at the foot of Skip's bed and read the paper clipped to it. "You'll probably be spending a couple of days with us. You have a mild concussion. Nothing to be overly alarmed about, but I do want to keep you under observation. You also have a fairly good-sized cut that required forty-seven stitches to close up, so you'll be parting your hair from the right side for a while."

Skip wasn't sure if he liked the doctor's bedside manner or not.

"Feel up to seeing your wife? She's been practically living at the hospital." The doctor saw Skip's eyebrows rise in question. "It's five-thirty, Tuesday afternoon. You were brought in to the emergency room around eight o'clock last night."

Skip nodded slowly. It was all he could do to concentrate on what the doctor was saying.

"Okay, I'll send her in, but only for a minute. I don't want you overdoing things. No sense pushing your luck any more than you have already." The doctor hung the chart back at the foot of the bed, patted him on the leg and left. A few seconds later Katie entered.

She was wearing a tan skirt with a white blouse, not the blue summer dress in the hallucination. Her outfit was wrinkled; she'd probably slept in it. She looked pale, and there were dark shadows under her eyes that yesterday's makeup didn't hide.

"Bill . . . honey." She grabbed his hand and sat lightly on the edge of his bed. Katie called him Bill only when she was upset. "How do you feel?" Her expression told him how he looked.

"Billy?" he whispered, flinching from the stiffness in his jaw.

"He's staying at Evelyn's. He wanted to be here with you, but I . . ."

Skip nodded. He understood. It was upsetting enough for her to see him like this; no sense terrifying the boy.

She leaned forward, resting her head on his chest. "Dear God, I'm so glad you're all right. You don't know how scared I've been."

Skip reached down and gently stroked his wife's hair. *Scared?* Could she possibly know the meaning of the word?

Chapter 11

Wednesday dawned cold and gloomy, the sky a lonely gray. Leafless trees stretched brown, skeletal fingers toward the heavens as if attempting to tear away the gray to reveal the bright blue of a summer afternoon. But summer was over, and such a melancholy day served as reminder that winter was on its way.

Skip sat up in his bed, staring out the window, watching the traffic that came and went from the medical center's parking lot. It was still early; visiting hours had just begun, so few cars were moving about. He watched a big Buick chug out into the street, vapor ghosts swirling from its exhaust pipe, and wished that he were leaving with it.

Turning away from the window, he thought about switching on the television but didn't. There wouldn't be much on except talk shows and soap operas, and he wasn't fond of either. He would have tried to read had there been anything worth reading. Someone, probably one of the hospital volunteers, had left a couple of dog-eared *Reader's Digests* on his nightstand, but Skip couldn't focus his eyes to read them.

There was a knock at the door. He looked up as Katie and Lloyd entered the room. Katie wore a white knit pullover sweater and a pair of brown slacks. Lloyd was in uniform.

"Good morning, hon," she said, setting a brown paper sack on the floor by the foot of his bed.

Skip glanced at the sack, trying to figure out the contents by its shape.

Books? Mysteries? Westerns, perhaps? Aspirin?

Katie leaned over and gave him a kiss. "How are you feeling today?"

"Bored shitless with a headache," he replied.

"Well, that's better than yesterday." She placed her right palm against his forehead, checking his temperature.

Skip removed Katie's hand, holding it in his. "I've got a concussion, not the flu."

She smiled. "You can never be too careful in a place like this."

Lloyd pulled up one of the two plastic chairs in the room and sat down facing Skip.

"When are you getting out of here?" he asked.

Skip shrugged. "I don't know. The doctor hasn't been in yet today. In fact, I only saw him once yesterday and that was just for a few minutes. He said he wanted to keep me under observation, but I don't see how he can do it if he's never here. If he doesn't show up soon, I'll sign myself out."

"Oh no, you don't," Katie cut in. "A concussion is

nothing to screw around with. You're not leaving until the doctor says you can. Lloyd can handle things for another day. If he can't, then call in the FBI, the CIA, whoever. But you're staying put."

Lloyd raised his eyebrows in an expression of shocked surprise.

Skip smiled. "See what I have to put up with? She's a regular warden."

"And don't you ever forget it," she said sternly.

Skip grew serious again. "Have you come up with anything yet?"

"Not a damn thing," Lloyd replied, moving his chair closer to the bed. "We've checked everywhere we can possibly think of looking. Nothing. That bear of yours is probably in Kentucky by now."

Yesterday, between one of his pain-pill-induced naps, Skip had found the strength to sit up long enough to tell Katie and Lloyd about the monster that had attacked him. They were the only ones he'd told. Katie believed him, but Lloyd, it was clear, did not.

"It wasn't a bear," Skip said, feeling a flush of anger warm his face.

"Oh Jesus, here we go again," Lloyd sighed. "Look, we've been through this before. It was dark. Everything happened fast. Your eyes can play tricks on you—"

"I know what I saw," Skip said.

"There were witnesses. They said it was a bear. Brown even got a couple of shots at it as it ran away."

Skip didn't like being called a liar. "Damn it, Lloyd. Could a bear wipe out a herd of cows and a Hereford bull? What about the Jerworski kid? Could a bear have hung him in that tree? I don't give a fuck what Brown says he saw. That asshole wouldn't know a bear from a kangaroo in the first place."

Skip was interrupted by a sharp knock at the door. They all turned to see who it was.

"I hope I'm not interrupting anything," Mayor Sonny Johnson said as he entered the room. He was followed by a tall, thin reporter from the Logan *Gazette*. The reporter carried a 35mm camera and a spiral notebook.

I knew I should have locked that damn door.

Skip forced a smile. "No, Mayor, not at all. Come on in. We were just debating, that's all." He shot a look of warning to be quiet to Katie and Lloyd.

Skip disliked Sonny Johnson intensely. He considered him a weasel. Without his glasses, he even looked like one: skinny, long neck, black hair greased flat against his head. The mayor had a way of coming across so nice it made Skip want to puke. Maybe it was the country boy accent he used, which was about as phony as his smile. How he ever got elected mayor of Logan was anybody's guess.

"Good, good." Mayor Johnson smiled, stepping farther into the room. He favored Lloyd with a nod before turning his gaze on Katie, where Skip noticed his smile became more of a leer.

Bastard's mentally undressing her.

"It's so good to see you again, Mrs. Harding," Mayor Johnson said. "You're looking lovely as ever."

"Thank you, Mayor," Katie replied, shifting uncomfortably under his gaze. "Good to see you again."

Skip cleared his throat. "Something I can do for you, Mayor?"

Mayor Johnson let his gaze fall away from Katie. Softening his smile, he turned to Skip.

"I was just on my way to Warrenton for a business meeting and thought I'd stop by to pay my respects and see how you were doing." He squeezed past Katie, stepping up to Skip's bed. "How are you feeling?"

"I'll live," Skip answered with something of a frown. He noticed the reporter positioning himself at the foot of the bed. Skip watched as he removed the lens cap from the camera.

"Glad to hear that." The mayor moved even closer. "I can't begin to tell you how much I appreciate the fine job you've been doing for this county . . . risking your life and all that. After you get out of here, and after that bear is rounded up—and I'm sure that will be very soon—I'm sure we'll all rest easier." He turned to Lloyd. "Right?"

Lloyd coughed. "Yes, sir. I've got extra men working on it now. We expect to nail it before sundown."

The mayor nodded in thought. "Good, good." He turned back to Skip. "Anyway, after this all blows over we'll have a little celebration over at my place . . . pass out a few citations for a job well done. That sort of thing. It'll be great for publicity. Speaking of which . . ." He turned and nodded at the reporter.

"I bumped into Phillip here on my way over. He's from the *Gazette.* He wants to take a few pictures of us together for tomorrow's paper. I said you wouldn't mind."

I do mind, you idiot, and you know it!

"It's okay, isn't it?"

No, it isn't okay.

"Sure. Why not?" Skip answered coldly.

"See, Phillip? I told you the sheriff wouldn't mind." Mayor Johnson beamed. He leaned over and put his arm around Skip's shoulders, striking a pose. Skip gritted his teeth to keep from flinching. The reporter raised his camera, focused and clicked off three quick shots. The camera's flash left colored dots swimming in front of Skip's eyes.

"There, that ought to do it," Johnson said, removing his arm from Skip's shoulders. The embarrassing photo, Skip clad in striped pajamas, would probably end up on the front page of the paper.

"Gentlemen, be sure and contact me the moment you find anything," Johnson said, moving toward the door. He had reverted back to his official, I'm-in-charge voice. Obviously, with the photo session over, he was anxious to be on his way. "I would stay and chat, but I've got an important meeting to attend."

With those parting words, the mayor turned and exited the room. The reporter followed him.

Katie sat down on the foot of Skip's bed and burst

out laughing. "He means he has a meeting with Janet Baker at the Oasis Motel."

"Shhh . . . he might hear you," Skip cautioned.

Lloyd sat back down on the yellow plastic chair. "It's almost as if the bastard's enjoying himself," he said, shaking his head in disgust.

"He's enjoying the publicity, that's for sure." Skip shifted in bed. "He thinks he's some kind of celebrity now that the cable news networks have picked up the story about the mutilations."

"Wait till *Hard Copy* does a story about it," Katie commented.

"Oh, God," Skip said. "You mean it's going to be on *Hard Copy* too?"

"Nothing definite, just a rumor I heard."

"Great, that's all we need—more publicity," Lloyd grumbled. "This town is filling up with tourists as it is. I swear, the next person I catch on Cemetery Road with out-of-county plates, I'm gonna lock them up and throw away the key."

Skip grinned. "Now, now . . . temper, temper. I thought you liked being sheriff."

"You know better than that," Lloyd said. "There's too much politics and paperwork involved. Damn phone never stops ringing. No, I've had a taste of what it's like at the top, and I don't like it. The sooner you get your heinie back to work, the happier I'll be."

"Oh, I almost forgot," Katie cut in. "I stopped by the library on the way home yesterday and picked these up for you." She picked up the paper sack she had brought and handed it to Skip. Opening it, he removed several library books.

"Books?" Lloyd questioned. He stretched his neck to read the titles as Skip removed them from the sack. Though the titles and authors varied, each book dealt with the subject of monsters and unexplained happenings in North America.

"Here we go again," Lloyd said.

Katie wheeled on him, her eyes bright with anger. "Damn it, Lloyd, what makes you so sure you're right? You weren't even there."

"I don't have to be there to know there are no such things as monsters, UFOs or abominable snowmen."

"And there aren't any bears in this part of the country big enough to kill a full-grown bull and half a dozen cows."

"Agreed," Lloyd replied.

"Okay, then you explain it," she challenged.

"I can't."

"Then why, for God's sake, are you so quick to put Skip down?"

"Put him down? I'm trying to protect him."

"Protect him?" She was puzzled.

"Do you have any idea what will happen if talk of a monster gets around? Not only will you have every looney-toon in the state showing up here, but there's a good chance of starting one hell of a panic. And what happens when election time rolls around next year? Do you seriously think anyone will vote for a man who claims to have seen a monster?"

"Not claims. Has seen," said Skip.

"Maybe," Lloyd clipped. "You want to end up in a rubber room, then you just start shouting monster and see what happens."

"What do you suggest I do?" Skip asked. "Keep my mouth shut until someone else gets killed?"

"If you shout monster, someone else *will* get killed. Every idiot this side of St. Louis will be out there looking for it." Lloyd got up and crossed the room to the windows, staring out at the parking lot and street beyond. "Monster, bear, whatever—we need to keep a lid on this thing." He turned back around. "Let us do our job. With the additional men we have helping from the state police, there's no way it's going to slip past us. Hobbs is not that big a county. If it's still out there, we'll get it. And if it does turn out to be some kind of monster, then you'll be a celebrity. If it doesn't, then you'll still have your reputation."

He glanced at his watch. "Listen, I'd love to stay and chat some more, but I've got to get back. I'll keep you posted on everything that's going on."

Lloyd said his goodbyes and headed out the door. Skip grimaced and laid back down. It still hurt to sit up for very long at a time, but he wasn't about to let Lloyd see his discomfort.

"He can be such a pain in the ass," Katie said.

"Yeah, he can. But he's still the best man I've got on the force. I guess I can overlook his other faults."

"But he doesn't believe you."

"Do you blame him? It's not something that's easy

to believe. If one of my men had come to me with the same story, I'd have sent them to see a psychiatrist."

Skip picked up one of the books and began thumbing through it. "Weren't there a few Bigfoot sightings in Missouri about ten years ago?"

Katie picked up one of the other books, flipping through the pages. "Here it is: Momo, the Missouri monster. Says the sightings took place on the outskirts of Louisiana, Missouri, back in July of 1972. Witnesses describe the creature as being about seven feet tall and completely covered with hair. Another person describes it as looking like a cross between a man and a gorilla."

"What color was it?"

"Black."

"Nothing about glowing eyes?"

"No, but it says monsters were also sighted in Fayetteville, Arkansas, and Peoria, Illinois, during August of 1972."

"Busy summer," Skip commented. "What else you got?"

"How about a story about the Ghost of Paris, Missouri?"

He laughed.

Katie turned the page and read a few lines. "Here's one dated 1947 from Piney Ridge, Missouri. It's about a creature killing sheep and goats."

Skip sat up, interested. "What else does it say?"

Katie scanned the page. "Not much, I'm afraid. It says that when hunters went after it, it killed their dogs."

"No description?"

"No."

"Damn."

"There's a couple more monster sightings listed from Union and Mountain View, Missouri, but they're just Bigfoot reports. Wait . . . here's another, but it's from Massachusetts."

"Read it anyway."

". . . In the summer of 1972, cattle and sheep around the town of Rehoboth were being mysteriously killed." She skipped to the next page. "Oh . . . never mind—they're talking about a mysterious panther."

"Scratch that. What attacked me is definitely not a panther. It's not a bear either. Hell, it's not like anything I've ever seen before."

"Could it be a mutation? You know, like in those science-fiction movies?"

"Like that thing in *Prophecy*?"

"That's the one."

Skip shook his head. "I don't think so. Don't ask me why, but I think what I saw was an original, not a mutation."

"But where did it come from?" she asked.

"I don't know, but I'm damn sure going to send it back."

Katie closed the book. "That's enough monster stories for now. You'd better get some rest."

"But I'm not sleepy!" he argued.

"Momma knows best," she said. "I'll leave these on the table. You can glance through them later."

She leaned over and gave him a kiss, mussing his hair slightly.

Lying back, he started to drift off as soon as he closed his eyes. The last thing he heard was the sound of the door gently closing as Katie stepped into the hallway.

The woods behind his grandmother's house were dark and mysterious. For a boy of six who had wandered off after supper and gotten himself lost they were downright terrifying. Skip would have cried had he not heard his grandmother calling for him. Her voice, though scolding, was like a foghorn to a storm-tossed ship, a beacon of hope to steer by.

Following the sound of her voice, he soon saw a flickering light moving between the trees in the distance. It was the light of a lantern, the one his grandmother always carried when she went out before dawn to milk the cows. But as he drew nearer to the light, it began to move away from him.

Skip cried out to his grandmother, begging her to wait for him, but the light drew farther away. He had to run to keep up. Sweat ran down his face and into his eyes; a stitch formed in his side.

He reached the clearing beside his grandmother's house in time to see her climb the steps to the front porch. She paused in the doorway, looking back at him, waiting for him to follow. It was funny, but the light from the lantern made her look ghostly, like she wasn't all there. He could have sworn that he could see through her.

His grandmother turned and entered the house. He called her name and raced after her. He reached the front door in time to see the glow from the lantern near the end of the hall. He followed.

The folding ladder to the attic had been pulled down. He watched as his grandmother climbed the rungs. The light went with her, leaving him in the dark. Skip wasn't allowed to play in the attic, but he didn't want to be left alone in the dark either.

"Grandma?" He touched the ladder, placed a foot lightly upon the bottom rung. "Grandma, is it okay if I come up?" There was no reply. The darkness closed in around him. He swallowed hard and started up.

Peeking through the opening, he saw his grandmother leaning over a large wooden chest. Reaching into the chest, she removed something wrapped in what appeared to be fox fur. She turned toward him, holding the bundle out to him. But as he reached out for it, the bundle disappeared. His grandmother vanished with it.

Skip awoke with a start, his heart beating madly in his chest. He was still in the hospital, not in the dusty attic of his grandmother's house—the house he now lived in with his family.

Jesus, what a dream.

Although a faded picture of her sat on the mantel, he hadn't really thought of his grandmother in years, let alone dreamed about her. What a dream. Strange. He had never gotten lost in the woods behind her house. And to his knowledge, she had never owned such a chest. So what did it mean?

It's just a dream, you dummy. It doesn't mean a thing. Just a side effect from all the junk they've been giving you. You'll probably be seeing pink elephants next.

At least that would be better than seeing monsters.

Wiping the sweat from his forehead, he rolled over and went back to sleep.

Chapter 12

Lloyd wet his comb under the faucet, shook it and ran it through his hair. He smiled at himself in the mirror. No . . . too happy. The serious look was better. He frowned. Perfect. That's the way he wanted to look on his election posters. Maybe he should put on a few pounds, touch up the gray a little.

He turned off the water and reached for a paper towel. It had all been so easy; Skip had believed everything. What a dumb ass. He could care less about Sheriff Harding's precious reputation. The only reason he wanted to clamp a lid on the situation was to prevent someone else from shooting his election-winning killer bear. Once Lloyd nailed it, which he would, he'd keep it on ice for a few days—long enough to let Skip scream monster to the papers. Sheriff Harding would look like a fool when he pulled up in front of the courthouse with the bear in the back of his truck. It would be political suicide.

Tossing the paper towel in the trash, he pocketed his comb and left the restroom. Walking past the nurses station, he almost collided with Jay Little

Hawk, who was coming around the corner from the opposite direction.

It was something of a rarity to see the game warden out of uniform; when he was off duty he rarely came into town. Little Hawk was dressed in faded blue jeans, scruffy brown cowboy boots and a gray flannel shirt. Around his neck he wore a five-strand choker of bone hair-pipes and red trade beads. Several of his fingers were adorned with turquoise rings. The Indian looked tired; deep shadows underlined his eyes. Maybe he had stayed out too late drinking.

"Hello, Lloyd," Hawk nodded. "I was just on my way to see the sheriff. Is he up?"

"He was," Lloyd said, "but he's resting again."

A troubled look crossed Hawk's face.

"Is there something I can do for you?" Lloyd asked.

Hawk shook his head. "No, it's something I need to see the sheriff about. I'll wait."

Lloyd didn't like that answer. It made him feel he was being left out of something. Had the Indian found where the bear was hiding?

"Listen, if it's something important, you can tell me. I'll see that he gets the message. And if it's something concerning the murders, then you should definitely tell me. I'm in charge."

Hawk shifted restlessly back and forth on his feet, apparently debating the choices offered. "Okay, I'll tell you, but not here." He looked around. "Can we go someplace private?"

"I think I can accommodate you on that," Lloyd replied, laughing.

They took the elevator down to the second floor, following the hallway to a small reading room operated by the ladies' auxiliary. Few patients ever frequented the room, so there was little chance of their being disturbed.

Lloyd closed the door and motioned for Little Hawk to sit on one of the four white plastic chairs that circled an equally white table, and waited for Hawk to speak.

Gazing downward, Hawk nervously flipped through the pages of a medical magazine on the table before him. "I want you to know that I didn't hear of the sheriff's attack until only a little while ago. I've been . . . away for the past few days. When I found out what happened, I rushed to get here."

"You know something we should?"

Hawk looked him square in the eyes. "I know the news reports are wrong. It wasn't a bear that attacked Sheriff Harding and killed the others."

Lloyd took a deep breath, trying to restrain a rising feeling of annoyance. "And how do you know that?"

"Let's just say I got my information from a very reliable source."

"Listen, mister," Lloyd said suddenly. "I haven't the time or patience to sit here and play games with you. Either you know something or you don't."

Hawk held up his hands. "I assure you, I am not playing games. What I have to tell you is difficult to put into words. If you will give me just ten minutes of your time, I'll make it worth your while."

Lloyd glanced at his watch, frowned, then fished a crumpled pack of cigarettes from his shirt pocket. "If you know something that might prevent another murder, then I want to hear it. Ten minutes? Hell, I'll give you ten days."

"Promise you'll keep an open mind and won't stop me until I'm finished?"

Little Hawk began reciting his story, a faraway look clouding his eyes.

"In the early eighteen hundreds, the white man was pushing westward across America like a swarm of angry locusts. Pushing the Indians back, settlers snapped up tribal hunting lands in Kentucky, Tennessee, Indiana and Alabama. Before they even realized what was going on, the Indians had their backs up against the Mississippi River, and still the cries could be heard for more land.

"There were some, however, who refused to give up their land without a fight. One that arose to stop the white man's advance was a Shawnee prophet named Tenskwatawa. His name meant 'the open door.' The whites simply referred to him as the Prophet. His brother, even more recognized in history books, was the great leader Tecumseh.

"In an attempt to create a great confederacy the Prophet traveled the land, instructing the Indians to renounce the white man's customs, thoughts and trappings. He urged them to return to traditional ways, never to touch whiskey, and not to intermarry with the whites. Their reward, he promised, would be the complete recovery of all Indian land.

"An Indian revival, naturally, was not in the best interest of the settlers. General William Henry Harrison—later President Harrison—hearing of the Prophet, challenged him to prove his powers. Tenskwatawa accepted the challenge, announcing that at noon on June 16, 1806, he would cause darkness to block out the sun as evidence of his supernatural powers. His prophecy came true.

"In 1807, another astonishing prophecy was sent to all the tribes by the Prophet. It warned that unless the tribes followed his example and turned away from the white man's way, there would be a great disaster within four years.

"By 1811, the prophecy was being repeated by Tecumseh, who was in the south seeking the support of the Creeks. Angered by their refusal to join the fight, Tecumseh warned Chief Big Warrior that when he returned to Detroit he would stamp his stick on the ground and cause an earthquake, destroying the Creek villages. On December 16, at two o'clock in the morning, his warning came true.

"Women screamed, children cried and old men prayed for the Great Spirit to save them. The sky glowed with a strange orange light as the ground began to shake. Lightning flashed and trees swayed like dancing warriors. Thousands of birds took to the air as the earth rolled like waves upon the ocean. Hills sank and disappeared, only to reappear elsewhere. Hundreds died as the great Mississippi, father of all rivers, reversed its course and flowed north for several hours, sending great waves of water charging into the villages. Upon the higher ground, great fissures split the earth's surface, releasing hissing clouds of sulphurous gas.

"Crowded upon a hill, the tribe of one of the smaller Creek villages looked on in despair as their homes were washed away. The nightmare had only begun, however, for as they watched something crawled from one of the giant cracks, freed from its subterranean home. The Chief knew what the creature was as soon as he saw it, though he had always believed it to be merely a legend, a story to tell noisy children. It was a creature from the dawn of time, known to the Indians as the Ancient One, the Sleeping Evil—the Crota.

"Knowing that they could not defeat the monster, the villagers fled in terror. They traveled westward, vanishing into the heavily forested hills of central Missouri. But the Crota, angered at being awakened from its sleep, followed and found them again. Night after night it stalked their village, leaving behind a freshly mutilated corpse each time. Finally, in sheer desperation, the tribal elders and medicine man held a great council. It was to be their last council ever, because in order to save the women and children, the men determined to sacrifice their lives.

"When darkness fell the following evening a lone warrior stood waiting for the Crota's arrival. Shouting words of power taught to him by the medicine man, the warrior threw his spear at the monster and fled. He did not run because he was afraid; he ran in order to lead the Crota away from the village. He ran as far and as fast as he could until, his legs no longer able to continue, he fell beneath the murderous claws and fangs of the creature. No sooner had the first warrior fallen than a second appeared to challenge the monster.

"On through the night the chase continued, eventually leading to a cave . . . a cave that was connected to a series of ancient underground tunnels. Warrior after warrior, the Crota was led deeper into the tunnels, while behind him the only exit to the outside world was walled up by the tribal elders. The young warriors knew they too would be trapped once the wall was complete, but they did not despair, for the sacrifice they made was for their people.

"The tribal elders also made a great sacrifice that night. Once the wall was in place, the medicine man made a magical bond upon the stones, sealing the exit forever. It was a bond written in blood—the blood of the medicine man and elders, who committed suicide before that great wall. They died so their tribe would live."

Little Hawk stopped talking. There was a silence. Then Lloyd shifted in his chair.

"Well, I appreciate you telling me all this—"

"You don't believe me, do you?"

"Should I? What you just told me is only a story . . . a legend."

The Indian leaned forward. "The murders started

Saturday. The earthquake was Friday. The wall sealing the tunnels must have fallen."

Lloyd snorted. "Your story has a hole in it: the people who've been killed aren't Creek Indians."

"The Crota *was* originally after the Creeks, because it believed they were responsible for disturbing its rest. But the monster blames all men for its imprisonment. The Crota is not a good sport; it won't rest until it avenges itself in blood. The creature will kill anything or anyone that crosses its path."

Lloyd started to stand up, but Little Hawk grabbed him by the wrist. "Listen to me; I'm not kidding. The Crota is a relic, a living fossil. It's been around since the age of the dinosaurs, perhaps even before then. It is a creature that lives for the hunt, the challenge of battle . . . to inflict pain and suffering on others."

Lloyd pulled his arm away. "I can't believe two grown men are sitting here discussing monsters and Indian legends. If what you're saying is true, then how come no one has ever heard of this thing until now?"

"But they have," Hawk answered. "The early white settlers knew the story of the Crota, that's why they named this area Hobbs County. *Hob* means goblin, devil. Even the name of this town relates to the story. A logan is a large balanced stone—the stones balanced in the wall sealing the tunnels."

"How do you come to know all this, anyway?" Lloyd asked.

"I was brought up in the traditional Indian ways.

As a child I learned all the legends and stories of the southeastern tribes."

Lloyd stared directly at Little Hawk. "You don't expect me to believe any of this, do you?"

"Everything I said can be easily proven."

"How?"

"I know where the Crota is hiding. I've found the entrance to the tunnels."

Lloyd was suddenly interested. He sat up straight in his chair. "Where?"

"The Devil's Boot," Hawk said matter-of-factly. "But I warn you, you must stay away from there."

The undersheriff frowned. "Why's that?"

"Because it would be suicide to challenge the Crota unprepared."

That did it. Bear, monster, whatever, no civilian was going to tell Lloyd what to do. "Listen, pal, I'll decide what's suicide and what isn't."

"You don't understand," Hawk protested. "You're not dealing with an animal. The Crota is a creature of darkness."

"I don't give a rat's ass what it is," Lloyd said. "Several people have been killed. More could die. I'm telling you—"

"And I'm telling *you*, if you go down after it you're a dead man." Hawk's voice grew calm. "Please, promise me you'll tell Sheriff Harding what I've told you. Then if you feel you must go down into the tunnels, wait a day or two first."

"Why?" asked Lloyd.

"Because I'll go with you."

"If what you told me is true, then why would you want to go?"

"As I said, the Crota cannot be defeated by conventional ways, but maybe I can come up with an unconventional way to kill it. It's going to take a little time."

"Time is something we don't have."

"The Crota hasn't been free for very long. It's probably still weak. Until it regains all its strength it won't travel far from its home."

Lloyd started to question Little Hawk about how he knew such things, but decided against it. He'd already made up his mind about what he was going to do, and he needed to get rid of the Indian.

"Okay, listen," he said. "I'll pass the information along to the sheriff. If a decision is made to go after that thing, I promise I'll contact you first."

Hawk smiled. It was a weary smile. "Thank you."

Sliding his chair back, Hawk stood up and shook hands. Lloyd watched the Indian leave, then leaned back and put his feet up on the table.

Of course, he had no intention of telling Skip what Jay Little Hawk had said. Nor was he going to wait as promised. Personally, he thought the whole story was preposterous—monsters, indeed—but all the better if it was true. Bagging a Crota might be just the thing to cinch next year's election. He could see it now: Sheriff Lloyd Baxter, monster hunter.

"Crota, my ass!" he said aloud. Throwing his head back, he laughed.

PART III

Chapter 13

THURSDAY, SEPTEMBER 20

Lloyd watched as Professor Steven Fuller pulled at his white coveralls and adjusted the straps of his chest harness. The four uniformed men standing before him mimicked his moves as they prepared to enter the eternal darkness of the Devil's Boot.

Each man wore one-piece coveralls and heavy duty clothing to prevent abrasions and provide warmth in the chilly temperatures of the cave. They also wore a caver's pack small enough to fit through tight spaces, yet roomy enough to hold a moderate supply of high energy food, a first-aid kit, compass, a space blanket and a canteen of water. Along with the carbide helmet lights they wore, they were packing additional flashlights and enough climbing equipment to scale a mountain.

The members of the sheriff's department would be carrying their personal side arms and Winchester 1200 riot guns. The shotguns had been adapted for the mission by replacing the wooden stocks with pistol grips and adding nylon rifle slings. In addition, each officer also carried a spool of thin cable wire that would link the party to the radio topside.

At first Steven Fuller had suspected Lloyd's phone call the previous day to be a joke, a prank played on him by fellow faculty members. It was well known among students and staff at Washington University that Professor Fuller was one of the leading speleologists in the state. He was quick to point out that explorers of caves detested the name "spelunker," which they considered old-fashioned, preferring instead to be called "cavers."

Even after Lloyd had identified himself, the professor still had doubts. He'd read about the bizarre killings (who hadn't?) but found a story about a possible labyrinth of underground tunnels hard to swallow. Still, the history teacher jumped at the chance to lead an expedition in search of them.

Lloyd had kept the rest of Little Hawk's story to himself, explaining to his men that they were following up a lead about a killer bear. He doubted the possibility of a "Crota," but if such a thing existed he wanted the credit for killing it. It was just the thing he needed to get elected. He also made certain the operation itself remained a secret by not telling his men what the plan was until they were actually at the cave. He explained that the tight-lipped secrecy was necessary to keep the press from dogging their trail, but the real reason was he didn't want Skip to find out about what was going on.

"A few more minutes and we'll be ready to go

in," Professor Fuller said, approaching the small folding table where Lloyd and a young deputy sat.

"Good, we're all set here." Lloyd adjusted the squelch knob of the radio before him. David Hays, the newest member of the sheriff's department, would remain behind to operate the base station, providing a secure link to the outside world in case the expedition ran into trouble.

Lloyd stood up. "I guess we'd better get started, Professor Fuller."

"Call me Steven."

"Okay, Steven. These are for you." He slid a dirty cardboard box across the table to the professor.

"What's this?"

"It's some stuff left over from last year's Halloween party."

Steven opened the box and pulled out a couple of foil-wrapped cylinders.

"They're lightsticks," Lloyd said. "We handed them out to all the kids who came around the station, but we still ended up with a bunch left over. I figured they might come in handy."

"Now this is what I call using your head." Steven grinned, obviously delighted with the gift. "You know, you might turn out to be caver material after all."

Picking up the box, Fuller headed toward the mouth of the cave. Lloyd smiled. He couldn't help liking the professor. Underneath the slightly graying beard and a complexion whitened by too many years spent inside a classroom was one of the world's last true adventurers. He watched with amusement as the wiry history teacher climbed spiderlike over a pile of loose rocks at the cave's mouth. His teaching job may have robbed him of his suntan, but Professor Fuller was still as agile as most twenty-year-olds.

Deputy Hays spoke up. "The professor's a card, isn't he?"

"He sure is," Lloyd nodded. He turned to the deputy. "Hays, I don't want you wandering off or taking a nap while we're down there. Understand? If you get bored, read a book. Whatever you do, make damn sure you stay within hearing range of this radio. If I have to call you more than twice to get your attention, I'll have you mopping piss out of the drunk tank for a month of Sundays."

The deputy withdrew a dog-eared paperback novel from his hip pocket. "Got you covered, boss. But what if I have to make a nature call?"

Lloyd frowned. "Turn the volume up and use the bushes."

"Right," Hays nodded. He glanced at the radio. "You sure you've got enough cable for this thing?"

"We've got enough." Lloyd turned and started walking away.

"Bring me back a bearskin," Hays called after him.

Lloyd snorted.

At the mouth of the cave Lloyd considered who he needed to keep an eye on in case something *did* happen on the inside. Sergeant Mitchell and Corporal Murphy had been with the department long enough to know how to take care of themselves. And if push came to shove he knew that Deputy Brown could hold his own. He wasn't so sure about Deputy Ferguson, who had been with the force for less than a year and hadn't had the opportunity to prove himself under pressure. Maybe he'd get that opportunity today.

The wooden ladder leading to the lower level of the cave was still in place. Lloyd shone his light down into the chamber below. Everything appeared exactly as it had the last time he'd been in the cave. Even some of the chalked graffiti could still be read. CINDY LOVES DARRELL . . . SEX, DRUGS AND ROCK & ROLL . . . GREG SUCKS—the usual stuff aspiring authors write in their teenage years.

Steven squatted next to him. "It'd be safer if we use the ropes to climb down. Cave organisms often attack wood, rotting it from the inside out."

He considered it, then shook his head. "Naw, the ladder's sturdy enough. You just gotta be careful of the rungs: the dampness makes them slick." He remembered the eleven-year-old boy who'd slipped and died. "If we go one at a time and don't rush, we shouldn't have any problems. I'll go first; it'll give me a chance to test the radio once I'm down."

Steven nodded. "I'll go last; that way I can lower most of the gear down by rope rather than have the men fumble with it on the ladder."

The descent into the second chamber took only a few minutes. While Steven lowered the gear down with a climbing rope, Lloyd clipped a field communication telephone onto the end of the first spool of wire. He was happy to learn that his voice could still be heard loud and clear on the outside.

In addition to the field phone, each of the officers carried walkie-talkies. None of them wanted to take the chance of becoming separated from the group.

Once on the floor of the second chamber, the men reslung their gear and weapons. The carbide helmet lamps were also switched on, casting eerie shadows across the walls. Fanning out, they moved toward the back wall, searching for a previously unknown opening or passageway, if such a thing existed. Lloyd was surprised that none of the men thought to question how a bear could possibly climb a ladder to get into or out of the cave.

"Hey, over here!" Sergeant Mitchell yelled, waving his flashlight to attract attention. He stood on a large pile of rocks, in front of what appeared to be an opening to a narrow passageway.

"Damn," Lloyd said, reaching Mitchell's side. "I've been in this cave dozens of times; this opening wasn't here before."

Steven stepped past the two men. "You're right; this breakdown appears recent."

"Maybe it collapsed during the earthquake," suggested Corporal Murphy.

Lloyd looked up at the ceiling. "Any chance of another cave-in happening while we're down here?"

"There's always that possibility," Steven answered. "It's one of the dangers of exploring subterranean worlds. But no, I don't think we have to worry, not unless we have another earthquake."

"Let's just hope we don't," Lloyd said.

The professor kneeled to examine the pile of stones. "That's odd. These stones are not consistent with the geological makeup of this cave."

Lloyd frowned. "If you don't mind, I'd prefer if you'd talk in English."

Steven grinned. "It means these stones were carried in from the outside." He broke a piece of hardened mud away from one of the rocks. "Look at this. These rocks were mortared together, but it was done in such a way that when the wall was standing it looked like a natural part of the chamber. Fascinating."

"Holy shit," Deputy Brown exclaimed. "Take a look at this!"

Brown was standing in the opening, shining his light through at the floor beyond. The others scampered up the rocks to see what had gotten the young deputy's attention. Their surprise was as great as his.

Just beyond the opening, neatly aligned along the right wall of a passageway, were ten human skeletons. The skeletons had been carefully positioned side by side, with arms extended and hands touching, forming a continuous chain of bones.

Lloyd pushed past and stepped into the passageway.

"I wouldn't get too close," Steven cautioned. "No telling what they died of or what kind of diseases you might pick up."

The undersheriff stopped where he was. Shining his light down at the feet of the skeleton closest to him, he spotted a small pile of flint arrowheads and a few polished stones. Each of the other skeletons had a similar pile of trinkets.

"What do you make of this, Professor?"

Steven stroked his chin in thought. "I'm not an archaeologist, but I'd say this was once an Indian burial chamber. Maybe Osage. When the Indians buried their dead, they often buried their possessions with them. The arrowheads and stones were probably stored in baskets, which have long since rotted. One thing's for sure, this ought to make the local historians happy."

Lloyd nodded, though he really wasn't paying much attention to what the professor said. Instead he thought about the story Jay Little Hawk had told him. The game warden had been right about the previously unknown section of the cave. Judging by the evidence at hand, he'd also been correct about the Indians erecting a wall. Whether or not the wall had been built to seal in a monster, however, still remained to be seen.

Thirty feet farther in, Professor Fuller paused to examine the wall on his right.

"Amazing," he said, running his hand over the stone. "It appears this tunnel is man-made. At the very least, an existing passageway was enlarged by someone." He pointed at a spot on the wall. "See these scratches here? They're tool marks. Could be this tunnel was part of an early mining operation—possibly Spanish. New Madrid was supposed to be the seat of the new Spanish empire."

Professor Fuller turned to the others. "I don't wish to excite you, but it appears we've stumbled onto a pretty important find, historically."

They pressed on, going deeper into the earth. Excited over their discovery, Steven Fuller talked almost constantly, pausing only to jot down a quick note or take a photo with his instamatic camera. Thirty minutes later the expedition came to its first real obstacle when the tunnel forked into two separate passageways.

"Looks like we'll have to split up," Lloyd said, shining his flashlight into one passageway and then the other.

Steven shook his head. "That may not be such a good idea. You never know what you might run into down here—pits, slides, rivers, any number of things."

"I appreciate your concern," Lloyd said, "but we've got a job to do. If there is a bear down here somewhere, we've got to find it and exterminate it before it kills again. I don't like the idea of splitting up any more than you do, but we don't have a choice. It'll take too much time to explore each passageway separately. My men aren't used to this much walking. They're patrol officers, not foot soldiers."

"I see your point," Professor Fuller nodded, "but that's exactly why we should stick together: your men aren't foot soldiers. Nor are they cavers. You're in a whole new ballpark down here. Not only do you have to worry about cave-ins, chokes, bottomless pits and breaking a leg on loose rock; there's also exhaustion, exposure, flash floods . . . You hired me to be a guide, now let me do my job."

Lloyd gave in. "Okay, Professor, you win. We'll stick together—for now, anyway. Before we continue any farther, though, I think it'd be a good idea to go ahead and divide up the lightsticks. Never know when we're going to need them."

While the lightsticks were being divided up each officer went through an additional inspection of his personal items, paying particular attention to the weapons. If there was a bear waiting for them farther down the line, then they had better be prepared. They'd already seen what their opponent was capable of doing.

Chapter 14

During the winter of 1934, a giant kangaroo terrorized farmers near South Pittsburg, Tennessee. Leaving a trail of killed and partially devoured geese, ducks and police dogs in its wake, the kangaroo was tracked to a mountain-side cave, where it disappeared.

Skip closed the book, tossing it with the others at the foot of his bed. His head throbbed with pain, his eyes ached from reading and he still hadn't come across anything even vaguely resembling what he had seen. The only thing reading the books had accomplished was to fill his head with enough useless trivia to last a lifetime.

He'd gone through chapter after chapter on the Sasquatch and other hairy denizens of the deep woods, the reports varying in description as much as they varied in location. The creature was sometimes tall, sometimes short, sometimes black in color, sometimes white, sometimes violent, other times friendly. In the end, he'd been led to believe that most if not all of the stories were concocted by people wanting to get their names in the paper.

Compared to some of the other stories, the Sasquatch reports were pretty tame. Within the last couple of hours he'd read about sea monsters, glowing green men, giant birds and UFO abductions. Closer to home came a story about several different "wildmen" inhabiting the Ozark hills.

The most interesting article he'd read so far was about a rocky hill—aptly named Mystery Hill—just north of Holstein, Missouri, in neighboring Warren County. Every year during the month of May, or so the story went, strange rumblings could be heard coming from the interior of the hill. No one knew what caused the rumblings, but the countryside around Mystery Hill was honeycombed with caves, one of which was reputed to have a bottomless pit.

Skip rubbed the back of his head, thought about taking a nap, but decided against it. Every time he dozed off he dreamed of his grandmother. Each time she tried to tell him something, but he couldn't understand the words. What was the bundle she offered him? Was the dream some kind of premonition, or just a sure sign that his stay in the hospital was getting to him? He suspected the latter. It wasn't like him to sit around and do nothing, especially with a monster on the prowl.

But was it a monster? Was Lloyd right? Had his eyes played tricks on him? Had it been a bear after all?

No, dammit. I know what I saw.

He closed his eyes and thought back to the night of his attack. Instantly, every detail came rushing back to him: the sound of dry grass crunching beneath his boots; the smell of fresh air, trees and dead cattle; the feel of the evening chill upon his face, and of being watched. And then the sight of a nightmare springing from the darkness of a creek bed.

Skip froze the action playing inside his mind, locking on the monster, enlarging the picture.

It was there, up close and personal, trapped forever on the movie screen of his memory: the muscular body rippling under a light layer of red hair. A mane of the same color framing a broad head accented by glowing eyes, a piggish snout and a mouth crowded with deadly teeth.

Skip remembered the creature's speed, its strength, the sound of its roar and the smell of its foul breath.

He opened his eyes; sweat had broken out on his forehead and under his arms. There was no reason to recall any more, no reason to relive the fear and pain of that night. He had seen enough to convince him that it wasn't a case of imagination.

Fuck you, Lloyd.

He made a grab for the telephone, dialing the number to the station. Forget what Lloyd said. He couldn't afford to worry about his reputation when there was such a creature on the loose. So what if some laughed? Enough would listen to do some good. And if the monster had left the area, it would only strike someplace else, kill another.

The telephone was answered on the third ring.

"Vicky, it's me," he said, pouring a glass of water

from the blue plastic pitcher on his side table. "Is Lloyd there? No? Then how about Murphy?"

Skip's fingers fumbled for his cigarette pack as he listened to the dispatcher explaining why neither Lloyd nor Murphy could be reached. As she continued he could feel his face becoming flushed and the big vein in his neck starting to pump harder. By the time he hung up he was mad, boiling mad.

"Damn him!" Skip cursed.

Lloyd had no business authorizing such an expedition without clearing it through him first. At the very least he should have told him what he was planning on doing. Obviously Lloyd had gone behind his back to keep him from finding out what was going on.

"That pigheaded son of a bitch!"

Lloyd, in his own feeble line of reasoning, was willing to risk his ass to prove that Skip's monster wasn't really a monster. But he hadn't stopped to consider that he might also be risking the lives of the other men as well.

Skip glanced at his watch. It was 5:35 P.M. He crossed the room to the closet. Flinging open the door, he reached in and snatched a clean uniform off a hanger.

Why had Lloyd picked the Devil's Boot as a starting point? Had he gotten a tip from someone? Perhaps. It didn't matter. Skip had to do something.

Quickly he stripped out of his hospital pajamas.

Yeah, I'm going to do something, starting with getting out of this place!

Chapter 15

A blind salamander scampered along a narrow ledge, anxious to escape the noisy intruders. Steven watched in silence as the tiny amphibian slipped into a shallow pool of crystal-clear water. The wall just behind the pool was decorated with golden curtains of almost pure calcite, while the surface of the water was dotted with circular mineral formations called cave rafts.

The pool and the ornate wall framing it were the first natural formations they'd seen in almost forty minutes. The rest of the time it was as though they were walking through a subway tunnel—minus the tracks, ticket booths and muggers. Steven didn't mind the absence of the usual cave decorations and oddities. He was too busy thinking about what their discovery would mean to the scientific community. Whoever dreamed a series of man-made passageways existed in Missouri? In the Southwest it might have been believed, even expected, but not here.

It made him dizzy to think of it. Hundreds of cavers from all over the world would be racing to Missouri. There would be newspaper stories, magazine articles, maybe even a television special or two. They'd probably name the tunnels after him. Imagine, the Fuller Tunnels. Better yet, the Fuller Passageways. It had a nice sound to it.

Steven checked his compass. They were still heading north, the tunnel's floor sloping ever downward. The incline wasn't steep, three or four degrees at the most, but it added up after covering so much distance. Pocketing the compass, he licked the end of his pencil and jotted down a couple of notes on a small spiral notebook. Lloyd joined him as he did.

"Well, Professor, what do you think?"

Steven closed his notebook. "I'm almost convinced that we've stumbled across some kind of Spanish mining operation. More than likely they were looking for gold. Hard telling what we're liable to find. I'd still like to know how you found out about all this."

Lloyd grinned. "You wouldn't believe me if I told you."

Half an hour later all thoughts of Spaniards and gold were forgotten—as forgotten as the city of stone spreading before them.

"Oh, my God," muttered Deputy Brown. He was the first to emerge from the tunnel into the cavern. The light of his carbide helmet danced off the squat stone buildings closest to him.

"What's the matter, Wayne? I thought—"

Steven stopped mid-sentence. Nothing in the world could have prepared him for the shock of seeing the city. Nothing. It was Machu Picchu, Tenochtitlán and a Pueblo village rolled into one. An Anasazi city, shrunk down and relocated deep underground. He pinched his left leg to see if he was dreaming. He wasn't.

The buildings were small, squat and square. Forty or fifty of them, crowded together and stacked on top of each other like the cells of a honeycomb. Some appeared to be constructed from mud and stone; others looked as if they were carved from the walls of the cavern. Between the buildings narrow avenues and alleyways crisscrossed each other, sometimes disappearing into the darkened opening of additional tunnels, other times ending at steps leading to higher levels.

Steven stood speechless before the mysterious city. There was something about it that made him feel uneasy. Maybe it had something to do with stumbling upon something so ancient, so forbidden and forlorn-looking. It was like stepping into a crypt.

It's impossible. How could a city like this exist underground? There must have been two, three hundred inhabitants. How did they live? How did they feed themselves?

He pulled the instamatic camera from his shirt pocket and clicked off several pictures. He tried to take notes, but his hands shook too badly to hold the pencil steady.

"This blows your Spanish mining theory all to hell," Lloyd said, stepping next to him.

As the professor took more pictures, Lloyd connected the mobile phone to the remaining few feet of cable on the last spool. The other spools had already been used. Switching on the phone, he attempted to contact Deputy Hays.

"Base. This is Unit One. Come in, Base."

There was no reply.

"Base. This is Unit One. Come in, Base."

Still no answer.

"Maybe there's a break in the connection," Steven suggested.

"Unit One, this is Base," came the fuzzy reply.

Lloyd smiled. "What took you so long, Hays?"

"I . . . eh . . . was taking care of business. What's up?"

"You're not going to believe this, but we just discovered a lost city."

"You're kidding."

"I'm as serious as a heart attack," Lloyd said. "I'm standing right here looking at it. Real old. I'd say at least a thousand years . . . maybe more. Listen, don't get upset if you can't get hold of me. I'm going to have a look around and I'm about out of cable, so I'll be off the air for a while."

"Right," Hays said. "Let me know what you find."

"You got it." Lloyd switched off the phone and set it on the ground. He unwrapped a lightstick, bent and shook it and set the glowing cylinder next to the phone to mark the spot.

Turning away from Lloyd, Steven approached an archway of black stone that marked an entrance to the city. Carved upon the arch were pictographs of strange symbols and animals. "Beautiful . . . simply beautiful," he said, tracing one of the symbols with his fingers. "What a find. A discovery such as this . . . unexplored, unexploited. It's a miracle. A dream . . . the dream of scientists everywhere."

He wheeled on Lloyd. "We must go back! We must go back right now! We've got to report this, to inform the proper authorities. A find of this magnitude will take years, decades, to unravel its mystery. Even then we may only scratch the surface. This isn't a page in history; it's the whole book! It's bigger than the discovery of Troy, bigger than King Tutankhamen's tomb!"

"I agree," Lloyd said. "But we can't go back."

"Can't go back! Why?"

"Because we're down here to do a job. We still have a bear to find."

"There's no chance of coming across a bear down here," Steven argued. "We've gone too far . . . too deep. A bear wouldn't come this deep."

"That may be," Lloyd nodded, "but I'm still going to check it out while we're here. If you want, we can split up and search. It'll take forever if we don't."

"Yes, I suppose we can do that," Steven said, looking up at the arch. He wasn't paying attention to what Lloyd was saying, his mind occupied instead on the historical treasure before him.

Lloyd turned to the others. "All right, listen up. We're going to split into pairs. Mitchell, you've got Brown. Ferguson, you're with me. Murphy, I want you to stay with the professor. You guys go slow and keep your eyes and ears open. Any trouble, you get on the radio. Understood? It'd also be a good idea to drop a lightstick every so often to mark your trail. It wouldn't be hard to get turned around in this place. Another thing—no souvenirs!"

"Aw, come on, Lloyd," Brown whined.

"I mean it! I'll bust any man I catch trying to sneak something out. If you come across an artifact, leave it alone. Where something is found is often more important to an archaeologist than the object itself. Ain't that right, Professor?"

Steven turned around. "Oh, absolutely. Lloyd's right. If you find something that looks important, please leave it alone. Just touching it might cause it to break or crumble. Some truly magnificent finds have been ruined that way. I promise you, if it's at all possible, each of you will end up with a little something for your efforts."

"What if there's nothing here?" Deputy Mitchell asked.

"Then the publicity alone will be souvenir enough," Steven said. "Gentlemen, you may not realize it, but you're about to become famous."

The statement brought a healthy round of smiles from the men.

"All right, ladies, let's get our asses in gear," Lloyd said.

They moved out.

Chapter 16

Deputy Wayne Brown was almost a foot shorter than his partner, Sergeant Eric Mitchell. The sergeant walked with a wide, loping gait that made Wayne struggle to keep up. After splitting up from Lloyd and the others, they turned left from the main avenue at the first side street they came to. Passing several unadorned, single-story block buildings and an empty reservoir that must have once held water from an underground stream, they reached a carved stairway leading up to the second level.

The steps emptied onto a rectangular courtyard measuring approximately twenty feet by ten. The courtyard was flanked by three singular block units similar to those on the lower level. Each building had a separate doorway opening onto the courtyard.

Sergeant Mitchell paused to look around. "Wayne, what do you think this used to be?"

"Oh, I don't know. A patio, maybe," Wayne replied, happy for the brief rest. He pulled a pack of gum from his shirt pocket, offering a stick to the sergeant.

Eric accepted the piece of gum. He kicked at the ground with the toe of his boot. "This sure will be something when they're finished."

"What do you mean?" Wayne asked, popping a stick of gum into his mouth and throwing the paper on the ground.

"Well, after the scientists get done excavating everything, they'll probably string lights across the ceiling like they did at Meramec Caverns. You ever been to Meramec Caverns? A hell of a tourist trap. This will probably be even bigger when they're through."

Wayne nodded. "It'll put Disney World to shame, that's for sure."

Eric looked around. "Somebody's going to make a pretty penny off of it."

"Somebody's going to make millions." Wayne glanced up at the cavern's ceiling.

"Damn shame it won't be us."

A thought suddenly hit Wayne. "Who said it can't be?"

Eric looked at him, puzzled. "What do you mean?"

Wayne stepped closer, lowering his voice. "As far as I know, nobody owns the property Devil's Boot sits on. Now, for the sake of argument, let's say someone went and purchased that particular piece of real estate. Then that someone would also have title to the only known entrance to the tunnels. The way I see it, the man who owns the entrance to the tunnels owns all this as well."

Eric smiled. "You know, I never looked at it like that."

"That's why you're only a sergeant."

"So who do we see about purchasing the Boot?" Eric asked.

"The best place to start would be the record section of the courthouse. We're going to have to act fast before word spreads about the discovery. How are you set for cash?"

"I've got a couple of thousand stashed away," Eric said.

"Good. Between the two of us, we should have enough to purchase the property. Like I said, we've got to jump on it before someone else decides to do the same thing."

"Or before the government steps in and claims it."

"But if they claim it, they'll still have to buy it from us, for a hell of a lot more money than we paid for it."

"True," Eric said. "I take it we have a deal then?"

"We most definitely do." Wayne grinned and shook Eric's hand.

"So what do we do in the meantime?" Eric asked.

"Try to find a bear, I guess," Wayne said.

"Hell, Wayne, there ain't no bear."

"Lloyd thinks there is."

"Maybe so, but if you ask me no bear is going to come this deep underground. I think Lloyd just wanted to have a look around before we went back. We ought to do the same. Maybe we'll find a souvenir or two. I mean, we've got a right to look the place over before we buy it, don't we?"

"We sure do," Wayne said.

Their lights casting eerie, dancing shadows before them, they crossed the courtyard to the first of the three block buildings. Peering through a doorway, they were greeted by an empty room, its floor littered with potsherds, stone chips and mollusk shells. Three symbols were scratched just above the doorway. Wayne guessed that the symbols were letters of an unknown alphabet. Perhaps it was the name of the former occupant.

"Not exactly the Ritz, is it?" Eric said. Removing his pocketknife, he kneeled and began to scrape at a section of the wall near the doorway.

"What are you doing?" Wayne inquired, peering over the sergeant's shoulder.

Pieces of hardened clay flaked away as Eric dug and chipped at the wall. The knife blade penetrated a couple of inches before hitting solid rock. Apparently satisfied, Eric closed the knife and stood back up.

"I was curious if the buildings were adobe or stone. They're stone, but whoever made them covered the walls with mud, probably as insulation."

"A lot of work went into this place," Wayne commented. "Must have taken years to build."

"Yeah," Eric nodded. "I wonder what they were scared of."

"What do you mean?"

"I can't see anyone going to all the trouble of building a city underground unless it's for protection. That's why the cliff dwellers in Arizona and New Mexico built their pueblos in such hard-to-get-at locations—for protection against their enemies."

"How'd you get so damn smart all of a sudden?" Wayne asked.

"My old lady subscribes to *National Geographic.*"

The second room they explored was a carbon copy of the first, with the exception of a square opening in the floor near the back wall. Shining their lights down into the opening, they discovered an even larger room than the one they were in. Unlike the other rooms, the walls of this basement room were decorated with vividly colored murals of lavishly dressed men and women.

"I'll be damned. A kiva," Eric said.

"A what?"

"A room used for religious ceremonies."

"Oh."

Two of the murals depicted scenes of battle between tan-skinned warriors. The third, however, showed a scene from everyday life. In the painting, women with flowing dresses carried great earthenware jugs down a narrow street, while naked children played what appeared to be a ball game.

In the center of the farthest wall, forming a central focal point for the murals, was a painting of a striking young woman whose beckoning arms were entwined with a pair of deadly looking serpents. Though she was by all means beautiful, her eyes were cold, cruel. Wayne figured she must have been some important leader, or a goddess perhaps, for she wore a spiked crown of gold and was depicted riding atop a monstrous two-headed turtle.

A massive altar of stone, appearing to be carved

from a solid piece of ebony rock, stood in front of the painting of the turtle woman. Several large earthenware jugs flanked each side of the altar, while a doorway was just visible in the wall behind it.

"Man, I've got to get down there!" Eric said, rubbing his hands together with excitement.

Wayne nodded. "There must have been a ladder once, but it probably rotted away. We can use the ropes."

While Wayne unwound his climbing rope Eric drove a bolt into the floor. He fastened one end of the rope to it with a spring-gate carabiner and dropped the rest down through the opening.

Descending to the lower chamber, they discovered an additional exit on the opposite side of the room from the altar. Unlike the square doorway behind the altar, the second opening appeared to be a natural formation in the rock.

Eric shone his flashlight into the opening. "Looks like another tunnel."

"There'll be plenty of time to explore it later," Wayne said. "First let's have a look in those jugs."

Reaching the altar, Wayne had to rise on his tiptoes to peer over the rim of the first clay jug. He was hoping for gold or jewels, but the jug only contained an inch or so of dust.

"Nuts, it's empty."

"This one too," Eric said, checking one of the other jugs. "Maybe they held water."

"Or the blood of sacrificed victims," Wayne replied.

Eric aimed his flashlight at the altar. "You really think they sacrificed people down here?"

Wayne shrugged. "The Mayans and Aztecs used to do it all the time. Why else would you have a stone altar this size?"

Eric looked up at the wall. The light on his helmet danced over the painting of the serpent woman. "You could be right. She doesn't exactly look like the Virgin Mary."

"Virgin *eater* would be more like it."

Eric turned away from the altar. "I'm gonna leave the rest of the jugs for you. I want to have a look in the tunnel."

"Okay, go ahead. Just don't wander too far."

"Got ya."

Wayne watched Eric start down the tunnel, then turned back to the task of examining the earthenware jugs. He was dismayed to find that the rest of the jugs were as empty as the first. Perhaps, he thought, they were only storage vessels for water. Whatever they were, he'd love to have a pair sitting in his living room.

Finished with the jugs, he decided to take a closer look at the stone altar. No bloodstains; maybe it was just a table after all. But he doubted it. It was much too elaborate to be anything other than an altar of some kind. Zigzag lines carved in the table's top ran at right angles to each other, forming a maze around a creature that looked something like a frog . . . a four-legged frog with tits.

Kneeling down, he tried to figure out how the top

was joined to the two slabs forming the legs. He failed to find any separation between the sections, further convincing him that the altar was carved from a single block of stone.

This must have taken years to make.

He stood back up as Eric reentered the room.

"Nothing down that way but tunnel," Eric stated matter of factly. "Any luck with the jugs?"

"No. They're empty."

"Listen, I . . ."

Eric stopped. Wayne started to ask what was wrong, but then he heard it too. A strange crackling, like the sound of wool sweaters being pulled hot from a dryer.

"What the hell is that?" Eric asked.

"Damned if I know," Wayne said. The hairs on his arms stood up and the air was pungent with the smell of ozone.

"Shit, Wayne, I don't like this."

"Me neither."

Wayne started to suggest that they leave when he spotted something moving in the tunnel behind Eric. A pair of funny yellow lights, like the headlights of an approaching automobile.

The lights came closer, grew in size.

Wayne opened his mouth to yell a warning to his partner when something exploded into the room. Sergeant Eric Mitchell never knew what hit him.

God Almighty!

The light of Eric's carbide helmet lamp winked out as his head disappeared into the gaping jaws of the

Crota. There was the crunch of bones, followed by the sound of brains splattering on the floor, as the monster bit off the sergeant's head just above his eyebrows.

Eric's eyes were wide, bulging, staring. Blood poured from his nose and streamed down his face. His mouth moved, but no words came out; his body spasmed and jerked. Before he could fall dead to the floor, the Crota flung him against the far wall like a child casting aside a rag doll.

His brain sending out a million messages at once, Wayne's legs finally got the signal they needed to get moving. With a howl of terror, he turned and ran for the opening under the turtle woman. The Crota roared and gave chase.

My God . . . My God . . . My God. What is it? What the fuck is that thing?

The lights of Wayne's helmet and flashlight bounced madly off the walls as he raced down the narrow passageway. His heart pounded like a jack-hammer, his breath came in short, painful gasps. Unless he could get back into the open he was a dead man. There was no hope of anyone coming to his rescue if he remained in the subterranean passageway. No sense calling for help on the radio. How could they find him if he didn't even know where he was? From behind him came sounds of pursuit.

The passageway took a sudden turn to the left. Wayne missed the turn and smashed into a wall, dropped his shotgun, spun off and kept running. The Crota gained on him.

Don't stop. Don't stop. Keep running.

He shrieked as the floor suddenly changed into a flight of descending steps. He couldn't stop in time. Head over heels he tumbled, his body bouncing off the stone steps.

He came to rest at the bottom of the steps, his back pressed tightly against a cold stone wall, his left leg bent painfully beneath him. He had lost his flashlight in the tumble. His helmet too. In the total darkness surrounding him all was silent. All was still.

Wayne gritted his teeth as he slowly unfolded his left leg. His knee was badly wrenched, but the bone wasn't broken. Pulling his revolver, he waited to be attacked. Time passed. His breathing slowed. Nothing happened. Had the monster given up the chase?

Where is it? Where did it go?

He grabbed two lightsticks from his pack. Removing their foil wrapping, he bent both sticks and shook them. A green glow instantly lit the corridor around him.

He was alone. The creature was nowhere in sight. Wayne let out a sigh of relief.

I must have lost it. Maybe it ran past me when I fell. Maybe it gave up and turned back . . .

Maybe it went back to the room to finish eating Eric.

Wayne tried to call for help on the portable radio, but it had been damaged in the fall. Like it or not, he was on his own.

He had no idea where the tunnel led, but he couldn't—dared not—go back the way he came. Then again, if he continued on, he ran the risk of becoming hopelessly lost in what could be an elaborate tunnel system. But he had no choice. Using the wall for support, he slowly got to his feet.

Keeping one of the lightsticks to light his way, he dropped the other one on the floor to mark his trail. His knee screamed in pain and threatened to buckle beneath his weight as he took a careful step forward. Wayne ignored the pain. He could make it—had to make it. He had to find his way out before that thing came back looking for him.

He shuffled along for about twenty minutes, dropping a half-dozen lightsticks in the process. Exhausted, the throbbing in his knee almost unbearable, he decided to stop and rest for a moment. If he didn't, he would surely pass out.

Leaning against the wall, Wayne looked back down the passageway. The corridor was long and straight, and he could still see the eerie green glow from three of the lightsticks he'd dropped. As he stood there looking, the farthest lightstick flickered and went out.

What the hell?

A prickle of fear danced from his temples to his testicles. "It just went out, that's all. Damn thing was probably defective. A dud."

Wayne really didn't believe that.

His hands beginning to shake, he slowly cocked the hammer back on his revolver.

The next lightstick also flickered and went out.

Legs trembling with fear, he started slowly backing

up. He stayed close to the wall, his gaze focused on the last lightstick.

The final lightstick was only about twenty feet away. Wayne watched as it, too, flickered and went out, leaving the corridor in complete darkness. In that blackness, two eyes suddenly appeared—two slanting yellow eyes—glowing with a light all their own. The eyes turned his way and stared at him with unblinking curiosity, watching him with an intelligence so strong he could almost feel it. Beneath the eyes a mouth appeared, lined with a double row of glowing green teeth. . . .

The son of a bitch is eating the lightsticks!

The Crota seemed to laugh in delight.

Wayne screamed.

Chapter 17

The stew hissed and boiled, chunks of carrots, potatoes and meat rising slowly to the surface to dance with the bursting bubbles. Outside the tiny cabin, the wind picked up, blowing stray tumbleweeds across the South Dakota prairie. Somewhere in the distance a coyote howled his lonesome cry.

Jay Little Hawk sat cross-legged on the bare wooden floor, his back resting against the wall. He tried to ignore the wonderful aroma of the stew, but it wasn't easy. He hadn't eaten since leaving Missouri. The plane out of St. Louis didn't serve meals and he'd barely had enough time to grab a cup of coffee while changing airlines in Sioux Falls. Thirty minutes later, he'd landed at the Pierre Municipal Airport. He had been met at the unloading ramp by two Lakota Indians, Lenorad Firekeeper and Lenorad's younger cousin, David White Cloud. Both followed the medicine path.

Almost ten years had passed since Little Hawk last saw either of the two men, so the reunion was a happy one with lots of hugging and backslapping.

The long ride back to the Rosebud Reservation gave the three of them a chance to exchange information about family and friends. Not wanting to cloud happy conversations with unhappy shadows, they deliberately avoided talking about what brought Little Hawk to South Dakota.

Hawk opened his eyes. David White Cloud and Lenorad Firekeeper sat across the room from him, their backs against the opposite wall. The blanket the men sat on was an interesting weave of bright reds, blues and greens. Their grandmother had made it when they were still toddlers, many years before her eyes yellowed and went blind. Lenorad and David shared the blanket equally, neither trying to claim total ownership. It was their most treasured possession.

Just to Hawk's right sat Charlie Grey. Charlie was a big man at six feet four inches tall and a little over two hundred thirty pounds, but he was easygoing. He always had a smile and a kind word for everyone, and he could tell a joke like no one else could. Even if he flubbed the punchline, his comical expressions made you laugh. But Charlie didn't seem so happy-go-lucky tonight. His shoulders sagged heavily, and he nervously tugged at his braids. It wasn't an occasion for joke making, so Charlie kept quiet. Maybe a few funny stories is what they needed.

To the right of Charlie, practically dwarfed in the big man's shadow, sat an Apache named Sam Golthlay. Sam was ten years older than Charlie, less than half his size, thin and wiry with a hooked nose and narrow face. He was considered an elder, but he never let age slow him down. Sam had already outlived three wives and fathered at least a dozen children.

The last man in the room, Jim Hightower, owned the house they were in. Like most reservation Indians, Jim was dirt-poor and couldn't afford much. Still, the two-room shack he called home was clean and comfortable. What little furniture he owned had been moved into the bedroom in preparation for the ceremony to come. Like the others in the room, Hightower was also a medicine man.

When he arrived earlier, Hawk had lent a hand in covering the windows and doors with heavy blankets. The smallest flicker of light was not to be allowed in once the ceremony started. Nothing shiny could be in the room either; therefore, all pictures and mirrors had been turned towards the wall, all eyeglasses and watches removed.

A large rectangle was drawn on the floor in chalk, leaving enough space between it and the walls for the participants to sit comfortably. A different-colored flag hung from the ceiling at each corner of the rectangle. At the western corner a black flag represented darkness and night. A red flag, representing the sacred pipestone and the blood of the people, hung at the south corner. The yellow flag at the east corner stood for the rising sun, while a white flag represented the north.

A wooden staff, standing in a clay pot, had been placed between the north and west flags. Painted red and black, with four eagle feathers fastened to its top, the staff stood before a small altar of powdered earth. To the left of the altar sat two gourd rattles.

As though an unseen signal had passed through the room, the quiet whispers died down and Jim Hightower hurried to open the door. The others rose to their feet. The one they were waiting for had arrived.

The man who entered might possibly have been the oldest man alive. His face was creased with rivers of time, and the braids hanging over his shoulders were white as new-fallen snow. The ends of those braids were wrapped with soft brown beaver fur, held in place with pieces of red cloth. A golden eagle tail feather hung from the left braid, the feather's quill beaded with turquoise and red beads. About his thin neck he wore a bone choker, while a blue and white blanket was draped carefully over his shoulders.

Though the man's body was old, his eyes burned with a fiery intensity. When he moved, it was not with the feeble shuffle of someone frail and weak, but with a straight-shouldered bearing that demanded and received respect.

There was no need for an introduction. Everyone in the room knew George Strong Eagle. There probably wasn't an Indian on the reservation who hadn't asked for his help at one time or another. Everyone knew Strong Eagle; everyone respected him. He was a tribal elder, a council leader, a chief and one of the last of the truly great medicine men. If there was a problem, he would know what to do about it.

Strong Eagle hugged Jim Hightower as he entered the room, handing him a leather-wrapped bundle to hold. He then hugged the other men, greeting each with a word or two in Lakota. Eagle didn't speak any English, and it saddened him how many of the younger people spoke only the white man's tongue.

Little Hawk, who could speak Lakota almost as well as he could speak Cherokee, was the last to be greeted. Strong Eagle not only spoke to him, but hugged him longer than all the others. There had always been a special place in Hawk's heart for Strong Eagle. They'd known each other for a very long time. After Hawk's return from Vietnam, Eagle had adopted him as a son. It was quite an honor. The act had been made official by a special ceremony in which they were covered with a buffalo robe and tied together with thongs, symbolizing their togetherness for life.

The others waited patiently for Eagle to sit down before taking a seat themselves. He sat midway along the end wall, in the place of honor, forming the central point of those gathered in the room. Across the room from him was the fireplace, where the stew boiled. To his left was the wall occupied by Lenorad Firekeeper, David White Cloud and Jim Hightower. To his right were Little Hawk, Charlie Grey and Sam Golthlay. Before sitting back down, Hightower returned Eagle's bundle to him.

Eagle carefully opened the bundle. It contained

three smaller bundles wrapped in soft deerhide. The first bundle was his medicine bag. In it were a necklace of bear claws, several different kinds of dried roots and plants, seven twisted braids of sweetgrass, sage and numerous things the Great Spirit had given him over the years.

He handed two braids of sweetgrass to Lenorad Firekeeper. Lenorad lit the end of each braid and walked around, waving the sweetgrass back and forth so the fragrance filled the room.

Next the old medicine man passed around a small tobacco pouch filled with sage, instructing each man to put a sprig behind his ear or in his hair to please the spirits.

While the sage and the sweetgrass were going around, Jim Hightower removed the pot of stew from the fire and set it next to the altar. Alongside the stew, he set a bucket of cold well water.

The Yuwipi ceremony was ready to begin.

Stripping naked to the waist, Eagle stood before the altar. Lenorad Firekeeper and David White Cloud stood just behind him. Placing his arms behind his back, Eagle told the two men to tie his fingers together with a length of rawhide cord, starting with thumb to thumb. After tying his fingers together, he had them bind his wrists and arms.

Strong Eagle was then covered with a large quilt and tied up with a rope. Once tied, he was placed face down on the floor within the chalked rectangle, his head to the altar. Technically, he was dead. Like his ancestors, who were wrapped in blankets and placed on scaffolds at the time of death, Eagle had ceased to be. With the symbolic death of his body, his spirit was free to wander, to seek answers to questions that could not have been answered otherwise.

Lenorad Firekeeper and David White Cloud stepped back out of the rectangle, resuming their places along the wall. They were not allowed to reenter the sacred area until after the ceremony. Jim Hightower waited until the two men took their seats and then turned off the lights. Blackness swallowed the room.

The darkness was an ally, helping each man to concentrate on what was transpiring, adding strength to their songs and prayers. Little Hawk started off the singing. Though he could speak the Lakota dialect, he sang in Cherokee:

In a sacred way I am living.
In a sacred way I am praying.
The spirits they are coming.
The spirits they are coming.
Come spirits, come listen to my song.

No sooner had Hawk finished his song than Charlie Grey started in with his deep-throated lyrics. And so it went, each man singing a different song or prayer when his turn came around. They were halfway through the second round when their songs were answered. The spirits had arrived.

Bright sparks of light twinkled and popped in the

inky darkness of the room. At times they appeared as little more than the soft winking of starlight on a balmy summer night. Other times, the flashes were as bright as the strobe of a camera.

The walls and floor groaned and shook as separate entities announced their arrival. Rattles shook and unseen objects flew through the air, crashing into the walls. Little Hawk heard the murmur of whispering voices. The voices grew in number until it sounded as if many people were crammed inside the tiny room. The rattles continued to shake, but now they were accompanied by the hollow beating of a drum. No one had brought a drum to the ceremony. The spirits must have brought their own.

Cries of different animals echoed off the walls and the strong, musty scent of dung and fur filled the air. A woman spoke, asking about the welfare of a relative.

Something flew into Hawk's left shoulder; a feathered wing brushed his cheek. Suddenly, a misty cloud of light appeared before his eyes. It began to swirl, grow solid and take on shape. As he watched, the patch of light formed into the head of a great buffalo. Hawk could feel the beast's hot breath upon his face, smell the dusty fragrance of the open prairie. The buffalo came closer, blurred and passed completely through him, leaving behind a longing for days long past.

"Hurry, turn on the lights!"

Hawk squinted at the sudden brightness. He looked to the spot where he had last seen Strong

Eagle, but the medicine man was no longer there. Instead, he was sitting cross-legged before the altar, completely unwrapped and untied.

Eagle smiled and nodded to those in the room. He listened carefully as each man spoke of his experience during the ceremony. Several also took the opportunity to ask personal questions which were answered by the medicine man. Little Hawk did not ask any questions; Eagle already knew what was on his mind.

Strong Eagle carefully unwrapped the piece of deerskin encasing his second bundle. Everyone was quiet as the old man spoke.

"It is customary that the Yuwipi ceremony be ended with the pipe, as are all our important ceremonies. The pipe used is always that of the person conducting the ceremony, but the spirits have told me not to use my pipe tonight. Instead, they have given me another to use in its place."

Hawk's mouth dropped open. Several of the others gasped as Strong Eagle revealed what was in the second bundle.

The pipe's bowl was pipestone, blackened with age, its stem the lower leg bone of a buffalo calf, wrapped in buffalo wool and red flannel cloth. Tied to the stem were eagle feathers, four small scalps and a couple of bird skins.

There was no mistaking the pipe, because there wasn't another one like it in all the world. The pipe was called Ptehincala Huhu Canunpa, Buffalo Calf Bone Pipe, and it was the most precious heirloom of the Sioux Nation. It was the same pipe that White Buffalo Woman gave to the tribe centuries ago, the original pipe of the spirit woman who taught the people how to pray.

Eagle carefully picked up the pipe and filled its bowl with kinnikinnick. Store-bought tobacco would never be smoked in such a pipe; it would be like drinking Kool-Aid in the name of Jesus.

Hawk sat to the right of Eagle, so he lit the bowl for the old medicine man. Once lit, the pipe was raised to the Great Spirit, then lowered to Mother Earth and offered to the four different directions. The pipe was then passed to Lenorad Firekeeper to start it on a clockwise journey around the room. Strong Eagle waited for the pipe to complete the circle back to him before speaking.

"The spirits have decreed that we were to use Ptehincala Huhu Canunpa tonight, because tonight's ceremony is of great importance." He turned to Hawk. "Little Hawk comes here tonight asking for help. He does not ask it for himself, but for the entire race of man. A great evil has been released upon our world, an evil not known since the times of our great-grandfathers. I know these things. The spirits have taken me to the dwelling place of this evil one. I have peered down into the dark and forbidden lair it calls home. I have seen it, and I know its name. So too did my grandfather know its name, but even then it was a very old name, an almost forgotten legend. But I tell you this: this evil one is no legend; it is as real as you or me. Its name is Crota."

Hawk stared at a spot on the floor. A few of the others shifted nervously under the intense gaze of the old medicine man.

"Little Hawk, I know that you seek a way to destroy this creature of darkness. I must caution you that this evil one is of stronger magic than you can imagine. It will not be easy to destroy a creature such as this. It will be very hard, but not impossible. Nothing is impossible as long as there is courage and faith."

Strong Eagle looked around the room, then continued: "Still, Little Hawk, I don't recommend that you challenge this creature by yourself. While you may have courage and faith—as I know you do—you lack the experience of wisdom that comes only with age. Unfortunately, the Crota will not wait for you to mature. And if we wait, while you will grow wiser, it will grow stronger. No, you cannot wait, but neither can you defeat this thing by yourself. That is why I am going with you."

You could have heard a snowflake fall, so silent did the room become. No one moved. No one swallowed. They were all in shock from what Strong Eagle had said. Not once during his long life had the old medicine man set foot off the reservation. Little Hawk started to speak, but the old man held up his hand for silence.

"Do not question what I have said or what I am about to do. We all know there are strange forces at work in the universe. The spirits have shown me the path I am to follow. I am not one to question the ways of the spirits and neither are you. Now, if you don't mind, I would like to eat. I am hungry and there are many things I must do before I leave, and there are only a few hours in which to do them."

Jim Hightower quickly served bowls of stew to each of the guests. The ceremonial stew was thought to bring good luck. Little Hawk and Strong Eagle each had seconds. They were going to need all the luck they could get.

Chapter 18

It was a good thing they were leaving a trail of lightsticks, otherwise Corporal Randy Murphy would have been hopelessly lost in a relatively short time. The narrow stone alleyways and footpaths they followed twisted and turned like a serpent, often ending at a courtyard or high wall, forcing them to backtrack and start again.

They were in the process of exploring what had apparently been a communal food-storage room, pieces of broken pottery lying everywhere, when a scream echoed through the cavern. Randy reacted automatically by jacking a round into the chamber of his shotgun. Professor Fuller turned away from the pictographs he was studying. He didn't speak. Like Randy, he was trying to determine which direction the scream came from.

"Unit Three, this is Unit One. Over."

Randy made a fumbled grab for his radio. "Go ahead, Lloyd. Over."

"Did you yell?"

"Negative."

"Can you tell where it came from?" Lloyd asked.

"No," Randy said.

"Me neither. Unit Two doesn't respond. The stone walls must be interfering with radio transmissions. What's your present position, Three?"

"We're . . ." Randy looked quickly to the professor.

"West," Steven Fuller whispered.

". . . on the west side of the city. I'd say about three or four blocks from where we split up."

"Roger, Three. I figure I'm about four blocks north of you. Get back to the main avenue. We'll rendezvous there."

"Roger, One. Out."

Randy looked around. He wasn't buying the part about the stone walls interfering with radio transmission. Unit Two not responding could only mean they had run into trouble. The scream meant it was serious trouble.

He turned to the professor. "You heard the man, let's go."

"We'd save a lot of time if we cut across the roof tops," Steven said.

Randy considered the suggestion. "What about falling through?"

"We'll stick to the outer edges, that way we'll actually be walking on top of the walls."

Randy nodded. "Sounds good. Let's do it."

With the city terraced as it was, they had only to scale a five-foot wall to gain access to the roofs of the second-tier dwellings. From their new vantage point the ancient city looked like a gigantic beehive.

Randy noticed that some of the buildings were not roofed, or were only half-roofed. Maybe it was deliberate, for many of the buildings had no doorways in their outer walls. Entrance into those particular habitats could be made only by climbing onto the roof of an adjoining building.

The first three buildings they crossed didn't present a problem, but the fourth was roofless. Though the walls were wide enough to walk on, Randy felt his mouth go dry as he started his trek to the other side. It was all he could do to keep from staring down into the room below. A slip would probably result in at least one broken bone, maybe two.

Three more of the roofed structures followed and then they came to the end of the block. Here they were faced with the problem of either climbing down, crossing the intersecting alleyway and climbing back up the wall on the other side or attempting to jump across from roof to roof. It was at least fifteen feet to the street below, which meant they would have to use a rope to make the descent, wasting valuable time. In addition, once down, there was no guarantee they would be able to climb back up to rooftop-level again. However, the alley was only about five feet wide and not much of an obstacle to jump across, provided nothing went wrong.

They decided to jump.

Steven Fuller went first, making the jump look easy as he landed lightly on the opposite side. Randy had suspected all along that the professor was half mountain goat. Still, his ego would not allow him to be outdone. Taking a deep breath, he prepared to follow.

"Here goes!" Randy shouted.

Steven backed up to give him room.

Sprinting to the edge of the building, Randy pushed off with a groan. His takeoff was good, but his effort was only halfhearted. He landed close to the edge on the opposite building. Too close. A stone in the rock wall shifted and gave way. Loose stones clattered to the rocky alleyway below.

Randy, feeling the weight shift under him, pinwheeled his arms, trying to keep his balance. The wall crumbled beneath his feet; he felt himself falling. Professor Fuller made a mad grab for him. He caught about two inches of fabric on the front of Randy's coveralls. The fabric stretched, ripped, and tore free.

Randy screamed as he fell backwards. Steven Fuller, eyes wide with fright, stood on the roof's edge, clutching the torn piece of fabric. Randy had a brief glimpse of the alleyway rushing up to meet him. Darkness followed.

Chapter 19

Skip stopped by his office long enough to pick up his revolver and to question the dispatcher further about the whereabouts of Lloyd and the other members of the department. Vicky couldn't provide any more information, except to say that none of the officers taking part in the Devil's Boot expedition had reported in yet. That tidbit of knowledge only added to the growing shadow of concern tugging at the back of Skip's mind.

Turning off Cemetery Road, he drove as far as possible along the rocky path to the cave. He might have gotten a little closer, but the way was blocked by three patrol cars not equipped for roughing it like his Bronco. Calling the station to let them know he was going to be out of his vehicle, he locked the door and continued on foot. Five minutes later, he reached the cave's entrance.

Seeing Skip, Hays jumped up from his chair. "Sheriff! . . . I thought you were still in the hospital. When did you get out?"

Skip pushed past the deputy and grabbed the microphone. "How long have they been down there?"

"A couple of hours . . . maybe longer."

"What call sign is Lloyd answering to?"

"Unit One. We're Base."

Skip nodded and keyed the microphone. "Unit One, this is Base. Come in, One. Over."

There was no answer.

Skip repeated the message. "Unit One, this is Base. Come in, One. Over." The silence hung heavy between the two men.

"God damn it, Lloyd, answer the fucking radio!"

The only answer was the quiet hum of the amp.

"Maybe he can't hear you," the deputy said.

"Maybe he doesn't want to."

Chapter 20

"Oh my God!" Lloyd whispered, his breath burning. Deputy Greg Ferguson took one look and retched.

If it wasn't for the gum wrapper lying in the doorway they would have walked past the building, for it looked no different from all the rest. But the wrapper had caught Lloyd's attention. Entering the unadorned building, they discovered an entrance to a basement room . . . a room with walls covered in exotic murals, and a floor splattered with blood.

They lowered themselves into the room by means of a climbing rope, left behind and anchored to the floor by one of the other members of the expedition. As they descended, their lights swept across the body of Sergeant Mitchell lying on an ebony altar.

Eric Mitchell was naked, the tattered pieces of his uniform scattered about the altar like pieces of brown crepe paper. He lay on his back, eyes staring, his mouth open in a silent scream. The sergeant's head ended just above his eyebrows in the front, and just below his ears in the back. The skull was empty, his brain removed by whoever had killed him.

Lloyd glanced down. Bloody footprints criss-crossed the floor. *Big* footprints, each measuring about fifteen inches long and five inches wide. The creature that left the tracks had to be enormous. The prints led from the center of the room to the altar, back to the tunnel on the opposite side of the room, and back again to the doorway beyond the altar.

As he stood studying the footprints, the words of Jay Little Hawk came rushing back to him. It would be stupid to continue believing they were dealing with a bear. There wasn't a bear on earth that left a track that big.

Sickened by the sight before him, Lloyd stepped away from the altar. Behind him, Deputy Ferguson had quit throwing up and was now sobbing uncontrollably.

Lloyd had just reached the center of the room when something changed in the air about him. Maybe it was only the tension of the situation, but he could have sworn the air was suddenly electrified. Looking around, he tried to determine where the sensation was coming from.

"Do you feel that?" he asked, turning to the deputy.

Greg Ferguson nodded.

Knowing whatever killed Mitchell might still be nearby, Lloyd turned and faced the doorway beyond the altar. With his flashlight held against the left side of his shotgun, he braced himself for what might appear from the darkness. The electric intensity in the room grew.

"L-Lloyd!"

Startled, he spun back around.

Because of the tracks, Lloyd had assumed that the creature exited the room through the doorway behind the altar. Maybe it had. If so, then the damn thing had circled around to come up behind them.

His body trembling in terror, Deputy Ferguson slowly backed across the room. His slow, shuffling movements were watched closely by a living, breathing nightmare. A nightmare with eyes of yellow fire.

Skip was right, so was Jay Little Hawk. It was true, all of it. There wasn't a bear, never had been. What there was instead was something almost incomprehensible, something straight out of a science-fiction movie. Only this was no movie. The creature was real.

The Crota shifted its gaze from Ferguson to Lloyd, then back to Ferguson. The creature was hunched, tensed, like a cat ready to spring, its hands slowly opening and closing in anticipation. The scraping of its claws sent chills up and down Lloyd's back.

He raised his shotgun and aimed at the monster, but his hands shook so badly he didn't dare fire for fear of hitting Deputy Ferguson.

"Get the fuck out of the way, Ferguson!" Lloyd hissed between clenched teeth.

The deputy didn't reply, didn't move. He stood there, looking up at the monster before him. His tremblings reached spasm level. Flecks of spittle flaked his lips.

"Damn you, Ferguson. Don't you dare go south on me now. Not now."

The deputy's flashlight fell from limp fingers. The shotgun followed.

Lloyd's finger tightened on the trigger of his shotgun. "Get . . . out . . . of . . . the . . . way."

Deputy Ferguson moaned. The sound started soft, grew louder, building into a scream.

"AaayyyeeeEEEE . . ."

The deputy's head tipped back. The scream climbed in volume, reaching the level of an air raid siren. Black claws sliced the air, seeking the source of the shrill noise.

"EEEEEEE—"

The scream stopped. A bubbling gurgle replaced it.

Deputy Ferguson's head pivoted backwards, fell back until it touched his backbone, hung upside down by a single thread of flesh. His eyes stared, unblinking; his mouth opened and closed like a fish out of water. A heartbeat later, the deputy's body fell in on itself like a deflating balloon.

Lloyd didn't shoot. He ran.

Chapter 21

Jay Little Hawk gazed out the tiny window. Somewhere below was the sleeping city of Omaha, though it was doubtful very many of the residents could sleep through the thunderstorm they were having. Bolts of lightning arced across the night sky, lighting up the horizon in a spectacularly fiery display. From thirty-five thousand feet the storm didn't look very frightening, nor was it much to worry about, especially considering the greater troubles he faced.

"Sir, would you care for a pillow?"

Hawk turned his head and nearly got a face full of breast.

The flight attendant's name was Julie, at least that was the name on her nametag. She was a tall brunette with a pair of legs that seemed to go on forever. Her smile was orthodontically perfect and her personality utterly charming. There was a fresh, clean scent about her guaranteed to wake up a few glands. Another trip, another time maybe, he might have been tempted to flirt a little, maybe even make a pass. But not this time. He knew he wouldn't be good company for anyone, except maybe for his unusual-looking traveling companion.

"No, thank you. I'm fine," he smiled back.

"Eh . . ." Her eyes looked past Hawk. "What about him?"

George Strong Eagle made quite a spectacle among the dark-suited businessmen spaced throughout the red-eye special. He wore faded blue jeans, a brown shirt and moccasins. The tips of his braided hair were wrapped with strips of red cloth. A golden eagle tail feather was tied to the left braid, his blue blanket draped loosely about his shoulders. He sat rigid in his seat, his eyes transfixed on an invisible point out the window. For an old Indian who'd never flown before, let alone been off the reservation, he was doing pretty well. During takeoff, however, he did startle a few passengers when he started singing his death song.

Hawk turned and asked Eagle in Lakota if he needed a pillow. The old man's reply made him laugh.

"He wants to know if you come with it."

Julie smiled. "Sorry. If you'd like, I can put this in the overhead compartment—"

She started to reach for the deerskin-wrapped bundle resting on Eagle's lap, but his left hand shot out like a snake, intercepting the attendant before she could touch it. She gasped. Hawk spoke quickly in Lakota. Eagle answered back and released the young woman's wrist.

Hawk translated: "He says he's very sorry if he

frightened you. He's a foolish old man. This is the first time he's ever flown in an airplane, the first time he's been away from his home. Please forgive his actions, but the bundle on his lap makes him feel less afraid. He would rather hold it."

Julie straightened back up. "It's okay . . . I understand."

There was a noticeable change in her voice. It was more metallic, more artificial than before. There was a white mark around her wrist where Eagle had grabbed her. She refrained from rubbing it, although Hawk could tell she wanted to.

Hawk sighed as he watched the attendant continue forward between the rows of resting passengers, heading for the galley. No doubt she'd give the rest of the flight crew warning to steer clear of their seats. Just as well; he didn't need the distractions of fragrant perfumes and pretty legs. He had too much to think about, too many things to plan out. Tomorrow was going to be a busy day, probably the busiest day of his entire life. Tilting his seat back, he returned to gazing out the window.

Chapter 22

Pain preceded the return to consciousness. At first Randy wasn't sure whether he was alive or dead, awake or not. Darkness lay before him like a blanket. Surely he must be alive; death was supposed to be painless. But was he awake? He never remembered having dreams of discomfort—nightmares, yes, but never physical discomfort. Perhaps if he tried to move he would be able to determine if he was still among the living. He did so, but very slowly, starting with his right arm. His actions brought a flash of pain intense enough to form colors in the back of his head.

Upward his probing fingers glided until they reached his face. He was surprised to find a dampened cloth covering his eyes. Everything came rushing back to him. Like a computer summoned on-line, Randy's memory came alive. He sat up.

"Professor?"

Dizziness slammed into him, forcing him back into the supine position. His head sank back into the softness of a pack.

"Shhh . . . I'm here," came a whispered reply from off to his left. A flashlight switched on long enough to allow Randy to see the professor's silhouette. He was sitting against a nearby wall, his ear pressed tightly against the radio.

"Don't try to move so fast. You took a nasty fall. Anything broken?"

Randy ran a quick mental check of all his body parts. "My back hurts."

"Can you wiggle your toes?"

With great effort he could. "Yes."

"Then it's not broken, only sprained."

Cautiously, he probed along the back of his head to the source of the painful throbbing. His head was bandaged; several wraps of gauze held a large patch in place. The hair around that patch was sticky with blood.

"I think some of my brains leaked out," Randy stated as he drew his hand away.

"No such luck," Steven Fuller replied sourly. "I scooped them up and packed them back in. I may have gotten them scrambled around and backwards, but they're still there. Can you walk?"

"No," Randy replied, picturing the professor packing his head like a suitcase.

"Come, come, I was only kidding about the brains. Lucky for you, you have an extremely hard head. You may have suffered a concussion. Nothing more."

"That's easy for you to say. How long have I been out?"

"About thirty minutes."

"Jesus . . ." Randy made it to his elbows. "I have to get in touch with Lloyd."

Steven came over and kneeled by him. Randy could hear the hissing static of the radio.

"I'm afraid that's impossible," he said. "It seems Lloyd has keyed his radio to the On position. There's no way to get through to him."

"Are you sure it's Lloyd? Maybe one of the others—"

"There are no others."

The professor's words were like a sucker punch to the stomach.

"What?" Randy asked in astonishment.

"There are no others," Steven repeated slowly. "We're the only ones left."

"That's impossible," Randy argued. "How? What?"

"Lloyd's radio was keyed, so I heard everything. Something killed Deputy Ferguson. I don't know what it was, but I heard Lloyd yelling for the deputy to get out of the way so he could shoot it. I heard Ferguson scream."

"What about Mitchell and Brown?"

"You heard the scream earlier. It had to be one of them. And they didn't respond to any of the calls."

"That doesn't mean they're dead!"

"No, it doesn't," Steven agreed. "But we can't stick around here to find out. There's something terrible walking around out there. What it is, I don't know, but it's not a bear. That much I'm sure of. You'd never find a bear this far underground: too deep, too dark, not enough food. Whatever this thing is, it lives here . . . probably has for years."

"What about Lloyd?" Randy interrupted. "You said his microphone is keyed. He's still alive, isn't he?"

"I don't know. It's hard to tell with the static. Sometimes I think I hear something, other times I'm not so sure. If he is alive, he's not talking. And there's no way to get through to him. Maybe he dropped the radio and what I'm hearing is only my imagination. Now do you see why we should get out of here?"

"I don't think I can make it."

"I'll carry you if I have to," Steven said. "I'm a caver, a history teacher. Nothing more. I did not agree to fight monsters, and you are no longer in any shape to do so. Once we get out of here we can send in the marines."

Bending over, the professor grabbed Randy under the arms and helped him into a sitting position. Randy nearly passed out from the pain. But gritting his teeth, he was able to stand up. He started to pick up the pack his head had rested on.

"Leave it," Steven ordered. "We're traveling light. I have more than enough gear for the both of us." He handed Randy a flashlight. "You're going to need this: you broke yours in the fall."

"What about my helmet?"

"Forget it. Your head survived, your helmet did not." He gave Randy back his shotgun.

"We're not going to cross any more rooftops, are we?" Randy asked.

"It's the quickest way. It's also the safest. Too many blind spots and hiding places along the alleys. Up topside we'll be in the open, less chance of anything sneaking up on us."

Reaching rooftop-level again was fairly simple. Locating a narrow passageway between two buildings, Steven made the ascent by chimneying upwards. He supported his back against the wall of one building while firmly planting his legs against the wall opposite it. Squirming upwards in small steps, he was on the roof in less than three minutes. Once up, he lowered a rope for Randy, anchoring the other end with a screw.

"Neat trick," Randy commented, joining the professor.

"That was nothing," Steven smiled. "I once chimneyed a forty-foot vertical shaft in the Spanish Pyrenees. Wouldn't have been so bad except the shaft was directly underneath a waterfall. Took me almost an hour to make the climb."

"I would have taken the elevator," Randy said.

"I never thought of that," Steven said. "My, what a brilliant caver you will make someday."

Randy shook his head. "Uh, no, thanks. I've seen all the cave I'll ever want to see."

They coiled the rope back up and readjusted their harnesses before setting out across the rooftops. Steven took the lead, setting a pace slow enough for Randy to keep up. He was also considerate by picking a route that made it unnecessary to jump a gap any wider than two feet. Even then, Randy felt his stomach knot up at the thought of what had happened the last time he attempted to jump from rooftop to rooftop.

Even with the moderate pace Steven was setting, Randy still lagged behind from time to time. Part of the time it was due to the intense throbbing in his head and the tightness in his lower back. Other times he held back deliberately, hoping to spot a beacon of light moving in the streets below. So far there was nothing but the darkness.

Randy didn't like the thought of leaving, not sure whether the others were alive or dead, but he didn't have much choice. As weak as he was, it would be stupid to stay and continue the fight by himself, especially not knowing what he was up against. And he was under orders to keep an eye on the professor, even if the professor was actually keeping an eye on him.

Seeing that Randy had again lagged behind, Steven decided to stop and take a break. He walked to the center of the roof they were crossing and lit a cigarette.

"How's the head?" Steven asked.

"Which one? I feel like I have two, and they're both killing me."

Steven opened his mouth to say something, when the section of roof he had just stepped on gave way beneath his feet. With a startled cry, he dropped straight down.

It was the ropes and bulky equipment attached to his chest harness that kept Steven Fuller from falling through the roof and possibly injuring himself on the stone floor in the room below. Instead his chest wedged tightly in the hole, like a cork in a wine bottle. Randy rushed to his aid.

"Stay back!" Steven warned.

Randy froze in place.

Steven took a couple of deep breaths to steady his voice. "Don't come near me. This roof is weak. We may both fall through."

"But I've got to get you out of there!" Randy said.

"Indeed you shall. But you will not do it by getting us both killed in the process. We've got to take it slowly. Don't rush. I'm not going anywhere. I'm wedged pretty tight."

"What'll I do?"

"First off, I've got to see if I can work one of these ropes loose. If I can, and if I don't fall through in the process, you'll be able to pull me back up."

Moving with slow, precise movements, Steven brought his left hand in to his armpit, hooking his thumb under the coil of rope wrapped over his shoulder and under his arm. He carefully slipped the rope off his shoulder and down his arm to his elbow. Then, like a circus contortionist, he worked his arm out of the coil. His left arm was free, but the rope was still wedged between his chest and the roof. Moving the rope might cause additional stones to tumble, plunging him to the depths below, but he had to take the chance.

Steven again took a couple of deep breaths. On the last one, he exhaled hard, forcing air from his lungs, decreasing his chest size. At the same time, he gave a steady, upward pull on the coil of rope. An inch moved upwards. Two inches. He gasped for breath, paused, rested. He tried again. More rope moved.

The rope came free on his third attempt. His body slipped down. Steven closed his eyes, held his breath, but the fall he expected did not come. He was still dangling through the ceiling.

He tossed one end of the rope to Randy.

"Quick. Find something to tie that to. You're in no shape to haul me up by yourself."

Randy scrambled across the roof, searching for some fixture to fasten the rope to. He spotted a carved niche in the far corner of the roof. He was tying the final knot when Steven called him.

"Randy?"

Randy turned, his fingers till fumbling with the rope. Steven's face was expressionless, his voice somber and collected.

"Randy, my lad, please hurry. Something just brushed past my legs."

Warning bells went off in Randy's head. Finishing the knot, he raced back to the trapped professor.

Steven Fuller was looking down, his face thoughtful, as if he was trying to see through the roof to the room below him. He glanced back up at Randy.

"It's back again . . . I believe it's sniffing me. I think you'd better pull me out."

Steven grabbed the rope in his left hand, wrapping

it around his arm. Randy took up the slack and started to pull.

"Please hurry," Steven said. "It's— *Aaaayyyyy!*"

The scream exploded from Steven Fuller. His head flew back, his face contorting in hellish torment.

"Nooo!" Randy cried. He pulled desperately on the rope, trying to free the imprisoned man.

Steven screamed again. His head snapped straight back. His eyes flew open. He was staring at Randy, staring through him. A thin trickle of blood started at each corner of his mouth. The flow increased, cascading over his lips and down his chin, staining the front of his coveralls. His mouth moved slowly, quivered. He gasped, coughed, and tried to speak, but failed. A roar echoed up from the room below. Then, in the blinking of an eye, he was gone.

There was no warning. One second Randy was looking at Steven Fuller's anguished face, the next he was staring at thin air. The professor was snatched from below, disappearing through the hole so quickly it was impossible to follow the movement with the eye. It was like a magic trick: now you see him, now you don't.

The rope slid through Randy's tightened fist, laying the flesh open on both palms. He barely had time to let go before he too was dragged through the hole.

Rolling to his left, he watched the length of rope uncoil and flash by like fishing line attached to a game bass. There was a sharp pop as it snapped free of its mooring. The piece of stonework to which the rope was tied flashed across the roof and disappeared into the hole. Silence followed, interrupted only by the hammering of Randy's racing heart, and the crunching of bones in the room below.

Chapter 23

Terror is a very personal thing. It seeps in through the pores of the body, turning everything icy-numb. Once inside, it grows like a living entity, feeds and takes on shape, pushing the soul back into a quiet little corner of the mind. Shadows become hideous monsters lurking in wait; the wind becomes whispered words, and the beating of one's own heart becomes the footsteps of things racing to attack from the darkness.

Lloyd tripped and sprawled, the flashlight sailing from his fingers. He tried to catch himself but failed, his elbows and then his chin striking the tunnel's hard rocky floor. Sparks of pain shot through both arms and danced from his jaw to his temples. Shaken but not seriously hurt, he got slowly to his knees. As he did his right hand came into contact with something cold and clammy. Something dead.

With a startled cry, Lloyd recoiled from what he had touched. Off balance, he fell against the wall, the beam from his carbide helmet light sweeping across what he had stumbled over. A body . . . Deputy Brown's.

Wayne Brown lay on his back, his legs crossed in an eternal figure four, his arms extended straight out from his sides. The deputy's chest looked like an empty sardine can. Peeled from throat to stomach, flaps of flesh hanging loosely to each side, his chest had been scooped out, robbed of heart, lungs and other internal organs. All that remained were the intestines, glistening wetly in the dead man's lap.

Lloyd looked away from the body. He had seen enough, more than he wanted to. Pushing himself off the wall, he recovered the dropped flashlight and stumbled onward. He wasn't sure how long he'd been running through the underground corridors. For him, time no longer existed. Everything had become the present, the here and now, measured not in minutes and hours but in footsteps and heartbeats.

Somehow, he had to get away. He had to get back to the surface and tell the others. That's what he'd do. He'd tell Skip. The sheriff would know what to do. With this brief glimmer of sane reasoning, a spark of determination flared back into him. His pace quickened, changing from a drunken stagger to a fast walk, then to a jog. Before he turned the next corner he'd gotten his second wind and was running flat out. And it was the next turn that finally brought him from the stuffiness of the narrow, lower-level passageways to the openness of the cavern and the empty streets of the ancient city.

Lloyd stopped and drew a deep breath. The air was slightly sour, but better than what he'd been breathing. It helped clear some of the cobwebs from his head.

Making a quick compass check, he turned and followed a path that would hopefully lead back to the main avenue of the city. He'd gone no more than half a block when he heard sounds of movement coming from an intersecting alley on his left.

Instantly, the fear was back with him, digging its icy fingernails deep into his bowels and blowing cold kisses up and down his spine. He unslung his riot gun, snapping off the safety. Too late to run, no time to hide. The only option was to stand and fight.

The movement came closer, grew louder. Lloyd braced himself. He took a deep breath, let a little out, then held it. His finger tightened on the trigger of the shotgun.

Something stepped before him. His finger squeezed. The shotgun roared.

Gut reaction, more than anything else, saved Randy Murphy's life. Had he taken time to think about his actions, his brain would have been plastered over the stone walls of several buildings. For some strange reason, when he entered the intersection of the two narrow alleyways, stepping directly into the beam of Lloyd's helmet light and his line of fire, he threw himself facedown on the ground. Randy heard the whistle of lead pellets as they sailed over his head. A half inch lower and he would have felt them.

Both of them remained frozen in place. Lloyd stood stiff as a statue as he clutched the smoking shotgun, finger still on the trigger, knuckles turning white. Randy lay on his stomach, unmoving, barely breathing, face pressed tightly into the dirt.

A long moment passed. Lloyd's shoulders slumped. The barrel of the shotgun lowered. "Jesus Christ . . ." He started towards Randy, faltered, and started again. "Jesus Christ . . ."

Randy pushed himself up on his elbows. "Lloyd?"

Lloyd was at Randy's side. "Don't move. Don't try to talk."

"I'm all right," Randy whispered, pushing himself up farther.

"Listen, you stay still. I'll go for help."

"Seriously . . . I'm okay. You missed."

"Missed?" Lloyd helped him into a sitting position. His hands raced madly over Randy's chest, searching for wounds. "Missed? How could I miss? I fired at point-blank range."

"I know," Randy nodded. "Believe me, I know. I heard the pellets as they went by. Sounded like a pissed-off hornet."

Lloyd's hands shook uncontrollably. He grabbed Randy by the lapels. "My God, that was double-aught buck. It could have killed you. I could have killed you."

Randy put his hands on Lloyd's shoulders. "Relax. You came close, but no cigar. I may need new laundry."

"Me too," Lloyd nodded.

Lloyd took a drink from his canteen, then passed it to Randy. They remained silent for a minute, each trying to regain his composure. It was Lloyd who spoke first.

"Where's the professor?"

Randy swallowed hard. "He's dead. That thing got him."

He quickly told Lloyd about their attempted flight across the rooftops and the death of Professor Steven Fuller. To validate his story, he showed the undersheriff the palms of his hands, still raw and bleeding with rope burn. He also recounted how it had taken him nearly an hour to work up enough courage to move from his spot on the roof. He had lain there and cried, listening to the snapping and cracking of bones from the darkened room below.

"What the hell is it?" Randy asked.

"I don't know." Lloyd shifted his weight and looked around. "Listen, we've got to get out of here. I think that thing lives down here."

"I'm all for getting out of here," Randy agreed. "I damn sure don't want to be around when it gets hungry again. Which way do we go?"

"If we head west we'll connect back up with the main avenue."

"Do we go by rooftop or alley?"

"Alley," Lloyd said.

"Thank God."

Gathering up their remaining equipment, they started out. Gone was the awe they had felt when first seeing the ancient city. Death had spoiled the sensation, tainted the feeling of childlike wonder. No longer interested in dusty ruins or forgotten civilizations, they cared nothing for the buildings and carved inscriptions they passed. Only one thing mattered anymore: survival.

They had been walking for about ten minutes when Lloyd suddenly stopped.

"What's the matter?" Randy asked.

Lloyd held up his hand for silence. "Listen. Don't you hear it?"

"What? Hear what?" Randy turned his head, straining to hear. There was nothing, only a soft wind moaning ghostlike through the alleys.

"It's just the wind," he said, realizing the foolishness of such a statement. They were in a cave, deep underground; there couldn't possibly be any wind—yet there was. With the wind came a peculiar crackling, like the crinkling of a cellophane bag.

"Do you hear it . . . that funny popping?" Lloyd asked. "I heard the same thing right before Ferguson was killed. That thing's coming. I know it."

Randy spun around, facing the darkness behind him. "Let it come. We'll give the fucker something to think about."

"No!" Lloyd cried. He grabbed Randy by the shoulder, frantically trying to drag him farther down the alley. "You don't understand! You can't kill it!"

Randy shook loose from his grasp. "Bullshit. Everything that lives can be killed."

"Not the Crota!"

"The what?" Randy turned and stared at Lloyd. When he spoke his voice was barely a whisper. "You know something about this thing, don't you?"

Lloyd took a step backward.

"Damn it. You know something, don't you?" Randy yelled. "You knew about it all along. You said it was a bear. A fucking bear! You knew it wasn't a bear all along, didn't you? Didn't you?"

"Yes," croaked Lloyd.

"Son of a bitch!"

Randy lashed out. His right fist nailed Lloyd on the left side of his jaw. Lloyd staggered back, collided with a wall and sat down heavily. He made no attempt to stand back up.

Randy stepped forward, his shotgun aimed menacingly at Lloyd's head. "You fucking bastard. You led us down here when you knew that thing was waiting for us. Why? Why didn't you tell any of us what was down here?"

Lloyd's lower lip trembled. "I didn't believe it."

"You didn't believe?" Randy shrilled. "You didn't believe? Hear that, world: he didn't believe. Try telling that to Mitchell, Brown and the others. Do you think they'd buy that? You got them killed because you didn't believe. Do you believe now?"

"Yes," he nodded. "I'm sorry."

Randy laughed. "Sorry! Is that all you can say? You—"

Randy's words died in his throat. Lloyd was no longer paying attention to what he was saying. Instead he was staring in bug-eyed terror at something just behind him. Randy didn't have to look to know what was there. He could feel the increased tempo of the popping in the air about him, feel the hairs on his arms and neck rise almost magically. There was a soft scraping as a heavy, taloned foot glided across the stones. Another sound that might have been a tongue darting wetly across hungry lips.

With a yell of defiance, he turned and fired. The shock of seeing the monster for the first time made his blood run cold.

The Crota crouched no more than twenty feet away, its glowing eyes carefully studying them. The creature's chest and mane were matted with dried blood—the blood of those who had already fallen victim to it. Lloyd was right and Randy knew it: they couldn't kill it.

The Crota roared and charged, running on all fours. Randy screamed.

The monster crashed into Randy, knocking him down. Powerful jaws closed about his right knee. He screamed again. The jaws bit down. Bones crunched and the leg fell free of the body.

Randy's brain flickered and died like the flame of a candle. His body acted on its own as it crawled slowly across the ground, seeking to flee from the Crota. Escape was impossible. His mind knew that; therefore, it had already given up. His body, however, a little slow about catching on, refused to give up the fight.

Lloyd dove to his right, rolling clear of the battle. He hesitated long enough to witness the pitiful sight of Corporal Murphy crawling helplessly across the alleyway, the stump of his right leg twitching and jerking with a life of its own.

Randy had crawled only about six feet when the Crota brought one foot forcefully down on the center of his back, snapping his spine like a thin, dry twig. Lloyd didn't stick around after that; there was no reason to.

He ran four blocks before reaching the place where they had first entered the ancient city. It was also the spot where he had left the portable field phone. Taking a deep breath, he grabbed the phone.

"Home Base, this is Unit One. Over."

Skip's voice responded instantly. "This is Home Base. Is that you, Lloyd?"

"Yeah, Skip, it's me," Lloyd answered.

"What the hell's going on down there? We've been trying to reach you for hours, but couldn't get through—"

"They're dead."

Skip hesitated. "Say again?"

"They're dead, Skip. All of them: Mitchell, Brown, Murphy, Ferguson and Professor Steven Fuller, Washington University, Missouri. All dead."

When Skip spoke again it was in a soft voice, like that of a mother to her child. "Stay where you are, Lloyd. We're coming down to get you."

"Negative," Lloyd responded. "You do not, repeat, do *not* come down here. You were right, Skip. You were right all along. It isn't a bear, and it's not some drugged-out, devil-worshiping cult. It's a monster."

"We're coming in."

"No!" Lloyd screamed. "Don't you understand? The others are dead. I killed them. They were my responsibility and I got them killed. I knew before I ever came down here that it wasn't a bear."

"Lloyd, you're not making any sense."

"Yes I am, only you don't know it. I tried to play the big man, tried to be the hero. I wanted all the cookies . . . wanted your job. Damn it, Skip, I was warned in advance. Everything he said was true."

"Who, Lloyd? Everything who said?"

"Jay Little Hawk. He's the one who told me about the cave, the monster. Everything. He warned me that it couldn't be killed. Go talk to him, Skip. Go talk to Little Hawk. Maybe he'll know what to do."

"We'll go see him together—"

"No, Skip, you'll have to do it alone. I'm not coming out. I'm going back."

"Lloyd, you get your ass back to the surface. Now! Do you understand?"

"Sorry, Skip. I left several damn good men behind. I'm not coming out without them."

"That's an order, mister!"

"Won't work, Skip. I've got a score to settle. Besides, I'm tired of running. I guess maybe it's about time I stood up for my actions."

Skip changed his tactics. "Lloyd, please come out."

Lloyd unpinned his star from his shirt, holding it in the palm of his hand. Tears streamed down his face. "Skip, promise me two things."

"What?"

"That you'll be the one to tell my wife what happened, and that under no circumstances will you let anyone come down here until after you go see Little Hawk."

There was no reply.

"Skip?"

"I'm here, Lloyd."

"Promise?"

"Please come out, Lloyd. Come out and we'll dynamite the cave's entrance . . . seal the thing up forever."

"I can't come out, Skip. Those men trusted me. They were my responsibility and I fucked up. You can understand that, can't you?"

Silence.

"Can't you, Skip?"

"Yes, Lloyd, I can." Skip hesitated. "Okay . . . I promise."

"Thank you."

Lloyd switched off the phone and set it down on the ground by his feet. He then gently laid his star on top of it. There wouldn't be any need for a star where he was going.

Straightening up, he took a deep breath, wiped a tear from his eye and jacked another round into the chamber of his shotgun. He had a score to settle. This one was for the boys.

PART IV

Chapter 24

THURSDAY NIGHT.

Deputy Hays kept his eyes downcast while he talked. Several times he had to stop, catch his breath and start again. When he was finally finished, he broke down and cried. Except for the deputy's sobs, silence gripped the tiny office like a black glove.

Driving back from the Devil's Boot, Skip had called ahead to arrange for the mayor, the police chief and Fred Granger to be waiting for him in his office when he arrived. He studied the faces of those three men, trying to read their expressions. It was Mayor Johnson who spoke first.

"This is a joke, right?" He uncrossed his legs and pulled nervously at his necktie. "That's it . . . some kind of joke."

"It's no joke," Skip answered. He'd already given his report, including a description of the creature that attacked him. "I think the coroner's report on the three bodies will back up what's been said."

Everyone turned to Fred Granger, waiting to see

what he had to say. Fred leaned back in his chair and looked at the ceiling, thoughtfully scratching at the back of his head. "That would explain the marks on the Jerworski kid and Hoffman." He looked at Skip. "Damn, no wonder I couldn't match them up with anything. All this time I thought I was losing my touch."

"What about the Owens's cattle?" Skip prodded, anxious to have Fred help establish a convincing argument.

Fred removed his glasses, wiped them with his shirttail, and put them back on. "There's no doubt in my mind that those cows were attacked by some kind of predator. In addition to teeth marks, several of the carcasses were missing internal organs. One was even minus a hindquarter. But while the bodies of Owens, Jerworski and Hoffman were also mutilated, there were no indications that anything had tried to eat them. In other words, they were ripped apart and left untouched. If we are dealing with some unknown creature, then the damn thing doesn't eat people, it only kills them."

Skip removed a fifth of Jim Beam and a stack of Dixie cups from his lower desk drawer. He set the bottle and cups down on his desk. Police Chief Alex Newberry and Mayor Johnson made a grab for the bottle at the same time. The police chief got to it first.

"No offense, Sheriff, but I'm finding this hard to believe." Chief Newberry opened the whiskey bottle, filled his cup halfway, spilling some on the carpet, and handed the bottle to Mayor Johnson.

Skip's jaws tightened. He had never been overly fond of Newberry, who was your typical thick-headed, hick cop. During the past week, he'd tried his best to get in on the investigation, but Skip and Lloyd had refused to tell him anything, deliberately keeping him in the dark, pulling rank to borrow his men for needed roadblocks. But now, like it or not, Skip had no choice but to work with the man.

"Damn it, Newberry, over half my department's been wiped out."

Mayor Johnson cleared his throat. "Skip, if what you're saying is true, then why didn't you tell anyone what you saw?"

"What was I going to say, that I saw a monster? You wouldn't have believed me, and you know it. Even Lloyd didn't believe me."

"He does now," Newberry said, looking down at the floor.

Mayor Johnson poured a double shot of whiskey into his coffee. "So what do we do?"

"We send for the National Guard," Chief Newberry answered.

"No," Skip disagreed. "That's the last thing we want to do. You go calling in the National Guard and you're going to have thousands of people pouring in here to watch the action. Besides, you send anyone down in that cave and they're going to end up dead. We've lost enough men as it is."

There was a brief pause as they thought of the men who had so recently lost their lives.

"Have you notified their families yet?" Fred asked.

Skip shook his head. "Not yet. I thought this meeting was too important to put off. And truthfully, I wasn't sure what to say to them."

"Are you going to tell them the truth?" Newberry asked.

Skip frowned. "What, that their daddies and husbands got torn apart by a monster?"

"No, I guess that wouldn't go over too good," he agreed. "Are you sure they're all dead?"

"I'm sure."

"Jesus." Newberry tipped his head back and belted down his whiskey in one gulp. It wasn't the booze that made his eyes water.

Skip looked to Mayor Johnson. "Mayor, it's your decision. You can call in outside help if you want. But the governor is not going to be happy about it, especially when you tell him it's for a monster hunt. Along with the bad publicity, there's a good chance more people will be killed."

"What about using dynamite to seal the cave?" Chief Newberry suggested.

Skip nodded. "That's another option. But there's no guarantee our monster won't find another place to tunnel out."

Fred Granger cleared his throat. "Skip, you can't seal the cave without bringing those bodies out; the families would be up in arms about it."

"What if we said there was a cave-in?" asked Newberry.

Fred shook his head. "No good. With a cave-in you wouldn't know if the men were alive or dead until you dug them out. Hell, you'd have thousands of volunteers showing up to help with the digging."

"And hundreds of reporters on the scene," Mayor Johnson added. Skip figured the mayor didn't like the idea of sealing the cave because the ancient city the team had apparently discovered was just the thing to put Logan on the map.

Deputy Hays raised his head and looked around the room. "I have an idea."

Skip paused and looked at the young man.

"You could say they hit a gas pocket. That happens . . . I've seen it on the news before. Coal miners sometimes hit gas pockets and blow themselves up. Maybe you can say the same thing happened this time and you can't go down because there might be more gas."

Skip looked to Chief Newberry, then to Fred Granger. Fred nodded.

"He's got something there, Skip," Fred said. "A gas explosion would be a good reason for not bringing the bodies out. It would also be a good reason to keep everybody away from the cave."

"But how long will the public buy that story?" Newberry said.

"Not long," Skip answered, "but it would give us some time to figure out what to do next."

"What *do* you suggest we do next, Sheriff?" Mayor Johnson asked. He obviously wanted to put the decision-making back on Skip's shoulders. That way, if anything else went wrong, he could also lay the blame on him.

"The first thing I'm going to do is pay a visit to Jay Little Hawk."

"What does he have to do with any of this?"

"I'm not sure. The last thing Lloyd said was for me to go see him . . . that he would know what to do. What that's supposed to mean, I don't know. I do know, however, that Little Hawk told Lloyd where to find the monster. That means he knows something."

"How long do you think we got before that thing pokes its head above ground again?" Fred asked.

Skip shook his head. "I don't know. I believe it's nocturnal, so we shouldn't have to worry about it in the daytime. In the meantime, I want the entire area, from Cemetery Road to Highway U, sealed off."

Chief Newberry spoke up: "If you want, I'll lend you a couple of my units."

"Thanks, Alex. I'm going to need as much help as I can get. If you can spare it, I would like to have a couple of your men stationed just back from the cave's entrance. If we're going with the gas explosion story then the fire department is going to be involved. I'd feel a lot better knowing they had some protection out there."

Skip turned to Mayor Johnson. "Mayor, I'll leave it up to you to handle the press."

Mayor Johnson nodded. "Don't worry, I have a silver tongue when it comes to reporters."

Skip said, "Gentlemen, I don't need to remind you that what is said in this room should stay in this room. If word leaks out about this, we'll have a panic on our hands bigger and faster than you can imagine. I suggest you don't even tell your wives about this."

"Hell, I don't tell my wife anything anyway," Mayor Johnson quipped.

"Smart man," said Fred Granger.

"Now, gentlemen, if you please . . . I've got some families to notify."

Everyone except Deputy Hays rose to leave. Fred Granger and Chief Newberry exited the room together. The mayor followed them. Skip didn't have to worry about Fred backing him. They'd been friends for years. He couldn't say the same about Newberry. There never had been anything in the way of a real rivalry between them, but they had locked horns in the past. Still, Skip doubted if the police chief would risk causing a massive panic just to get even over a couple of minor disagreements.

Deputy Hays remained seated in the straight-back chair by the side of the desk. Skip handed the bottle of whiskey to him. "That was a pretty good idea you had about the gas pocket."

The deputy didn't bother with a cup. Unscrewing the cap, he tilted the bottle back and swallowed three good chugs.

"They don't believe us, do they?" he said, passing the bottle back to Skip.

"Fred does."

"What about the others?"

Skip wiped his hand across his mouth. "It's not so much that they don't believe, it's just they're having a hard time dealing with it. Can't blame them; if I hadn't seen it with my own eyes, I wouldn't be so quick about believing it either."

The deputy's face looked drained. "Sheriff, I know I haven't been with the department for very long, but those guys who died down there were my friends, probably the best ones I've ever had. We're going to get that thing, aren't we?"

"Yeah, we're going to get it."

Deputy Hays nodded. He stood up, stuffed his hands into his pockets and headed for the door. Then he turned back around. "It must suck having to call their families. I wouldn't want your job for anything in the world."

"Right now, I don't want it much, either."

Chapter 25

FRIDAY MORNING.

They were expecting him.

Jay Little Hawk was sitting on his back porch. To his right sat an elderly, white-haired man. They faced the west, watching the last patches of mist hugging the valley struggle against the overpowering warmth of the rising sun. Neither man turned to look when Skip pulled the Bronco to a stop beside the cabin. It was as though they already knew, without looking, who he was and why he'd come.

Putting the pickup in park, Skip killed the engine and stubbed his cigarette out in the ashtray. Little Hawk still hadn't looked his way. Skip frowned; he didn't like being ignored. Grabbing his hat, he eased out of the cab and closed the door behind him.

"Good morning, Jay," he said as he walked around the front of the truck.

Hawk slowly turned his head in Skip's direction and nodded. "Morning Sheriff. Grab a seat. Coffee's still hot, if you're interested." He motioned to a vacant wooden chair in front of him.

Skip quickly climbed the five short steps to the porch. A small wooden table had been placed strategically between the three chairs. On it sat a chipped and battered metal coffeepot, a sugar bowl and some loose packets of instant creamer. He noticed that three cups had been set out when there were only two of them drinking coffee.

They really were expecting me. The thought, though nonsense, made him uncomfortable.

Hawk didn't speak until after he'd filled the sheriff's cup. "I heard about the accident in the cave. I'm sorry."

Skip accepted the cup of coffee. "It wasn't an accident."

The Indian paused and looked thoughtfully at him. "I know it wasn't. Cream?"

"No, thank you." Skip cast a quick glance over at the old man, then looked back to Little Hawk. "What *do* you know, Jay?"

Hawk ignored the question. "Sheriff, this is George Strong Eagle. He doesn't speak any English . . . he's come here to help us."

"Help us?" Skip set his coffee cup down and leaned forward. "Listen, I've never been one to beat around the bush, so let's get to the point. The last thing Lloyd Baxter said to me was that I should come see you . . . that you might know what to do. Please tell me, what in God's name *is* that thing?"

Hawk lowered his head, took a deep breath and looked back up. There was a sudden sadness in his eyes, as though a great and terrible burden had been placed upon his shoulders. Slowly, with deliberate actions, he began to recite the legend of the Crota.

When Jay Little Hawk finished with his story he leaned back in his chair, waiting for the sheriff's response. Perhaps he expected a chuckle, a laugh or a snort of amusement. Skip didn't even crack a smile.

"Is that what you told Lloyd?" he asked.

Hawk nodded. "I was coming to tell you, but he intercepted me in the hallway. After I left the hospital I went straight to the airport. If I knew then what I know now, I never would have left town."

"It's not your fault," Skip said. "Lloyd knew better. He should have come and told me what you said. I guess he was just trying to prove a point. He didn't believe me about the monster."

"One thing bothers me, Sheriff. The Crota attacked you too, yet you live. How?"

Skip pulled his butane lighter from his pants pocket and handed it to him. "It's a birthday present from the guys at the station."

Hawk took the lighter, thumbed its wheel a couple of times, then passed it to Strong Eagle, translating what Skip had said. As Eagle turned the lighter over to examine it, the clothes of the curvy redhead on its side began to disappear. The old medicine man burst out laughing. He spoke rapidly to Hawk.

"What'd he say?" Skip asked.

Hawk smiled. "He says it's pretty funny that your life was saved by a girlie lighter. Either the Crota doesn't like fire or it doesn't like pretty women."

Skip smiled at the old Indian's humor.

"But I don't think it was the lighter." Hawk leaned forward and touched the shell gorget that Skip wore. "I think this saved your life."

"My necklace?"

He nodded. "Were you wearing it the night you were attacked?"

"Yes, but . . ."

"It is obviously a medicine piece. Very old. The spider and rattlesnake are considered godlike by most southeastern tribes." He held out his hand. "Do you mind?"

Skip untied the gorget and handed it to him. Hawk examined the shell disk closely before passing it to Strong Eagle. The old man turned the necklace over several times before speaking.

"Strong Eagle also thinks that your necklace is a medicine piece." Hawk handed the gorget back to Skip. "Where did you get it?"

"I found it along the banks of Lost Creek when I was a kid. My grandmother said it would bring me luck. I guess it did."

Hawk nodded. "Perhaps it was made by the same people who sealed the Crota underground." Hawk was thinking it might even have been dropped by one of the Creek warriors who had led the Crota to the cave.

Skip retied the shell disk around his neck. "So . . . what do we do now?"

Little Hawk laid his hands flat on his lap. "That all depends on how much you're willing to believe."

"What do you mean, believe? I believe there's a

monster, because I've seen it. Whether or not it's the same monster from your legend, I don't know. I do know, however, that it's got to be stopped before it kills someone else. Maybe we could dynamite the entrance to the cave and seal it up again."

Hawk shook his head. "You could seal it up, but for how long? Another earthquake might set it free again. No, sealing it up again would be a waste of time. We've got to kill it."

"How?" Skip asked.

Hawk turned to Eagle and exchanged a few words in Indian, then turned back to Skip. "Sheriff, at first we had no intention of including you in our plans—too many have died already. But Strong Eagle feels your defeating the Crota may be a sign—"

"I didn't defeat it!" Skip exclaimed.

"The fact that you are still alive is in some way a small victory, is it not? By already beating it once, you may have shaken its confidence a little. I hope so; we're going to need any advantage we can get. Like I said, I didn't want to involve you, but it seems you are already involved. Kill it? Yes, we may have a way to kill it."

Skip glanced at Strong Eagle. The old man was staring at him, his eyes hard and cold amidst a sea of wrinkled flesh. There was something about his penetrating gaze that made Skip feel giddy when he maintained eye contact for very long.

Hawk leaned forward in his chair, his face only inches away. "Sheriff, the Crota cannot be killed with modern weapons. It is a creature of power, so it can be killed only by an equal or stronger power. Only if we walk the right path can we hope to defeat it."

"The right path?" *Jesus, what sort of mumbo jumbo is this?* Skip wiped a hand across his forehead. He was starting to sweat. Why? It wasn't hot. Must be the coffee.

Hawk continued, "The right path is a way of doing things—a spiritual way—that leads to a higher plane than the one we are on now."

Skip wiped his forehead again. He was feeling a little nauseous. Maybe he was coming down with something—the flu, perhaps. It could be stress. He glanced toward Strong Eagle. The old man was still staring at him, his eyes wide. Skip didn't like being stared at; it bothered him. He turned away, but could still feel the eyes of the old man burning into the side of his head. He tried to straighten up in his chair, but couldn't. He had never felt so weak before.

"Are you talking about magic?" Skip croaked. His lips felt heavy, his face rubbery.

"If you'd like to call it that, then that's okay," Hawk replied with a wry smile.

Skip was beginning to panic. Something was wrong. He felt weak, dizzy. He tried to stand up but couldn't. His vision blurred. What was wrong with him?

The coffee! That's it. They've drugged the coffee. My God, they're trying to kill me. But why? I have to get away.

A voice seemed to come from somewhere behind him. He couldn't understand what was said, nor could he turn his head to see who spoke.

Hawk's face drew closer. His eyes looked like twin

moons of shimmering light. "Eagle says not to worry. We have not drugged your coffee."

Why did I come? What are they doing to me? They're going to kill me. I don't want to die. I have a son who needs me . . .

No, that's not it. They're not trying to kill me; they're trying to show me something.

What?

They're giving me an example. . . . An example of what?

Power! They're giving me an example of power to show me forces beyond my comprehension.

The thought came to him with crystal clarity. Somehow, the old Indian was holding him captive with an unknown power. He was doing so to prove a point—to demonstrate the forces at work in the universe—as well as to make Skip realize what he was up against when facing the Crota.

Suddenly, like someone flicking off a light switch, it was gone. The invisible bond holding Skip disappeared so quickly he almost pitched forward on his face. He would have gone for his pistol, but knew his arm would refuse to obey. Hawk poured him another cup of coffee.

"Please forgive us for our little demonstration," Hawk said, handing Skip the filled cup. "We could think of no other way to convince you that the Crota is to be fought our way or no way at all."

Skip's hands shook as he took a sip of coffee. "I would have believed you."

Hawk smiled. "You say that, but your subconscious would have resisted. It is only to be expected. You are a white man."

"But my grandmother was Indian. Full-blooded," Skip said.

Hawk's eyebrows rose in surprise. "Oh? That would make you one quarter. What tribe?"

He shrugged. "I'm not sure. Cheyenne, I think. I didn't know her very well; she died when I was young. I remember she used to spend a lot of time in her garden, growing herbs and things like that. She's the one who said my necklace was good luck."

Hawk exchanged a few words with Eagle, then turned back to Skip. "Eagle thinks that maybe your grandmother was a medicine woman."

Skip considered it. "Maybe. Mom and Dad used to say that Grandma had a cure for just about everything."

"It's interesting that your grandmother would be a medicine woman."

"Yeah," Skip nodded. "Maybe that's why I've been having so many dreams lately."

"Dreams?"

"Real strange ones. I'm wandering through the woods at night, totally lost. I see a light up ahead and start walking toward it. Turns out to be a lantern held by my grandmother. She leads me back to her house and into the attic where she shows me this big wooden chest. She takes something out of the chest. I don't know what it is because it's wrapped in fur. She tries to hand it to me, but when I reach for the bundle it disappears."

Hawk scratched his chin. "It sounds like your

grandmother is trying very hard to give you something, or to tell you something. Have you thought about trying to locate the chest?"

"I wouldn't know where to begin," he said.

"What about your grandmother's house?"

"No good. The house I live in now used to be hers. It was left to my parents and they left it to me. I've been in the attic hundreds of times. There's no such chest."

"Pity," Hawk said, shaking his head. "The chest may have contained something important."

Eagle spoke briefly. Hawk listened and nodded.

"By the way, Strong Eagle says you'll find that our demonstration has been somewhat beneficial." He ran his index finger down the left side of his head. "A warrior cannot afford to be weak or injured when facing his greatest challenge."

Skip failed to grasp what Hawk meant, so the Indian repeated the gesture by touching his finger lightly against the sheriff's left temple. Skip gasped.

It was gone! The throbbing pain that had been with him for the past few days was gone. Startled, he gingerly touched his forehead. There was no pain, not even any discomfort. Skip turned and looked at Strong Eagle. The old man was smiling.

"There are many things the white man does not know or understand," Hawk said. "Like myself, Strong Eagle is a medicine man—perhaps one of the most powerful to ever live. It is a great honor that he's here with us today; he's never even been off the reservation before. This should be an occasion for a celebration, but there's no time for that now. Perhaps we can celebrate later, if any of us are still alive."

At that, Skip turned to face Hawk.

"Sheriff, we're going to need your total cooperation to defeat the Crota. Can we count on your help?"

Skip nodded slowly as though in a daze.

"Thank you." Hawk smiled. "Now go home and see your wife. Tell her you will be away for a day or two, nothing more. Do not tell her, or anyone else, where you are going. Be back here no later than two hours from now. We have much work to do and very little time."

He leaned forward and grabbed Skip by the arm. "The Crota has been cautious so far. It has stayed away from populated areas, attacking only in the rural countryside. But it defeated your men, and knows now that large numbers of people pose no threat to it. The next time the Crota leaves the cave it may decide to travel even farther. Maybe it will head toward Logan."

The thought of the monster reaching town scared the hell out of Skip. Visions of Katie and Billy lying dead on a slab at the morgue flashed through his mind. He started to say something, but Little Hawk held up his hand for silence.

"Relax, your family is safe. We feel the Crota is resting now, but not for long. When you come back you will begin your training. When you come back, we will show you how to walk the right path. Go now."

Chapter 26

Skip arrived back at his house at a quarter to eleven. Nobody was home. Billy was still in school and Katie was working. He was glad. He didn't want to tell her that he might be gone for a couple of days without offering an explanation. Sure, he could make up some excuse, but Katie could usually tell when he was lying to her. He thought about calling her at the office, but he wasn't much better at lying over the phone. Instead, he left a note on the kitchen table saying he had to go out of town on official business and didn't know when he would be back.

Finished with the note, he entered Billy's room and laid a new pitcher's mitt, purchased on the way home, at the foot of the child's bed. God willing, he would be back to help his son break in the glove properly.

Crossing the living room on his way out, Skip's attention was drawn to the framed black-and-white photo of his grandmother, on the mantel above the fireplace. The picture, taken sometime in the late 1800s, showed a young woman with long black hair, wearing a weathered buckskin dress, beaded leggings and moccasins. She looked nothing at all like the wrinkled, gray-haired lady he knew from childhood. Only her eyes were the same. Even in youth they looked old and wise, appearing to gaze through him. Questioning. Demanding.

"Dammit, Grandma, what is it? What are you trying to tell me? Why am I having dreams about you now, after all these years?"

He glanced at his watch. Little Hawk and Strong Eagle expected him back soon, but they would just have to wait. There was something he had to do first. Turning away from the mantel, he crossed the room and headed down the hall. At the end of the hall Skip pulled down the folding ladder that led up into the attic. Flipping on the light, he started up the steps.

The attic was dry and dusty, smelling faintly of mothballs and roach spray. Sheets of plywood covered the floor, so Skip could move about freely without falling through. But there was no point in walking around because he could see everything there was to see. Except for a few boxes of books and broken toys, the attic stood empty.

"Okay, Grandma. You've gotten me up here, now show me what you want me to see."

He stood still and waited, almost expecting to receive some miraculous message from the spirit world—the visit of a ghostly apparition, a disembodied voice or a little spectral knocking. He was disappointed when several minutes elapsed and nothing happened.

"I'm wasting my time here."

He turned to leave when the single lightbulb lighting the attic flickered and went out.

"Great, now I'll probably break my neck in the dark."

But it wasn't completely dark. On the far wall a faint patch of light shimmered.

Must be sunlight coming through a crack.

What crack? Skip turned his head, seeking the source of the glow, but found no crack or hole that sunlight could have been shining through. Looking back across the room, he was startled to see the light dance along the wall and then return to its original spot.

She carried a light in the dream.

Chills raced down his arms. Marking the spot on the wall to memory, he crossed the room and climbed down the ladder. He returned a few minutes later with a flashlight and crowbar.

The flashlight wasn't necessary, however, for when he returned the attic light was back on. Reaching the spot where he had seen the mysterious glow, he wedged the crowbar between two boards in the wall and pried, ripping the nails loose from the studs.

As the boards came loose, it became apparent that what he had thought to be the outer wall of his house was in reality a false wall. Behind it were an additional seven feet of attic space. Two boards later he found what he was looking for.

The wooden chest scraped loudly against the floor as he dragged it into the light. It was the cedar chest of his dreams, three feet long two feet wide and a little over two feet deep. His hands trembled with excitement as he slowly raised the lid.

The smell of dust, mildew, spices and dried flowers rose up to greet him as he lifted the lid. He covered his nose to keep from sneezing. Inside the chest were things that had once belonged to his grandmother: a dress made of leather, stiff and brittle with age; a second dress of faded cotton. The beaded leggings and moccasins worn in the picture were also in the chest, though the leather was quite brittle and many of the beads had fallen off. Beneath the leggings, he found two butcher knives and a shawl.

The shawl was the last item in the chest. Skip sat back in disappointment. He expected to find much more, at least something of importance, something worth dreaming about. He started to replace the items when he noticed that the interior of the chest was only about half as deep as its actual size. Reaching in and giving the wood a rap with his knuckles confirmed his sudden suspicion.

I'll be damned. A false bottom.

A hole at each end of the panel allowed him to slip a finger in and lift out the false bottom. Inside he found an object wrapped in fox skin, tied closed with lengths of rawhide cord. It was the same bundle offered in his dream.

His heart pounding with excitement, he carefully lifted the bundle from the chest. He thought about opening it but decided against it. Mysterious forces beyond his understanding had led him to discover the chest and its contents. If his grandmother was a medicine woman, then she might have had powers equal to those of Strong Eagle or Little Hawk. Skip was no fool; he knew better than to play around with things he didn't understand. He would leave the bundle opening to the experts.

The sheriff stood up and crossed the room. Reaching the ladder, he stopped and turned back around. Nothing had changed; the attic was as empty as ever. Still, he could almost feel his grandmother's presence watching him, a smile upon her face. She had somehow crossed back across the great void called death to enter his dreams, guiding him to a chest she had hidden long ago. He didn't know what was in the bundle, but he knew it was important, something she wanted him to have.

"Thank you, Grandma," he said, acknowledging the gift and the woman who had given it to him. Turning, he started down the ladder.

Chapter 27

Deciding to wait for an opportune time to bring the subject up, Skip slipped his grandmother's bundle behind the seat of his truck and turned off the engine. Hawk greeted him as he climbed out of the pickup.

"Eagle had doubts you would return," he said, a faint smile touching the corners of his mouth.

"His little performance more than convinced me." Skip looked around. "Where is he, anyway?"

"He's waiting for us in the sweat lodge."

The sheriff was not impressed with the squat, dome-shaped sweat lodge, which resembled something a transient might live in. He was even less impressed by what Hawk said next.

"Take off your clothes."

Skip was taken back. "Everything?"

Hawk laughed. "We're not savages." He pointed at a pair of red swim trunks lying next to the sweat lodge. "Those should fit you. Don't worry, there are no women around, or any reporters lurking inside."

"Is this really necessary?"

"Do you want to destroy the Crota?"

"Yes, but—"

"Then it is necessary. Now hurry, there isn't much time. We still have a lot to do today. We must finish before night, because when darkness returns the Crota may leave the cave."

Laying his pistol and gunbelt carefully on the ground, Skip started removing his clothes. Hawk did likewise but with less hesitation, so he was completely stripped and already into his own pair of shorts before Skip was even half undressed. Skip's slowness made Hawk laugh.

"Embarrassment over nudity is something only whites suffer from. Most Indians find nothing shameful or dirty about the human body. If the body were something to be ashamed of, we would have been born with clothes."

Put on the defensive, Skip quickly removed his clothes and slipped on the trunks.

Hawk grinned. "You're learning."

George Strong Eagle sat just inside the doorway of the sweat lodge. He wore only a pair of baggy yellow gym shorts. Skip couldn't help noticing that, for a man of his age, the old Indian was in pretty good shape. Despite the wrinkled face, Eagle's muscles were still taut and firm.

Little Hawk entered the lodge first, sitting down directly opposite Strong Eagle. He motioned for Skip to sit to his immediate left. There wasn't much room inside the tiny sweat lodge, so when Skip sat down cross-legged his right thigh touched Hawk's left leg, while his left leg was no more than eight inches from Eagle's.

Besides being cramped, the sweat lodge was hot—damn hot. He had been in steamrooms before, but they were never like this. As soon as he sat down sweat started rolling off his body. He had to make his breathing slow and shallow, for too deep a breath burned his lungs. He would be lucky if he didn't singe his nasal hairs.

Hawk must have read his mind. "If the heat gets too unbearable for you, we can open the flap and let some air in. But try to stand it as long as possible."

"I'm okay," he lied.

Hawk closed his eyes against the steam. Skip did likewise. Strong Eagle started in with an Indian prayer. Though Skip didn't understand the words, they seemed to take on a life of their own as they flowed from the lips of the old man. The tempo picked up and the words vibrated with energy as they bounced off the walls and ceiling of the sweat lodge. The sheriff could almost feel the words penetrate his skin, carrying their strange vibrations deep inside his body. Eagle paused to slowly sprinkle water over the glowing bricks, creating a hissing cloud of steam.

Hawk leaned closer and whispered in his ear, "Strong Eagle is reciting a very sacred prayer. He is asking the spirits for knowledge, strength and, most importantly, their help. Each of us will also have to ask the spirits for help."

"But I don't know how," he protested.

"Shhh . . . you will know how to ask when the time comes. For now, close your eyes and let your spirit soar. The whole universe is inside this sweat lodge. We are part of that universe."

Skip closed his eyes and tried to relax. He wasn't as nervous now. His breathing grew shallow and his heart rate slowed to a steady, relaxed beat. His eyes no longer burned from the steam, and he found the heat slightly more bearable. As he relaxed he felt the vibrations begin again. They seemed to start in his abdomen and spread in short pulses through his body. He concentrated on the vibrations and was startled to find his heart keeping beat with them.

As he studied what was going on inside his body, Little Hawk started with a prayer of his own. The words were different from those of Eagle, because Hawk was praying in Cherokee. The two prayers created a strange stereo effect inside the lodge. It seemed to Skip that he was hearing the words of Eagle in his left ear and those of Little Hawk in his right. Both Indians had their prayers timed perfectly so neither spoke at the same time.

When Skip tried to concentrate on the prayers he became dizzy, and it was only when he relaxed his mind that the words made any sense—which was odd, seeing how they weren't being spoken in English. Rocking gently back and forth to the rhythm of the prayers, he discovered words to a prayer of his own forming in his head. How they got there he couldn't imagine, for they were far too alien to be anything he might have thought up. He felt he should share his words with the others. Opening his mouth, his new prayer tumbled out.

O Great Spirit hear my plea.
O Great Spirit hear my plea.
I come to you in a sacred manner.
Long I have lived in a sacred manner.
I come to you to ask for your help.
Please Great Spirit grant me courage and strength.
Grant me the courage to face my enemy and the strength to destroy him.
Long I have lived in a sacred manner.

The prayer surprised him, for as soon as Skip opened his mouth he realized he wasn't speaking in English. This didn't upset him. On the contrary, he liked his new prayer and enjoyed saying it. Each time he spoke his voice grew louder, his words blending with those of Strong Eagle and Little Hawk. The praying grew louder, faster, reaching a point where it was more vibration than sound—vibrations that made Skip's body tingle, caused his head to feel funny, allowed him to see things. . . .

A vast plain of green stretched before him, fields of weeds and tall grasses, peppered with wild flowers of yellow and white. In the distance rose rugged mountains, deep purple against the light of a setting sun.

Skip did not stand upon the plain but viewed it from a lofty vantage point, though he couldn't tell what he stood upon, if anything at all. He felt like he was flying, soaring high above the earth, dancing among the clouds on feathery wings.

Directly below him was a village of eleven brightly painted tepees. At one end of the village several men were engaged in the task of butchering a young deer, while others were hard at work making tools and weapons. Of the women to be seen, most were cooking, preparing the evening meal over small fires.

Children laughed and frolicked through the village, some participating in games of strength and skill, and some just being kids. They all looked so tiny to Skip, like something from a fairy tale. He would have liked to watch the tiny people for a while, for they made him happy, but he felt himself being pulled by the wind.

What do you see? a voice asked. *Look and remember. What do you see?*

The village passed below him as he soared toward the distant mountains. He sailed over a twisting river, its glassy surface reflecting the colors of the sky and clouds. The river looked peaceful, but something about it filled him with dread. Some unknown danger lurked deep within the flowing waters, waiting, watching.

Beware the river.

The level plain gave way to rolling hills and forests of evergreen trees. The trees reached out to him, waved silent greetings to his passing, their branches alive with a multitude of songbirds. Carried upon the wind, the songs reached his ears, filling his heart with happiness. He too was a bird, flying, soaring, sailing, viewing the earth as he never dreamed possible. He also wanted to sing, to offer thanks for the beauty he beheld, but when he opened his mouth he found he could not speak.

Beneath him a narrow valley ran through the middle of the hills. Skip spotted a small herd of buffalo grazing in the valley. His flight halted directly above the herd.

Look. See. Remember. It is all important.

As Skip floated there, gazing down upon the herd, the sun slipped behind the mountain range. As it did a brilliant ray of sunlight shot from between two peaks. Racing across the sky, the ray hit Skip straight in the eyes. At the exact moment the light struck him, an enormous bull buffalo below raised his head and sounded a lonesome bellow.

A feeling of intense fear suddenly gripped Skip. Without knowing why, he looked to the west. He waited with breathless anticipation, for he knew something was about to happen.

A dark spot appeared on the western horizon, a tiny black dot that streaked through the crimson sunset, dragging the night behind it. The object came closer, grew larger, took on shape. It was a bird, a gigantic black bird, easily measuring sixty feet from wingtip to wingtip. With a voice that was thunder, and eyes that flashed lightning, the bird swooped over the countryside. Mountains trembled at its passing and entire forests were laid low.

The bird's feathers were as black as moonless

night, glistening with a bluish sheen, but its claws and beak were as red as the fresh-drawn blood of a slaughtered lamb. As it drew nearer, he could see that the bird had four eyes, two rows of two, one row on top of the other. Those eyes never blinked, not once, as the bird raced toward him, legs outstretched, talons poised to rip him to shreads. Skip tried to scream but couldn't. He could only watch as death rushed toward him on silent wings.

The bird was only thirty feet away when it was attacked from above and below. Four eagles came at the giant black bird from four different directions. With piercing cries of anger, they attacked like dive-bombers going after a battleship. Two of the eagles grabbed the giant bird's wings, one on each wing, while the other two grabbed its legs. The black bird struggled to free itself, but the eagles fought back, pulling the bird in opposite directions, ripping it apart.

There was a brilliant flash of light as the black bird was torn apart, brighter than the blast of an atomic bomb. Within the midst of this ball of light a face appeared. It was the face of evil, of death and destruction—the face of the Crota.

Skip's eyes snapped open. Gone was the giant black bird. Gone too were the four eagles. He no longer floated above the earth. Instead, he found himself back inside the tiny sweat lodge. The flap had been raised, allowing a cool wind to enter the lodge. He was grateful for the breeze, and took deep breaths to slow his racing heart.

Little Hawk and Strong Eagle silently watched him. Both men exchanged knowing glances. They seemed to be waiting for him to say something. He felt a momentary sense of panic as he tried to figure out what he was supposed to say. Little Hawk offered a reassuring smile. The smile turned into a frown, however, when a minute passed and he still hadn't said anything.

"What?" Skip said defensively, knowing he had somehow disappointed the other.

Hawk shook his head. "We were hoping you could tell us. You have obviously had a very powerful vision, for you have been away from your body for almost thirty minutes. What have you seen?"

Strong Eagle spoke and then laid a twisted braid of sweetgrass on the pile of burning coals.

Hawk smiled. "Eagle said maybe you were sleeping."

Skip felt his face flush with anger. "I wasn't asleep."

"Oh?" Hawk said, raising his eyebrows in mock surprise. "Then tell us about your vision. It is important that you remember every detail, no matter how small."

Wiping the sweat from his eyes, Skip described what he'd seen. He took his time, making sure nothing was left out. When he finished, Hawk translated the story for Eagle. Strong Eagle listened, then interpreted the vision. Hawk translated:

"He said your vision is truly a good sign, if a confusing one. The circle of tepees means we can only accomplish our goals through traditional methods. You see, a circle is a shape occurring naturally in nature. A rock is round, so is the trunk of a tree, the stem of a plant, the earth, the moon and the sun. The Indian respects the circle, acknowledges its power. Its shape is the shape of the sacred hoop. That is why tepees were always set in a circle, why our dance arenas are always round."

"What about the river?" Skip asked.

Hawk shrugged. "Eagle's not sure about that part of your vision. The Crota does not live in water, so maybe it has some other meaning. He will have to pray about it."

Strong Eagle spoke. Hawk listened and then translated:

"The most important part of your vision is seeing the giant bird. Being black, it stands for something evil, something of darkness. In this case I'm sure that it represents the Crota. You even said that you saw the face of the Crota when the bird was destroyed."

Skip nodded.

"You also said you saw four eagles attack the black bird. This is good, because four is a sacred number, standing for the four directions from which the wind blows: north, south, east and west. Four is also the number of the four races of man: white, red, black and yellow. The eagles coming to your rescue could also mean that the spirits are willing to help us.

"Strong Eagle also feels, however, that the vision

is trying to tell us something—that in order to destroy the Crota there must be four of us to complete our circle."

"Four?" Skip said.

Hawk nodded. "Who this fourth person is I have no idea. I think Strong Eagle already knows who it is, but he won't tell me. We'll just have to wait and see."

Chapter 28

A storm was brewing. The weather service wasn't calling for rain, but the eastern horizon rolled with thick, ugly thunderheads. Black tentacles stretched across the sky to do battle with the orange and purple of the setting sun. In a sense, the weather forecasters weren't wrong. It was no natural storm that approached. Little Hawk could sense the power of the storm the same way he could sense the fear in the forest creatures around him.

That the storm came from the east could be taken as a good sign. If it approached from any other direction, it would be a bearer of evil and their mission was sure to fail. Still, he wondered about the storm. Could it be a sign that the spirits were coming to help, or were they just coming to watch what was about to happen? He glanced to his left. Skip sat cross-legged on the ground, a fox-skin bundle resting on his lap.

At first, Hawk had had his doubts about Sheriff Harding accompanying him into the tunnels. Serious doubts. After hearing the sheriff's visions those doubts had disappeared. The three men's paths were now one and the same. But where did that path lead, and would any of them reach the end?

Clearing his throat to get their attention, Strong Eagle began to speak in a soft whisper. Little Hawk translated for Skip:

"The hour has come. Before the sun sets you must begin your journey. I will go with you, but only in spirit, for I am too old and brittle to make such a trip." He opened the buckskin medicine bundle lying at his feet, removing a tiny leather pouch attached to a length of cord. "Since you do not have one of your own, I have prepared a medicine pouch for you to wear. It will help keep you safe."

He handed the pouch to Skip, motioning for him to slip it over his head. Once in place, the medicine pouch hung in the center of his chest. Skip thanked Eagle for the gift, though he felt a little uncomfortable wearing it. The pouch had a funny odor to it, like a cross between witch hazel and muskrat.

"Sheriff, I feel you have something you wish to ask about, but are hesitant to do so. Why? There is no such thing as a dumb question, only an unanswered one."

Skip cleared his throat. "Remember the dreams I've been having, the ones I told you about?"

Hawk nodded.

"Well, when I went home I decided to have another look around the attic, just in case there was more to it than a mere flight of fancy. Turns out I found the chest in my dreams."

Hawk's eyebrows rose in surprise.

"Yeah, it was hidden behind a false wall. Wasn't much in it—not anything that could be useful—a few old garments, a pair of leggings and moccasins. But I found this hidden beneath a false bottom. Thought it might be important."

"What is it?" Hawk asked.

"I don't know," Skip replied. "I haven't opened it. I thought I'd leave that to you." He handed the bundle over to Hawk.

"Why didn't you mention this earlier?"

Skip shrugged. "I wasn't sure if it was important or not. And I guess I felt that the time wasn't right."

"And do you feel that the time is right now?" Hawk asked sarcastically.

"I wouldn't have given it to you if I didn't."

Little Hawk handed the bundle to Strong Eagle. A look of surprise came over the old medicine man as he carefully untied the leather cords. Inside the bundle were three arrows, their wooden shafts black with age, the sinew cords holding the flint points and feather flights nearly frayed. Strong Eagle noticed Hawk's puzzlement. He grinned.

"I did not think you would recognize them. Few would."

Lighting a sprig of sage, he picked up the arrows and passed them through the smoke. He handed one to Hawk, another to Skip.

Skip gasped. The arrow felt cold to the touch—icy

cold. It was a cold that burned, like touching frozen metal. The arrow obviously contained some kind of magical power.

Eagle continued: "Judging by the marking on the shafts, plus what you have told me about your grandmother, I would say that these arrows are Cheyenne. Perhaps they are three of the four medicine arrows brought down from the mountains by Motzeyouf, the Arrow Boy, though I have heard that those arrows are cared for by the Arrow Keeper of the Southern Cheyenne in Oklahoma. Either way, your being led to these means that the spirits aren't just watching anymore. They're helping."

The old medicine man allowed Hawk time to translate before continuing.

"I have told you before: the Crota is very powerful, but it is not invincible. While it cannot be killed with white man's weapons, it *can* be destroyed with these. Take these arrows. Let your heart be strong and your aim true."

He wrapped the arrows back up and handed them to Hawk, which was a good thing because Skip was a lousy shot with a bow. The sheriff noticed that Little Hawk's hands shook when he took the bundle.

Strong Eagle picked up his pipe. "Now we smoke once more before you leave. Perhaps we smoke together for the last time."

Eagle slowly filled the pipestone bowl as he had several times before. Nobody said anything, but Skip sensed a strong feeling of sadness between the two Indians. Maybe Strong Eagle's words rang truer than he let on; maybe this was the last time the three of them would smoke the pipe together. In the distance, a whippoorwill cried out; he could have sworn it called his name.

Chapter 29

There wasn't a moon, and the sky was covered with fat, foreboding storm clouds. The wind howled like a wounded animal as it rattled the branches of the trees, gathering leaves and tiny twigs in its grasp. Thunder rumbled and lightning reached skeleton fingers across the sky. The only thing missing was the rain. A storm so powerful should have been drenching them to the bone, but not a drop fell from the swollen clouds. Perhaps what Little Hawk said was true—perhaps it was no ordinary storm that roared overhead. Maybe the spirits had come to watch the show.

They took the back way to the Devil's Boot, leaving the truck parked in a turnaround just off Cemetery Road. Neither of them wanted to run into anybody else and have to explain what they were up to. By hiking in, they avoided the roadblocks.

Skip was amazed at Hawk's ability to move through the woods. The same vines and branches that tugged at his clothes and raked his skin seemed to magically step aside to let the shaman pass, quickly snapping back in place behind him. When they finally reached the ledge above the mouth of the cave, Skip was fatigued, his hands and face stinging from dozens of tiny scratches. Little Hawk, on the other hand, didn't have a scratch on him. Nor was he even breathing hard.

Squatting in the darkness, they waited to see if their approach had been seen. About a hundred yards from the cave's entrance sat a city police car and a fire engine. Since it was pitch-black outside, and the clothes they wore were dark, Skip doubted if they would be spotted before making it inside.

He glanced at Hawk. The Indian was wearing his traditional blue jeans, cowboy boots and a work shirt. A length of rope was coiled around his left shoulder, an elmwood bow slung across his back. In his left hand he carried the fox-skin bundle containing the three arrows.

The sheriff was dressed in a similar fashion, but instead of a bow and arrows he carried his revolver and a shotgun. Strong Eagle warned him that guns would be ineffective against the Crota, but Skip felt more secure bringing them along. They both carried powerful, lantern-type flashlights and canteens of water. Skip had also brought a flare gun and three flares.

"Let's go," Hawk whispered. He slipped catlike down the steep path leading to the cave's entrance. Skip followed close behind. They didn't stop or turn their lights on until they were safely inside the cave.

"Hold still," Hawk said. Stepping closer, he placed a pinch of dried sage in Skip's left ear.

"What's this for?" Skip asked.

"It will help you to hear things you normally can't," Hawk said.

Skip didn't argue. He'd seen enough during the past twelve hours to convince him to believe in and follow the Indian's advice.

"Do you know which way to go?" Hawk asked.

"I think so."

"Then you should take the lead."

"What if I get us lost?"

"Don't worry," Hawk smiled. "I am sure the Crota will still find us."

Neither of them had any trouble climbing down the old wooden ladder to the lower level. Once down, Hawk took one of the arrows from the bundle and slipped it through his belt. Skip unslung his shotgun and slid a round into the chamber.

They walked slowly as they crossed the second chamber, listening carefully to the sounds around them, alert to any possible danger. Skip climbed the pile of fallen stones and entered the tunnel, stopping short when he spotted the skeletons.

"Looks like we found the place," he said.

Hawk stepped past him and looked around. "Do you feel it? Power lingers here."

Skip tried to feel what the shaman was talking about. "I don't feel anything."

Hawk turned around and looked at him coldly. He made a clicking noise with his tongue. "That's because you're trying to feel it the way a white man feels things, with only his five senses. You must do as an Indian would do: you must look inward in order to see out."

"I don't follow you."

"Shhh . . . be quiet." He placed his fingertips on Skip's lips. "Now, relax your mind. Slow your breathing. Think of nothing. Let your spirit become the calm of a lake's surface, the mist of morning, the emptiness of space. Listen to what you hear through your left ear."

Skip closed his eyes and willed his muscles to relax. He forced his breathing to grow calm, slow. Pushing aside all thoughts, he finally managed to turn off the internal dialog of his mind. Only then did he reopen his eyes. The scene before him had changed.

The skeletons still lay in their neat row along the wall, half buried in the accumulated dust of eons past. Only now he noticed a faint blue mist floating in and about them. The mist was like a thin layer of fog, bright blue in color.

"Do you see it now?" Hawk whispered.

"Yes," Skip answered. "What is it?"

"It is the lingering trace of the power that was once worked here. If you were really sensitive—psychic, as people call it nowadays—you might feel a slight chill when you passed through the tunnel."

"Can you always see such things?" Skip asked.

"I can, because I'm a shaman," Hawk replied. "I've been taught how to look at things differently from most men. Many times I've seen spirits when most doubt the existence of such things."

The sheriff looked around. "Do you see any spirits now?"

"No. They might have been here once, trapped by the magic they wove, but they're gone now. They fled when the wall crumbled. They did not want to be eaten by the Crota."

"Eaten?" A chill touched his spine. "How can the Crota eat spirits?"

"There are many things a creature of darkness can do. The Crota would gladly catch and trap the spirits of those that tricked it before—trap them and keep them down in the darkness forever."

Skip was confused. "But if the spirits were trapped by their own magic, then they've already been down here for over a century."

Hawk nodded. "True, but a century is merely the blinking of an eye to a spirit. An eternity of darkness is another thing entirely." He picked up a small stone lying at his feet and handed it to Skip. "Feel this."

"It feels cold."

He spoke three quick words in Cherokee. The stone Skip held grew warm, a glowing red letter suddenly appearing on the side of it.

"See. There—" Hawk pointed. "Something was once written there with the blood of a medicine man. He must have been very powerful for the magic to stay around this long."

"I thought Indians didn't have a written language back then," Skip said.

Hawk looked at him funny. "Who said that?"

"It's in the history books."

Jay Little Hawk smiled, as if speaking to a child who didn't know any better. "Oh, I see. And doesn't it also say in the history books that America, a land already inhabited for thousands of years, was discovered by Christopher Columbus, a man so totally lost that he thought he had landed in India so he called the natives Indians?"

"Yeah, well—"

"So, tell me, who wrote those history books?"

"I don't know," Skip shrugged.

"Well, I do. Your history books were written by white men. Can you imagine a white man writing about the history of Indians? Pretty funny, huh? Someone who probably never even saw an Indian, let alone sat down and talked with one, writing all about them. The same ones who wrote the history books were the ones who called the Indians savages."

Little Hawk's face grew hard. Skip took a step backward as Hawk continued.

"Savages! Let me tell you something, friend. Long before the white man came to this country with his whiskey and his greed, we had our own form of government. The Cherokees were farmers. We respected the land, taking only what we needed from it. There were no jails because we didn't need them. An Indian would never steal from another. If he needed something, then others would give it to him.

But now we can pay taxes, get drunk and go to jail, just like the white people. Pretty civilized, huh?"

Skip held up his hands in a sign of surrender. "Remind me to keep my mouth shut unless I know what I'm talking about."

Hawk's features softened. He slapped Skip on the shoulder and laughed. "You're learning."

Before continuing, Hawk said a short prayer for the spirits of the Indians who had died in the cave. He wished them eternal rest and happiness, and thanked them for the noble sacrifice they had made. As the shaman spoke, Skip noticed the bluish mist grow faint and finally fade out completely. The magic of those before was gone.

It wasn't difficult to figure out which passageway to follow. Lloyd and the others had left a trail even a Cub Scout could follow. In addition to the thin cable wire that had connected the base station to the mobile phone, the tunnel was littered with candy wrappers and discarded wads of gum.

Onward they marched, the tunnel sloping gradually downward. How deep they would eventually go they could only guess, but they were both willing to follow it to the center of the earth, if need be. One way or another, they were going to find the Crota. One way or another, they were determined to destroy it, or die trying.

Chapter 30

Little Hawk held his hand for silence. A wasted motion. Skip opened his mouth, but no words came out. He could barely breathe.

The city was old, so very old. Never in his life had Skip seen anything so shrouded in antiquity, so wrapped in the very mystery of time itself. And somewhere amongst the twisting alleys and buildings of crumbling stone and adobe mud stalked the thing they had come to destroy. Deep within the very midst of that long-forgotten metropolis walked the Crota.

Hawk stood still and straight, his eyes closed. If Skip didn't know better, he would have thought the Indian was asleep on his feet. A full minute passed before the shaman finally stirred.

"What we seek is close," he said, opening his eyes.

Skip glanced around him. "How can you be sure?"

Hawk smiled.

"Never mind . . . how close is close?"

Little Hawk pointed at the city spreading before them.

"I was afraid of that," Skip said. "That thing could be anywhere. No way you could narrow down its location a little, is there? I don't like walking into a trap."

"You will not be going blind. Remember, the spirits are with you, for now you walk the path of your ancestors—"

"Please, spare me the philosophy," Skip interrupted.

Hawk looked annoyed. "We have all the advantages available to us. Anything else will be just good fortune and dumb luck. We must hurry; we are expected."

Skip wondered what he meant by *expected*. Before he could ask, Hawk turned and started walking away. Not wanting to be separated, helpful spirits or not, Skip hurried to catch up.

Hawk paused momentarily to study the pictographs on the arch guarding the entrance to the city.

"Indians?" Skip asked, joining him.

Hawk shrugged. "Maybe. I'm not sure. If it is, it's older than anything I've ever seen."

"Mound Builders?"

"Older than that. The people who built this city might have been related to the Aztec, or Mayan. It's often wondered what happened to the people who built the great cities of the jungle. Then again, there are legends, ancient ones, that tell of races of men long lost to time."

"Oh?" Skip said, curious.

Hawk turned and cocked an eyebrow. "Surely you've heard of the lost city of Atlantis."

"Everyone has."

"Well, the Indians too have their stories of an island nation that was destroyed centuries ago. But that is just one story; there are many others. Several legends of the Cherokee, in fact, tell that the first people came from the star system known as the Pleiades—"

Skip held up his hand. "You're starting to sound like Erich von Daniken."

"Who?"

"The guy who wrote *Chariots of the Gods.* You know, ancient astronauts, that sort of thing."

"Maybe Mr. Daniken is a clever man," Hawk said.

"Maybe he's a nutcase."

"Maybe," the Indian nodded. "But it never hurts to keep an open mind. Man doesn't know all the answers; he only thinks he does." He moved his arm in a sweeping gesture. "This in itself is proof that we have a lot to learn."

They walked beneath the stone arch, stepping through a portal into another time. Tiny windowless houses watched their passing with mute fascination. Courtyards that had served as arenas for social gatherings now lay sleeping under layers of dust and shadows. Murals, once bright and colorful, were nothing more than faded patterns of chipping pastels. Covering it all was a feeling of sadness and loss so great it almost brought tears to their eyes. Here a great city once thrived, a city left abandoned and unloved by the harsh mistress of time.

Skip looked down. The ground was littered with potsherds, stone chips, flint slivers, shells and bone fragments, the refuse of those who had lived in the underground city.

"Looks like a primitive fallout shelter," he said.

Hawk turned and looked at one of the buildings. "They—"

His sudden pause got the sheriff's full attention. "What's the matter?"

"We're being watched," he said calmly.

Skip clicked off the safety of his shotgun. Looking around, he tried to peer deeper into the shadows surrounding them. If they were being watched, it could be from a dozen different directions, in a hundred different hiding places.

"Are you sure?" he asked. He didn't doubt Hawk, he just felt the sudden need to talk, to say something to help disperse the fear building inside of him.

"Yes. Don't you feel it?"

"No," Skip replied.

"Then you are not looking inward," Hawk whispered. "Look inward, not outward. Relax. Let the spirits guide you."

Skip began taking deep breaths, willing his mind and body to relax. It wasn't easy, especially in the present situation. Slowly, however, he felt himself grow calm, becoming more aware of his surroundings, more in tune with the things around him. As his mind reached a state of heightened awareness, he too felt the sensation of being watched.

"I feel it," he said. "But I can't tell which direction it's coming from."

"It comes from behind us. Whatever it is, it's following us."

"Is it the Crota?"

"Perhaps. I'm not sure," Hawk shrugged. "It's hard to tell. I almost get the feeling there are two of them."

"Two?" Skip was alarmed.

"Yes. If it is the Crota, then it's being very cautious . . . trying to disguise its energy. Perhaps it senses we are somehow different, so it is puzzled, maybe even a little frightened."

"It . . . frightened of us?" Skip laughed.

"Maybe a little," Hawk said. "Remember, the Crota was tricked before. I imagine a century of imprisonment has made it leery. Another thing: you've already beaten it once. Maybe it remembers you, knows who you are."

The feeling of being watched increased. Skip wiped his hand across his forehead. He was sweating profusely. He always sweated when he was scared, and he'd never been so scared in his life as he was at this moment. He tried deep breathing, trying to focus his attention inward as Little Hawk had told him. It didn't work. He still had the feeling of being watched, but his inner calm was way out of order.

He allowed Little Hawk to take the lead as they wove their way through the twisting, narrow alleyways. Although he didn't ask, Skip suspected Hawk knew exactly where he was going. Either way, he was perfectly content to follow. Looking behind him as he walked, he didn't notice the shaman stop suddenly, and he accidentally bumped into him.

"You have all the grace of an old woman!" Hawk snapped.

"Yeah, well I think you ought to have your brake lights fixed. Why are we stopping?"

"Why not?"

"What do you mean, why not?"

"I think this is as good a place as any."

"For what?" inquired Skip.

"Why, to face our destiny, of course."

Skip hated it when Hawk talked around a subject. Still, he had a pretty good idea what the Indian meant. They had stopped in the center of a large courtyard, by far the largest they had yet seen, measuring about forty feet by sixty feet. The courtyard was open only on one side, the other three sides closed in by the windowless walls of single-story buildings. Only one way in, only one way out. The perfect spot for a showdown.

"So what do we do now?" Skip asked.

Hawk pointed at the closest wall. "You sit here. I will sit over there." He indicated a point about twenty feet to the left of where Skip would be sitting. "We will turn off our lights and wait. The Crota will come."

"How can you be sure?"

He smiled and touched the gorget Skip wore

around his neck. "I forgot to tell you. Because of your necklace, the Crota probably thinks you are one of those who stole its freedom. The creature will not rest until it finds you. It will come."

"The Crota thinks I'm a Creek Indian?"

Hawk nodded.

"How could you forget to tell me that?" Skip started to get angry, then realized what was going on. "Wait a minute. You son of a bitch, you didn't forget. You've been using me as bait. Haven't you?"

"Something like that," Hawk grinned.

The sheriff let out a sigh. "Good thing I've got a friend. Any last-minute words of advice?"

"Don't fall asleep."

Hawk stepped closer and stuck out his hand. Skip, thinking he wanted to shake hands, stuck his out too. Before he could react, the sharp blade of a knife nicked the palm of his right hand.

"Ow! What the hell are you doing?" Skip looked in shock at the bright red trickle flowing down his fingers.

"If I am to die with a man, then he should be my brother—even if he is already my friend." Little Hawk sliced his own palm, then offered his hand again. Skip didn't hesitate to take it. Their blood mingled—blood of a red man, blood of a white man—and joined together, became one. Brothers. The way it should be. The way it should always have been.

Chapter 31

Curious eyes of timid forest creatures watched the still form of George Strong Eagle. Before him the fire laughed and danced as it consumed crackling logs of cedar and pine. The darkness around the old Indian seemed to close in, held at bay only by the flames. His lips barely moved as he voiced silent prayers to unseen spirits. His eyes were closed, yet he saw.

It wasn't the orange of the flames he saw, nor the twisting black clouds above. Though Strong Eagle's physical body sat in the tiny clearing, his spirit was many miles away, deep within the bowels of the earth. And what he saw, the visiting spirits also saw. Spirits don't usually take an active interest in the affairs of men, but tonight was different. Tonight the spirits shrieked and howled, causing creatures of fur and feather to cower together in fear. Thunder rumbled and roared as lightning split the sky. There was going to be a battle, a veritable war between the forces of light and dark, between good and evil. The spirits had come for the show. They weren't to be disappointed.

* * *

Billy Harding lay awake in his bed, looking out the window, watching the limbs of the oak tree next to the house swing and sway. Though he couldn't hear the wind, he could feel the house shake from the force of the storm. With each flash of lightning, shadows formed on his bedroom ceiling. Long, dark shadows stretched across the room like the arms of a giant scarecrow, snatching at him with hooked fingers.

Pulling his covers up around his chin, he wished that his father was home. He wouldn't be afraid then. His dad was the sheriff; he'd protect him from anything that walked or slithered in the darkness of the night.

Another flash of lightning caused Billy to close his eyes tightly for a second. When he opened them again, he found that he was no longer alone.

His first thought was to jump up and run, but he was too scared to move, too frightened even to hide beneath the covers. He could only lie there and tremble, wondering how the old man with the long hair had gotten into his room. He hadn't come through the door, because it was still closed, and there was no way he could have walked across the room in the short time Billy had shut his eyes. He couldn't have climbed in through the window either, for it was closed and locked.

As Billy pondered these things, the old man slowly walked toward him. Reaching the side of his bed, he looked down and smiled. It was a warm, friendly, loving smile. Billy smiled back.

* * *

Skip would have moved to ease the discomfort in his back, but he dared not. He might have taken a drink of water, but his fingers refused to leave the shotgun resting on his lap. Instead he remained motionless, as he had for what seemed like hours, his gaze focused on the entrance to the courtyard. A lantern flashlight had been placed halfway between where he and Little Hawk sat, its glow giving just enough light to see by while still allowing them the concealment of darkness.

The waiting was the hardest part. Twice already his fear and nervousness had grown to an almost unbearable level. Each time that had happened, however, words of a prayer had popped into his mind. Spoken in a language other than his own, in the voice of George Strong Eagle, the prayer had calmed his fears, giving him strength and courage.

During those moments of calm, he followed Little Hawk's advice and focused his attention inward in order to see out. It wasn't an easy thing to do; the simple act went against everything he'd been raised to believe in. Still, he found his thoughts slowly clearing, as though a translucent screen had been carefully pulled away. Letting his mind relax further, he discovered that all his senses had increased dramatically. His nose detected dusty, foul odors previously unnoticed, and his ears picked up the sounds of insects scurrying in the darkness. But most startling of all was what he could see. He saw spirits!

At first, Skip had no idea what he was looking at.

Cloudy patches of blue mist drifted and danced about the courtyard. Some of the clouds floated lazily by like thunderheads on a warm summer day; others chased each other around and around in a constant whir of motion. A few of the patches vanished into the ground while several others rocketed toward the cavern's ceiling. When they came close Skip noticed a strange humming inside his head. But it wasn't until he grew tired of watching, focusing his attention instead on what he heard, that he realized the humming was actually a blending of many voices, like the sound of a crowd of people all talking at once.

He was trying to pick out an individual word or two, when another sound caught his attention: the soft, gentle scraping of something moving very slowly, very cautiously.

Skip's grip tightened on the shotgun. His eyes opened wider in an effort to penetrate the darkness beyond the flashlight's glow. He heard it again. Something had definitely moved. Along with the muffled sound came a feeling of electricity in the air. He'd experienced a similar sensation the night the Crota attacked him.

The hair on Skip's arms stood straight up as a tingle of terror walked up his spine on spider legs.

Sss-scrape.

His palms beginning to sweat, he rested the shotgun tightly against his thigh to keep his hands from shaking. The floating blue mists had vanished, leaving only the empty courtyard and the darkness beyond. In that darkness something moved, came closer. . . .

Sss-scrape.

A tiny sprinkling of dust and pebbles rained down upon him. He brushed it away with his left hand. . . .

Skip's bowels turned to ice. Slowly, very slowly, not making any sudden movements, he raised his head and looked up.

Sighting along the wall his back rested against, he looked straight above him. More pebbles sprinkled down. A head appeared, peeking over the wall, watching him. An enormous head with eyes of yellow fire. *The Crota!*

Skip screamed and pushed himself away from the wall. Stumbling, off balance, he turned and fired. He missed. The Crota roared in rage and sprang from the roof.

The air sparked and popped in a thousand different places as the Crota landed in the courtyard. Gusts of wind appeared from nowhere, stirring up miniature dust devils.

"Sheriff, get back!" Little Hawk yelled. He notched an arrow to his bow, pulled the string back, and released it.

Whoosh . . .

The arrow burst into a bolt of searing blue flame as it streaked toward the Crota. A flame so bright it left its image permanently etched on the back of Skip's brain.

For an instant the battle stood out in sharp contrast as darkness was turned into day. But Hawk fired too quickly, not taking time to aim. The arrow went wide, missed, bounced off the far wall and shattered. The blue fire vanished. Little Hawk fumbled madly to refit a second arrow to his bowstring. The Crota roared in anger at the shaman but turned its attention back to Skip.

Still partially blinded by the arrow, Skip stumbled backward and fired. The Crota kept coming. He worked the shotgun's slide, fired again . . . and again.

Claws lashed out, sliced through the air. Skip tried to get out of the way, but he wasn't quick enough. Pain ripped through his right thigh, spread like fire up and down his leg. He fell against the wall, the Crota towering over him.

Little Hawk's face was a mask of determination as he drew back the bow's string. His arms quivering, he took careful aim and then released the wooden shaft. The arrow exploded into a flash of blue.

The Crota sensed it coming. The monster turned its head at the exact moment the arrow was launched, twisted its body as the bolt of blue streaked across the courtyard. But the Crota didn't move fast enough. The arrow hit home, its flint head burning deep into the monster's shoulder. For the second time when facing the sheriff, the Crota felt pain.

Skip rolled just in time, escaping the heavy, clawed foot that lashed out to end his life. His back against the wall, he got slowly to his feet. There was a dark wet patch where the Crota's claws had sliced through his jeans, and he could feel blood running down his leg and into his boot. Using the wall for support, he edged away from the enraged monster.

Hawk notched the last arrow and took careful aim. He couldn't afford to miss, but the Crota refused to cooperate and stand still. The creature roared and shrieked, striking blindly at the area around it. Before Hawk could fire the monster turned and bolted for the open end of the courtyard. With a final wailing cry, it disappeared into the darkness.

Skip watched the Crota's departure with passing interest. His leg burned in agony, pushing all other thoughts from his mind. The sudden loss of blood also made him lightheaded, causing him to fall back against the wall. Seeing him slump into a sitting position, Hawk raced to his side.

"Nice shot," Skip said as the Indian reached him.

"It was luck," Hawk replied. Setting his flashlight on the ground beside him, he pulled his knife from its sheath and cut the seam of Skip's pants leg. "Ahhh . . . that doesn't look so bad," he said, pulling the fabric away from the wound.

Skip disagreed. The wound looked plenty bad to him. A deep gash ran from mid-thigh to knee, blood covering his leg.

Hawk reached into the medicine bag tied to his belt and pulled out what looked like a plug of green chewing tobacco. He broke the plug into two pieces, giving half to Skip. "Chew this, only don't swallow and don't spit."

The sheriff coughed, nearly gagging, as he put the plug into his mouth and started chewing. Whatever it was, it damn sure wasn't tobacco. The stuff tasted like dogshit—peppery dogshit. Hawk grinned at Skip's discomfort, then popped the other half of the plug into his own mouth.

Hawk chewed for a few seconds, then spat the wad back into his hands. Much to Skip's surprise, the shaman began spreading the chewed mush over the wound. Almost instantly, the pain began to fade as a cold numbness seeped into his thigh.

He held his hands in front of Skip's mouth. "Spit."

Skip spit the wad into the waiting hands. "Hey, that stuff works pretty fast. What is it?"

"You don't want to know," Hawk said.

Skip frowned but didn't press the issue. Maybe it was best he didn't know. Truthfully, he didn't care what it was as long as it worked.

After covering the wound with the greenish goo, Hawk wrapped the injured leg with pieces of cloth torn from his white undershirt. "You got off lucky," he said, putting his work shirt back on. "The wound isn't deep, no muscles are cut. You should be as good as new in a day or two. At least you're not going to bleed to death." He started gathering his things together. "I'll change the dressing when I get back."

"Whoa . . . hold on a minute," Skip said. "What do you mean when *you* get back?"

"The Crota is only wounded. I have to finish the job I set out to do. I have to kill it."

"You mean the job *we* set out to do. I'm going with you."

Little Hawk clicked his tongue. "You can't walk on that leg."

"The hell I can't. You just watch me."

"Sheriff, this is no longer your fight."

Skip sneered. "Listen to me, you thickheaded son of a bitch. This is still my fight, always has been, always will be. That thing murdered my men . . . my friends. It nearly got me. Twice. I owe it. You're not leaving me here. I'll follow you if I have to."

Hawk stared at him for a moment. "Very well, you can come. But do not expect me to carry you or help you to walk. If you fall behind, I will leave you."

"Agreed," Skip said.

Chapter 32

Skip's right leg sent an endless succession of dull throbs to his brain, but still he kept up. He would have kept up even if it killed him. Little Hawk cut him no slack; his pace was fast. The Indian looked neither left nor right as he followed the broad avenue bisecting the ancient city. The sheriff didn't possess the confidence Hawk did. He continued to watch the shadows on each side of the road, as well as throwing occasional glances behind.

"What makes you think the Crota has left the city?" Skip asked as they neared the last of the buildings.

"I just know it."

"So how come in the courtyard you didn't know it was sneaking up on us?"

Hawk wheeled on him. "I didn't know it was sneaking up on us because it didn't want me to know. It knew I could feel its presence, so it was being careful to guard its thoughts. The Crota blocked its mind the same way someone would lock a door."

"So how come its mind isn't guarded now?"

"Because it's in pain, that's why. The pain has maddened it, made it careless. The creature is apt to make mistakes now, mistakes that might work to our advantage. We must hurry; we cannot afford to let it get away."

Skip looked at the tunnel entrance they were heading for. "So why is it going this way? Why not go the other way, the way we came in?"

"I don't know. Perhaps there is more than one way in or out of the tunnels. Perhaps it panicked and made a mistake."

"Maybe it's leading us into a trap."

"You don't have to come with me."

"Just try leaving me behind and see what happens," Skip scowled.

A smile touched the corners of Hawk's mouth. "I don't know which is the hardest to deal with—you or the Crota."

Skip returned the smile. "*I* am. The Crota's a piece of cake."

The tunnel they followed appeared to have once been a natural passageway, widened over the years by the inhabitants of the city. After walking for an hour, Skip was having serious doubts about Hawk's tracking abilities. Still, he said nothing. Which was a good thing, because a few minutes later they came across a small puddle of blood.

Hawk knelt and put his finger into the puddle. "It's fresh."

"The Crota?" asked Skip.

Hawk nodded, wiping his fingers off on his pants. "It must have stopped here to rest. Stay alert and keep your eyes open."

"Believe me, I plan to do just that."

About half an hour later, there was a noticeable change in the tunnel. The temperature was suddenly much cooler, and damp. Water dripped from the rocky ceiling and collected in puddles, while patches of fungus grew along the walls. Curious, Skip walked over and placed a hand against the rock wall.

"It feels wet," he said.

Hawk touched the opposite wall. "Cold, too. Maybe we're under the river."

Skip was shocked. Though they had been walking for some time, he never dreamed they'd come far enough north to reach the river. There was something a little discomforting about the sudden realization that he was standing directly underneath the Missouri River.

"Damn, a tunnel under the river," he said. "Can you imagine what this could have meant to the early pioneers?"

Hawk nodded. "It would have been a great discovery to pioneers or Indians. But with the bridges of today it's worthless, except maybe as a conversation piece."

Avoiding the bigger puddles, they continued on, passing two smaller tunnels that branched off from the one they followed. There was a noticeable boundary as the rock wall went from wet back to dry again. Though the smell of dampness still lingered, the puddles and moisture were gone. They had crossed under the river.

They'd gone no more than twenty yards beyond the river's edge when Skip spotted a carving etched upon the wall to his left. He stopped, unable to believe his eyes. The carving was of a large bird, its wings spread in flight—a bird with four eyes.

It's the bird from my vision.

Little Hawk had stopped too, but he wasn't interested in the carving. Instead, he was looking around, a look of concern on his face.

"What's the matter?" Skip asked.

Hawk quickly explained that all through the tunnel he had been able to detect the Crota's presence in front of them, but he had lost contact with the creature back at the river and was no longer sure where it was.

The river . . . beware the river.

Skip remembered his vision and the message that had been given to him. There were other tunnels back at the river, places to hide. Little Hawk was right: the monster was no longer in front of them. It was behind them.

He turned around to yell a warning to Hawk, but it was too late. The Crota crashed into the shaman like a runaway freight train.

Hawk went down, his bow and arrow flying from his hand. He ducked, skidded and rolled, desperately trying to keep himself behind the Crota's hind legs, the only place where the creature couldn't get to him easily. Skip rapidly fired his shotgun, pumping five rounds into the monster.

The Crota roared and turned toward Skip. Seizing the opportunity, Hawk jumped up and tried to make it to his fallen bow and arrow. He'd taken only two steps, however, when the monster spun around and slapped him across the back, knocking him headfirst into the wall.

Skip discarded the empty shotgun. He thought about drawing his .357 but doubted if the revolver would have any effect on the Crota. Instead, he pulled the flare gun from his belt, sighted quickly and fired.

There was a loud pop as a brilliant ball of red fire exited the barrel of the flare gun. The burning ball streaked across the tunnel, striking the Crota high on the back. The monster spun around and hissed, its lips curled back to reveal deadly fangs.

Oh shit! Now you've done it.

Hands shaking with fear, Skip snatched the spent cartridge out of the gun and reloaded. In one movement, he raised and fired the pistol.

Pop.

The second flare hit the Crota on the end of the nose and traveled upward, the ball of burning fire exploding into brilliance between the monster's hideous amber eyes. The flare's brightness left Skip temporarily blinded, but it was far worse for the Crota.

While he could no longer see the monster, he could clearly hear its scream of rage. The Crota screamed a wail to end all wails, a cry of pain and anguish to chill the bones.

Skip jumped back out of the way and tried to stay clear of the thrashing monster in a tunnel grown terribly small. He almost made it, but the Crota lashed out with a foot, catching him just below the calves, sweeping his legs out from under him. He landed on his back at the creature's feet, staring straight up into the eyes of death.

He had no time to reload the flare gun, no chance to roll free. Skip's jaws clenched as he waited for death to claim him. He was determined to die like a man; he would not scream, would not give the thing towering above him the satisfaction of hearing him cry out.

There was a sudden rush of movement from his left. Shots rang out, white flashes framing the scene in the tunnel like the negatives of a photograph.

The Crota roared and turned to face a new challenger. Skip seized the opportunity and scurried backwards until he collided against the wall. There he stopped, his chest hitching in pain, watching the events unfolding a few feet from him.

Lloyd watched with satisfaction as Skip crawled to safety. Had he arrived a few seconds later, the sheriff would have been dead.

After ending his conversation with Skip, Lloyd had spent hours wandering through the city in search of the Crota. Unable to find the monster, he'd succumbed to fatigue and despair, curling up to sleep in a tiny alcove near where the tunnel passed beneath the river. He would have been there still if the blast of a shotgun hadn't awakened him.

"All right, you ugly son of a bitch," he said, ignoring the sweat rolling into his eyes. "Let's see how fucking bad you really are."

He pulled a fresh clip out of his pants pocket, ejecting the empty one from his .45. He was surprised the creature hadn't already attacked him. Maybe his sudden appearance had left it a little confused, or leery. Lloyd had another theory: he felt the thing recognized him from their previous encounter. Perhaps it was wondering what he was doing here; perhaps it knew exactly what he was doing here.

The Crota dropped to all fours and lowered its head, watching him with eyes that never blinked. A deep rumbling came from the back of the creature's throat, a growl so low it was barely audible. Lloyd was reminded of the sound a Doberman makes right before it rips your fucking leg off. There was a wet metallic click as he released the slide of his .45, sending a bullet into the chamber.

"Come on . . . come on, you bitch. I owe you. This one's for the boys."

The growl changed into a snarl, the snarl into a roar. The Crota exploded off the starting blocks. The monster's charge was met by the deadly accuracy of Lloyd's shooting. Seven searing-hot slugs slammed into the Crota's chest, but the bullets might as well have been spit wads. Lloyd knew even before he pulled the trigger that the .45 would be useless against the monster. He knew, but he still fired, still stood his ground. He didn't flinch, didn't move a muscle. Even when the Crota bore down on him like a Mack truck he held his ground, arms outstretched, hands clutching the barking automatic.

As Lloyd fell beneath the murderous jaws of the Crota, Skip crawled along the wall as fast as he could. He paused briefly at the crumpled form of Jay Little Hawk to check for a pulse. The Indian still lived. Thank God. He quickly checked for wounds, but the only thing he found was a nasty bump on his head. Hawk was unconscious but not seriously hurt.

His eyesight almost back to normal, Skip spotted the bow and arrow lying near the opposite wall. Jumping up, he made a run for it. He was halfway across the tunnel when the Crota spotted him. With a roar, the monster charged.

Skip made it to the bow and arrow a few feet ahead of the Crota. Scooping them up, his heart nearly stopped as the bow fell apart in his hands.

The bow was broken, useless; its wooden shaft had probably snapped when the Crota attacked Little Hawk. There was no time to fix it, no time to flee. The Crota was upon him!

Maybe he knew all along that it would come down to this. Maybe Little Hawk and Strong Eagle knew it too. Perhaps this was the reason they had picked him to face the Crota. Call it karma. Call it faith. Call it what you will. Skip didn't try to understand it. He only knew that something beyond his control had put him here at this exact moment in time.

Faces flashed through his mind like images in a slide show, the faces of those killed by the Crota. Some of the people he knew quite well, others only in passing, some not at all. They all had one thing in common: their spirits begged him to put a stop to their endless torment, to avenge their deaths. He wasn't about to let them down.

The Crota lunged, jaws spread wide. Skip stood his ground, didn't flinch. His grip tightened on the tiny arrow clutched in his right hand as the Crota went for the kill.

"Eat this, you bastard!"

He pivoted to the left, striking upward with his right hand. The arrow pierced the Crota's throat, the point penetrating deep into its scaly flesh.

Upward the tiny stone point traveled, through the creature's throat and into its mouth. The arrow flashed blue, the icy flame encasing Skip's hand. Blood spewed hot and steaming from the wound, splattered his arm and chest.

He pushed harder, pushed with all his might. The arrow skewered the Crota's tongue, burying itself deep into the roof of its mouth.

Skip released the arrow and jumped back out of the way. The Crota tried to scream but couldn't. It snatched madly at the arrow in an attempt to tear it free.

Blood spurted bright red from the Crota's throat, spilled down the monster's chest and over its legs.

A shudder traveled through the creature's body as it sank slowly to its knees. A hand reached out toward Skip, trying to grab him with claws that still dripped Lloyd's blood.

The Crota tried to crawl, desperately attempting to reach him. One foot. Two. Muscles strained; its chest heaved. A gasping sound came from deep within its throat, followed by a cascade of blood frothed with white foam, like waves upon the ocean.

The monster raised its head to look at him, and Skip saw intelligence in its eyes. The Crota knew it had lost the battle, lost the war. To the victor went life; to the vanquished, only death.

The amber glow of the Crota's reptilian eyes slowly faded, then flickered out like a candle in the wind. The creature collapsed, and died.

How long Skip stood there staring down at the lifeless monster he did not know. Tremors of fear rolled up and down his body as tears raced down his cheeks. The nightmare was finally over. They had won. The magic arrows had killed the beast.

"Thanks, Grandma."

A soft moan came from behind him. He turned.

Little Hawk pushed himself up on his elbows and looked around. His eyes opened wide in astonishment as he spotted the body of the Crota. He turned toward Skip and nodded. "You did good, for a white man."

Skip put his hands on his hips. "I'll have you know I'm one quarter Indian and damn proud of it."

Hawk smiled.

Skip walked over and knelt beside him. "Anything broken?"

The shaman thought for a moment before answering. "Nothing serious. I have a good-sized bump on the back of my head, but I think I'll live. Lucky for me I have a hard head."

"The Crota snuck up on us," Skip said. "My vision told me to beware the river. I guess I should have listened."

Hawk nodded. "In the teachings of the Indians, water has power. It is the home of the manitou, and the manitou can be either good or evil. The Crota must have known this. It used the energy of the rushing water to mask its power, making its presence undetectable." He spotted Lloyd's body. "Four. The circle is complete."

"You knew about this?" Skip asked.

Hawk shook his head. "I knew only what Strong Eagle said—that there would be four of us." A look of insight crossed his face. "That would explain why I was picking up two presences back at the city."

The sheriff nodded absently. "He saved my life."

"His actions will be remembered. Songs are always sung about the brave."

"So what do we do now?" asked Skip.

"We go home."

"What about Lloyd?"

"We will send someone back for him."

Skip stood up. "It's a long walk back to the Boot."

"Yes, it is," Hawk agreed. "We'd better get started."

Chapter 33

It was early afternoon when they emerged from the Devil's Boot. The sun shone hot and bright, the previous evening's storm just a memory. Their sudden appearance gave the deputy guarding the cave quite a start. Not wanting to go into details about what had happened, Skip merely told the deputy and the two men from the fire department to go on home, that the situation was under control.

They arrived back at Hawk's cabin a little after two P.M. George Strong Eagle was waiting for them on the back porch. A full pot of coffee sat on the small wooden table. Next to the table a six-pack of beer chilled in a washtub filled with ice. The old Indian rose and happily embraced each of them. He said a few words of greeting to Hawk, then turned and spoke to Skip. There was humor in the medicine man's eyes. Hawk translated what was said.

"He says he is very proud of you. You acted very bravely and followed the right path. He feels the blood of your Indian ancestors runs strong in your veins. With time, and the right teacher, you could one day become a great warrior, maybe even a medicine person like your grandmother."

Strong Eagle reached up and removed the choker of blue and white beads from around his neck.

"He wants you to have his choker. It is a great honor to receive such a gift; wear it proudly. He says that you and your family will always be welcome in his home and that he hopes you will someday come to visit us."

"Us?" Skip looked at Hawk.

Hawk nodded. "I'm going back with Strong Eagle. I will stay with him for a while, then I will return to the reservation of my people, in Oklahoma. My work is finished here. I am needed there."

"But what about your home . . . your belongings?"

"Some of my things I will keep, some I will sell, most I will give away. The cabin will stand for a time, but after a while it will be taken over by the forest. Eventually no one will know where it stood. Like all things, it too will return to the earth."

Little Hawk stepped closer, taking Skip's hand. "It has been an honor knowing you. Before I take you back to town we must smoke the pipe together one last time. Maybe afterwards we will get a little drunk; I think we both need it. Who knows, if we are lucky, Strong Eagle will sing for us."

Skip didn't arrive home until late that night. Like Little Hawk predicted, they had gotten a little drunk together—not to the point of staggering or falling down, just enough to make the nightmare of the past few days seem like a bad dream. Slipping quietly into the darkened kitchen, he removed his mud-caked boots and set them by the door. He dropped various other articles of clothing as he made his way down the hallway towards the bathroom.

The hot shower seemed to do him as much good as the beer. He didn't shut the water off until his skin turned a nice shade of pink. Drying off, he wrapped a towel around his waist and doused his clawed thigh with a good helping of disinfectant. The wound looked pretty good, considering. The stuff Little Hawk smeared on it had worked great. In a couple of days the old leg would be as good as new.

Slipping out of the bathroom, he retraced his steps back down the hallway until he came to his crumpled trousers. Removing his billfold from the back pocket, he slid his sheriff's badge into the palm of his hand. Stepping into the kitchen, he raised the lid on the trash can and tossed the badge in with the leftover food scraps and empty milk cartons.

There would be other jobs, other towns. Logan was getting just a little too crowded lately. With the discovery of the lost city it would probably boom into a first-rate city—a city packed with cheap hotels, bargain stores, tourists—and crime. Skip guessed it was time to move on, time to find someplace a little quieter, a little more restful, a place where a man could settle down and spend some time with his family. Maybe they'd open that flower shop Katie always wanted. He could just see himself, down on his knees, talking to a rosebush or two.

As he started down the hallway, he noticed that the light was on in the bedroom. Katie must still be up. He was about to open the door when he heard singing—a soft, sweet melody—coming from inside. He stopped and listened.

"Old McDonald had a farm . . ."

Skip slowly opened the door. Katie was kneeling on the floor, tears flowing down her cheeks. Standing in front of her was Billy, singing. They both turned in his direction as he opened the door.

"Billy . . . he's . . ." Katie tried to talk but couldn't.

Billy looked up at Skip, his eyes bright as silver dollars.

"Hello, Daddy." He held out something in his right hand. "See what the old Indian gave me, Daddy? It's an eagle feather!"

The feather was a golden eagle tail feather, its shaft beaded with turquoise and red beads, a length of leather attached to it so it could be tied to the hair. It was the same feather Strong Eagle had worn tied to his braid.

"He says he likes you, Daddy," Billy continued. "He says you're a good friend. He made my ears all better. I can hear now, Daddy. Honest. I can talk, too. Would you like to hear me sing, Daddy? Would you?"

Tears flowed down Skip's face. He wiped his eyes and nodded. "Yes, Billy. I'd like to hear you sing."

He slowly closed the door behind him, shutting out the blackness of the night, shutting out the outside world, leaving behind all the hurt and suffering.

Crossing the room, he kneeled before his son and listened, listened as one would to a songbird for the very first time, as Billy sang:

"Row, row, row your boat. . . ."